"Rusty Whitener weaves a deft tale of young friendship and the curve balls of faith, the whole story seasoned with sunshine and the leathery scent of baseball gloves!"

—Ray Blackston, author of *Flabbergasted*

"*A Season of Miracles* is a heartwarming, all-American story of small town boys and Little League baseball. You'll be cheering this captivating bunch of characters all the way home both in their game of baseball and the bigger game of life."

—Ann H. Gabhart, award-winning author of *The Outsider*

"*A Season of Miracles* is a triumphant debut novel with a heart of gold. Laced with wit and wisdom, the story had me chuckling out loud one minute and wiping tears the next. Highly recommended!"

—Deborah Raney, author of *Almost Forever* and *Beneath a Southern Sky*

"A very special book. Baseball, inspiration, and childhood memories—a great combination. I couldn't put it down!"

—Richard Sterban, bass singer for The Oak Ridge Boys and former owner of the Nashville Sounds AAA baseball team

A Season of
Miracles

RUSTY WHITENER

Huntington City Township
Public Library
255 West Park Drive
Huntington, IN 46750
www.huntingtonpub.lib.in.us

A Season of Miracles: A Novel

© 2010 by Rusty Whitener

Published by Kregel Publications, a division of Kregel, Inc., P.O. Box 2607, Grand Rapids, MI 49501.

All rights reserved. No part of this book may be reproduced, stored in a retrieval system, or transmitted in any form or by any means—electronic, mechanical, photocopy, recording, or otherwise—without written permission of the publisher, except for brief quotations in printed reviews.

Scripture taken from the King James Version or the New King James Version (copyright © 1982 by Thomas Nelson, Inc. Used by permission. All rights reserved.).

The persons and events portrayed in this work are the creations of the author, and any resemblance to persons living or dead is purely coincidental.

Library of Congress Cataloging-in-Publication Data
Whitener, Rusty
A season of miracles : a novel / Rusty Whitener.
p. cm.
1. Male friendship—Fiction. 2. Southern States—Fiction. 3. Nineteen seventies—Fiction. I. Title.
PS3623.H5846S43 2010 813'.6—dc22 2010016906

ISBN 978-0-8254-4191-2

Printed in the United States of America

10 11 12 13 14/ 5 4 3 2 1

To the real Rebecca,
the love of my life.
And to Mr. Evans,
my Little League coach,
who had the heart and the guts
to play a little kid like me.

PROLOGUE

I pulled the 4Runner close to the broken chain-link fence. Setting the parking brake, I opened the door and stepped out into the hazy, early March dusk of Silas, Alabama.

Walking slowly, I reached the opening and stopped at the low outfield fence, hanging loose and separated from the poles set in the ground. That fence had been tight as saplings during another early March.

How are you doing, Rafer? I'll be running those fields again with you. One day.

The years of our lives are not evenly weighted. Childhood is heaviest, sinking us deep in the space that will be our field of running, falling, and rising again. Middle age pushes the borders, straining the field's limits. Then come the later years, lighter than we had imagined, until the final seasons when we step like sparrows on the earth. In the end, we are without weight.

That was you, Rafer. I thought you and I were the same age. But you were almost weightless even then, when I saw you for the first time…

CHAPTER 1

I didn't set out to believe in miracles. Nobody does. That's what makes them miracles.

The year 1971 would pick me up in a tornado of changes and set me down in an amazing place of grace. Like Dorothy in *The Wizard of Oz*, it would be a kind of homecoming, except that I would be coming home for the first time.

Around the middle of March, about the time my hometown of Silas started to escape the gray Alabama winter, Little League baseball would crowd out everything else for my attention.

I wasn't alone. Those days, Little League in our county was akin to a small-town parade down Main Street. Everybody went, not really expecting to see the remarkable so much as the familiar. Pretty near every boy in town played the game. And most every player's parents went to watch, clap, groan, and cheer.

Little League is a game played by Charlie Browns and Joe DiMaggios. Most children that age are Charlie Browns, still struggling with how to handle an oversized pencil, let alone how to grip a baseball and hurl it a particular direction. They are likely to throw the ball farther from their target than it was when they retrieved it. They even look like you imagine Charlie Brown would, running in preadolescent distress to recover the ball they just threw in the wrong direction. On the weaker Little League teams, Charlie Browns mosey around the outfield, and DiMaggios man the infield. Players who hit the ball over the infielders' heads usually have an easy double. Stronger teams have a DiMaggio anchoring center field, or maybe left. If anyone better than Charlie is in right, then either the team is stacked with talent or something magical is going on. Maybe both.

I don't remember ever not being able to hit the ball hard. I didn't think much about it, really. Relax, breathe, bring the bat to the ball, and drive it on a line. I was a little tall for my twelve years, but I also had something much better than size. Confidence. I knew I could hit the ball, and hit it hard. Not every time, but most of the time. And batting over .500 with power will scorch any league.

I was the best hitter I had ever seen. Until 1971.

It was a cool Saturday in mid March. I called my best friend, Donnie White, and he called Batman Boatwright and Jimmy Yarnell. I really didn't spend a lot of time with Batman and Jimmy the rest of the year. Just spring and early summer. When Little League season came into focus, so did Batman and Jimmy.

I always took the back way to the old field, cutting through woods so thick and dark it was like traveling and hiding at the same time. My wicked cool Sting-Ray, with butterfly handlebars and a fat banana seat covered in leopard spots, gave me an edge in races with the guys. But in woods that thick, I'd just get to pumping the pedals hard before I'd have to dismount and negotiate the bramble bushes and low hanging, cobwebbed pines that duped nature by growing with so little sun.

Sawdust wasn't real keen on those woods. A hound-collie mix, he had followed me home two summers before and decided I needed him. Through these woods, along the rough path of moss and bracken, he got nervous when I had to stop the bike and walk. He looked back and forth and around, seemingly wary that something might sneak up on us. He barked his approval when we climbed the last ridge and tumbled out of the sun-spun shadows crisscrossing our wooded trek and into the sun's soaring shine over the ancient baseball field behind Mill Creek Fire Station.

It wasn't a real baseball diamond anymore, just a big space of worn-down grass. But it was enough of a practice field for us. There was even an outfield fence of sorts, a lot of chain no longer linked. A backstop someone put up years before helped us out. If the ball got by the hitter, it caromed off the chain links and dribbled in the general direction of the pitcher. If it didn't get a good enough carom to send it close to the mound, the batter picked it up and tossed it back to the pitcher. Who needed a catcher?

Donnie, Batman, and Jimmy were already there, tossing the ball in a triangular game of catch.

"It's about time, Pardner!" Donnie raised his arms in a "What's the deal?" gesture. "We're startin' to take root here." He dropped his arms and threw the ball too high in Jimmy's direction. Jimmy threw his glove after the ball, and then turned to look at Donnie like he couldn't believe he put up with a friend who threw that poorly.

"Sorry," said Donnie with a big smile. "Too high, I guess."

"Zack," Jimmy said, turning to me, "can you tell this guy about cool?"

"What do I know about cool?" I said, not really asking.

Sawdust barked at Jimmy and Batman, darting between the two. He made quick little circles around Jimmy, like they were old friends. They weren't.

"Whaddya always have to bring the mutt for?" Jimmy sounded seriously miffed.

"Sawdust likes chasing the balls," I said.

"I know *that*," said Jimmy. "He gets 'em all slimy."

Batman drawled, "He's got your glove now, Hoss."

Jimmy gave a squawk and bounded after Sawdust, who was running in large circles back and forth across the field.

"I'll make a glove outta you, ya mutt!" Jimmy's threat broke us up, and I laughed pretty hard until I saw the new kid. At first, I thought something was seriously wrong; he was so still. He sat at the base of a tree, his back ramrod straight against the trunk, his legs straight out from his body, arms at his sides. He looked almost unreal, not moving his head, stock-still, eyes frozen. Not moving anything.

"Whatcha looking at, Pardner?" Donnie gave nicknames to people he really liked, and people he struggled to like. Come to think of it, that's just about everybody. He once told me it was hard to call someone by a good nickname and still not like them. Donnie wanted to like everybody.

"That boy," I said, "over there."

"Oh man, he don't look so good." Donnie stared. "He even... is he alive?"

"What kind of a question is that?" I said, staring at the kid under the tree, who still had not moved. "Of course he's alive. I mean... don't you think?"

Batman jogged up to us. "Are we gonna play or what?"

"Look at that kid over there." Donnie pointed with his gloved hand.

"I see him," Batman said. "So what?"

"Is he alive?"

"Whaddya mean?"

"I mean he doesn't look alive." Donnie said the words slowly, as if he were announcing something important, like the moral at the end of a story.

"Well he's not dead," said Batman.

"How do you know?" I asked.

"Because he sits there like that all the time. I've seen him before, when we come here to play."

"Really?"

"Lots of times," Batman said. "I think he's a retard."

"Come off it." Donnie looked at Batman and shook his head, like he was disappointed in him.

"It's the Forrester kid," Batman said. "Everybody knows he's touched." Batman was blowing massive bubbles and struggling to move the gum to the side of his mouth so he could talk. "Don't tell me y'all haven't seen him at school."

"I seen him," said Donnie.

"I don't think I have," I said. "How come, you reckon?"

"Maybe 'cause you're always looking at Rebecca Carson," Batman joshed. "Anyway, he's touched."

"Okay, he's got some problems... ," Donnie started.

Batman decided to pluck the wad of gum out of his mouth and hold it in his free hand, a rare move he reserved for emergencies. "*Serious* problems," said Batman.

"Okay," said Donnie, "serious problems, but we don't have to call him—"

"Hey guys," I said. "Guys, I think he's coming over here."

The Forrester kid was on his feet, walking toward us.

"Holy metropolis," Batman whistled. "Look alert, Batfans."

Jimmy ran up, holding his glove away from his body, between a thumb and forefinger, the leather shiny with Sawdust drool.

"This is so foul, y'all. I can't play with this nasty thing. Do y'all... do y'all know that fella is coming over here?"

"Yeah Jimmy, we know," I said.

"Do y'all... do y'all know he's a retard?"

"He's *not* a retard. He has some problems, that's all," said Donnie, loudly.

"His problem is he's a retard—and his dad's a drunk, 'cording to my folks."

I really don't think Jimmy meant to say anything mean. That's just the way he was. Shoot from the lip and take no prisoners.

"Shut up, Jimmy," Donnie's voice was a sharp whisper now. "There's nothing wrong with his ears."

Rafer Forrester walked straight up to me, stepping up close, his face no more than a foot from mine. The other kids instinctively took half-steps back, clumsily trying to give me more space. Sawdust sauntered into the picture, sat down razor close to Rafer and put a paw on the boy's shoe. Without looking, Rafer put his hand on the dog's head and stroked it.

"Hey," I said quietly. "How's it going?"

I guess I hadn't really expected an answer. But I did expect him to say *something*. After some long seconds, he did.

"Hit."

"You wanna hit?" I asked.

Silence.

"You wanna hit?" I said again.

"Hit. Rafer hit." His face was still void of expression.

I heard Jimmy's voice behind me. "I think the fella wants to try to hit the baseball."

"You mean the ball?" I held it up in front of me, about six inches from his eyes.

"I don't think he's blind, Zack-man," Batman said, his voice joining Jimmy's in a nervous flutter of laughs.

"All right, guys," said Donnie. "Hey, Pardner, why don't you let him try?"

"Oh, come on, Donnie," Batman said. "Jimmy and me gotta go in about thirty minutes. We don't have time."

"Let him try, Pardner. Just a couple of tosses." Donnie was already walking toward home plate. "I'll catch so we don't have to keep fetching the balls."

I looked right in Rafer's eyes. "You want to hit the baseball a little?"

"Rafer hit."

"Okay, Rafer. Do you wanna take the ball yourself"—I pressed the ball gently in his hand—"and just toss it up in the air and hit it?" I figured he could do that. Hitting a pitched ball didn't seem plausible, no matter how slow I tossed it.

"Rafer hit." He pushed the ball back at me.

Batman moaned and sat down on the ground. "C'mon guys, we're wasting time."

"Okay, I can pitch it," I said.

Rafer walked slowly toward home plate and picked up the bat. Donnie was already crouched behind the plate calling to me. "Okay, Pardner. Toss it in, and Rafe here is gonna knock the cover off the ball. Here we go, Pardner."

Rafer stopped in front of Donnie and said, loud enough for everyone to hear, "Zack pitch. No Pardner."

Behind me I heard Jimmy's chuckle. Batman, sitting on the ground behind the pitcher's mound, laughed so hard his gum started slipping down the back of his throat. "Oh ... oh, my gosh. I almost swallowed it, y'all," he managed to say.

Donnie just smiled real big at Rafer. "That's right, Rafer, my buddy. He is Zack." Then, rocking back and forth in a low catcher's crouch, he called to me. "Okay, Zack, just toss it in gentle-like."

So I did. I tossed the ball underhand, as slow as I could, across the plate. As fat a pitch as I could make it.

Rafer didn't swing. He watched the pitch the whole way and the bat never left his shoulder. Donnie threw the ball back to me, and I tossed it again. Again, no swing.

From his spot now reclining on the ground, his head resting on his glove, Batman's groans were like a sick boy's. "Oh, guys. We're gonna be here all day. And we gotta go home soon."

"Batman," said Jimmy, "if we gotta go home soon, then we can't be here all day."

Jimmy crashed on the ground next to Batman, resting his head on his glove. An odd expression invaded his face. He bolted upright, frantically wiping dog spit from the back of his head. "Oh, that's stinking! Oh, that's so raw!"

Batman just groaned again.

Donnie called to me, "Maybe you need to get closer, Pardner ... I mean Zack. You know, toss it from a shorter distance."

I started to step off the mound. Rafer bellowed, "No!"

I froze.

"No!" he said again. "Zack pitch. Rafer hit."

"Okay, okay." I got back on the mound. I tossed it again,

underhanded, only this time as the ball was crossing home plate, Rafer caught it with his right hand. He dropped the bat. For several seconds he did not move. "Zack pitch," he said again as he started moving through an elaborate windup, turning his body like Tom Seaver and kicking his leg high like Juan Marichal, coming down with his throwing hand over the top. The ball rocketed from his hand to my glove, which I reflexively raised to protect my face.

Dead silence.

Then Jimmy drawled, "Well, good night, y'all."

Donnie, barely audible, said, "He wants you to pitch it fast, I guess. God help us." I wasn't sure what to do. I had a strong arm from playing third base.

"Come on, Zack. Fire it in here." Donnie was suddenly confident about the situation.

"Can you catch it?" I asked him.

"Oh, come on, of course I can catch it. You're not *that* fast, you know."

That was all my adolescent ears needed to hear. I wound up and released, letting the ball spring naturally out of my grip. The ball, a white blur, crossed the heart of the plate.

At least it would have.

Rafer dropped the head of the bat, quick like a cat, just in front of the ball. Coaches tell hitters to focus on getting the barrel of the bat on the ball, and let the pitched ball do all the real work, ricocheting off the bat. That's what Rafer did. And my perfect strike was now a perfect line drive, streaking into the gap in left center field. It had just started to drop when it banged off the old outfield fence.

"Throw him another one, Pardner!" yelled Donnie.

"He Zack," said Rafer.

"I know, I know, he Zack! I mean, he's Zack. Throw him another one, Pardner! And put some real zip on it this time."

I wound up and put everything I had into the pitch. Again, Rafer swung as if he were simply dropping the bat onto the ball in one quick, measured motion. The ball left his bat and left no doubt. It cleared the fence in left field, disappearing in trees ten or fifteen feet past the fence. We had never seen a ball travel that far off this field. Not even when Jimmy's brother, a starter on the high school JV team, had tossed a few in the air and socked them as far as he could.

"Don't throw him any more," Jimmy hollered, climbing over the fence with Batman after the ball. "These are my brother's balls, and he'll kill me if I don't bring 'em all back."

Donnie ran out to me at the mound. "Are you thinking what I'm thinking? We can get him. I bet he ain't on a team... I bet my silver dollar he ain't. We can get him."

I walked up to Rafer, still standing in the batter's box, expressionless. "Rafer, how old are you?"

"Rafer twelve."

Donnie went into a silent victory dance, a kind of jump and twirl.

"Do you wanna play on our team, on our Little League team, the Robins?"

"Yeah. I play."

"Great," I said, trying to stay calm. "Great, Rafer. We're going to have tryouts, right across the street, at McInerney Elementary School." I pointed in the direction. "Right on that field, this coming Monday after school. Can you be there?"

He didn't seem to get what I said. Just when I thought he wasn't going to say any words, he said three.

"Mack... and Ernie."

"Who are they?" said Donnie. "No, no, you tell him we just want him."

Donnie was standing right next to both of us. I didn't know why he thought I was Rafer's interpreter, except that I kind of felt that way too. Like I was a bridge between Rafer and Donnie and whomever.

"Who are Mack and Ernie, Rafer?" I asked.

"Mack and Ernie School."

"Oh." I smiled. "I get it. Hey, that's pretty funny, Rafer."

Only Rafer wasn't smiling, and I worried about him not showing up for the tryouts.

"Rafer, can you be here"—I pointed to the ground—"next Saturday?" I figured I could walk across the street with him to the actual tryouts.

"Mack and Ernie," he said without expression.

Donnie started to laugh and I gave him a sharp look. I was trying to get something important done.

"Rafer, I will meet you right here, next Saturday, by your tree." I pointed. "Then you and me will go to tryouts… I mean, play some baseball together. All right? Saturday morning. Is that okay?"

"Rafer hit."

"That's right. Saturday morning, you'll hit."

"I hit Saturday." I probably imagined it, but it looked like his mouth was turning at the corners in a small smile. Then he turned and started to walk. He passed his tree.

Watching Rafer disappear into the woods, I heard Donnie's anxious voice. "We can't let the other coaches see him bat. We gotta find a way to make him a Robin without, you know, without the others seeing him bat."

"I know," I said. "I'll think of something."

From a long ways off we heard Jimmy, sounding like someone you hear hollering when you're in your house with the windows closed.

"I found it. Hey guys, I… found… it."

CHAPTER 2

Sixth grade. You're a tweener. You're on the edge. You haven't crossed into teenage wasteland. Anxious to be older, you believe the teen years will bring better things. It's almost impossible as a twelve-year-old to recognize the beauty of childhood. You're so anxious for what's coming, you can't appreciate what you will have to leave behind.

In sixth grade, I still read schoolbooks at the little desk in my room. A lot of times, I'd roll a baseball back and forth slowly on the desktop. Next year, in junior high, the ball would graduate with me and my schoolbooks to a new site for homework—my bed. But in that last year of grade school, my desk still functioned as something more than a big flat shelf.

I was reading a world history textbook at my desk. Ancient Romans staged scenes for me.

I felt Sawdust saunter leisurely into my room, so I started to read aloud. He might be interested.

"While the Greeks were known for great ideas, the Romans were feared for their great armies."

Without looking, I dropped the baseball into my lap and reached backward with my hand, feeling for Sawdust's head.

Nimble as a jewel thief, he ducked around my hand, snatched the baseball out of my lap, and started slinking away.

"Hey, hey, hey. Come back here, boy."

His eyes shining at the thrill of the game, Sawdust brought the ball back and dropped it in my lap. He wagged his tail peaceably.

"I hit this ball over the fence twice in one game last year. Twice, Sawdust!"

He appeared marveled by my words, as if this were the first time he'd heard about such an incredible feat. Dogs are great that way.

"So we won... third place. Third place is where us Robins live. The Hawks play somebody else in the really big game. Usually the Eagles."

Out the corner of my eye, I saw Mom at my open door. "Third place is pretty good, ya know." She walked across the room, pausing to drop a stack of clean clothes on my bed, then put her hands on my shoulders and affectionately laid her chin on the top of my head. I always thought she was the one who had shown Sawdust that thing about resting your head on someone else.

I frowned. "Third place is third place."

"That's very profound. What's it mean?"

"You know," I said. "Third place feels like I failed."

My dad came in the room. "What's going on in here?"

Sawdust bustled up to him, a furry ball of celebration. It's not that he especially liked Dad, or was his dog. He wasn't; he was mine. He just liked having the whole pack together. And in Master Zack's room, too!

"Sawdust," said Dad, "did you call a family conference without me?"

"Zack's disenchanted with third place," Mom sighed.

"Good! Always go for first place or nothing, son. That's the American way!" His enthusiasm was infectious enough to convert Sawdust, who let out a yelp.

"Easy boy," Dad patted the dog's side and flanks. "First place, Zack," he said again. "Vince Lombardi would be proud, and so am I."

"Genghis Khan would be proud too," Mom said with a straight face.

"Play to win." Dad didn't quite catch Mom's comment. "Nice guys finish last."

"Nice guys finish last." When Mom said it, it sounded like a eulogy. "Is that Lombardi's genius too?"

"Leo Durocher," Dad announced. Mom was not impressed. "C'mon Paulette, Durocher's a baseball *legend*, for crying out loud."

I broke in, smiling. "You can't argue with a legend, Mom."

"A *legend*? If he's such a legend, how come I've never heard of him? Babe Ruth is a legend. Willie Mays is a legend."

"Mays is still playing," Dad announced.

"Okay, so he's a living legend," she sighed. "But the only Leo I know is the butcher at the Piggly Wiggly."

"Leo Durocher played on the same team with Babe Ruth," Dad said, pressing his pointless point. "And he was Willie Mays's first manager."

Mom put her arm around Dad's shoulder. "Well then, he brushed up against legends. But he himself remains a non-legend."

"What's a non-legend?" I asked for fun.

"A non-legend," Mom smiled, "is anybody who goes to the Piggly Wiggly to get their meat from another non-legend named Leo."

I laughed. Dad and Sawdust did too. Mom was sharp. And Dad loved that she was sharp, which made Mom love Dad even more.

Mom pulled a small trophy down off the little shelf over my desk.

"See this, honey?" She held it in front of me. "You hit two home runs in that game, and you and Donnie and all the boys played the best you could, and you got third place. That is a big, brilliant, start-the-parade accomplishment, honey."

Behind her, my dad shook his head. He put up an index finger and mouthed a silent "first place" to me. Of course, Mom turned sharply and saw him. She poked him hard in the ribs.

"Ooowww," Dad winced.

Sawdust cocked his head at this mini display of domestic agitation. Mom set the trophy down on the desk in front of me and walked out, head high.

"Ow again," said Dad, holding his side. "That was a good one." He straightened up, walked to the door, and said before leaving, "Third place is ... third place. First place ... well, that would be better, wouldn't it?"

I put the little trophy back on the shelf. Just over its spot, I had taped a poster of the Pirates' Roberto Clemente on my wall.

"The Pirates come in third all the time," I said to my canine confidant.

I looked at the schoolbook, still open on my desk, and read aloud.

"The Romans were feared for their great army, laying waste to any country threatening the rule of Rome."

I looked earnestly at Sawdust, who returned my sincere gaze. "You think nice guys can finish first, boy?" I asked him. I read aloud again. "The Robins were feared for their great plays, laying waste to any team threatening the rule of the Little League."

I took the baseball in my right hand and held it high overhead so Sawdust could see it. He got interested right away. I dropped it. He jumped to catch it, and bounded out of the room with it. When I didn't follow, or even call after him, he peeked back inside my room, the ball protruding from his snout.

"You can have it," I said. "It's a third place baseball."

CHAPTER 3

It was cold, windy, and seriously threatening to rain hard and heavy. March still thought it was coming in instead of going out. But I was excited. Tryouts had always seemed kind of silly to me before. This time, though, if I worked it right, something really neat was going to happen for my team. We would be getting a twelve-year-old Hank Aaron to play for us. I just had to figure out how to keep other coaches from picking him so our coach could take him.

All us returning Robins knew we were Robins no matter what happened in tryouts. It was really only the new kids that had to find a team to call home. They would be Blue Jays, Cardinals, Eagles, Falcons, Hawks, Ravens, or Robins.

Every new player had to try out. It was a rule, we were told, designed to protect kids. Looking back, I think the real purpose was to protect coaches from each other and from scheming parents. Everybody wanted a clear view of how a player really performed. There were to be no surprises once the season started. No hidden Sandy Koufax. No "tryout Jerry Lewis" transformed suddenly on Opening Day into a young Mickey Mantle, rocketing balls off his bat that only he could catch had he been in the field.

"See that tall, red-headed guy with the orange jersey? He looks pretty good, don't you think?" Donnie leaned next to me against the chain-link bordering the right field side of the diamond.

"He's not that tall," I said. "He's just thin. He's got some pop."

"Some pop? He's got Pentecostal power in his bat!"

That was a new one. "What kind of power?" I looked at my best friend.

"You know." Donnie smiled big. "Firepower!"

"You mean *mis*fire," I corrected. "Like when the rifle jams. He just missed two pitches. And they're putting them right there, right in the zone."

"Yeah but when he got it, he got it all!" said Donnie, raising his cap overhead like a rally flag. Everybody liked Donnie. I envied him, his easy talk and easier smile. His dad, a Baptist preacher, loved Silas and the town loved him back. A gentle, quiet man of practical faith. A servant. Donnie had his dad's heart and his mom's quick mind and mouth.

Words and laughs didn't come as easy to me.

We walked to the bleachers to sit near our coach, Mr. Hornbuckle. He was scribbling on a clipboard with his right hand, slowly turning his cap backward with his left, and chewing four full pieces of Bazooka gum. I knew it was four, because I'd asked him once.

"I always use four, Zack. Can't really taste just two or three. Can you?"

I told him my mom didn't want me chewing gum.

"Zack, I am sure you will live a long, happy life. Not because you don't chew gum, but because you do what your mom says." He was right.

"How's it looking, Coach?" Donnie asked. We took a bleacher spot a few seats away, figuring he wanted to take some private notes.

"Hey, Donnie. Zack, where's your shadow, guy?" Coach smiled. "Never seen you without Sawdust."

"He's off somewhere, in his world," I said. "He'll show up."

"How's it looking, Coach?" Donnie asked again.

"Well... I don't have to tell you two we need at least one more big stick if we're going to win it this year."

Donnie and I weren't about to say exactly what we both thought. *Coach, we need about four or five or six more big sticks if we're even going to smell first place this year. Maybe we should just let the Cincinnati Reds show up in our uniforms to give the Hawks a real run for their money.*

"And the only stick I've seen is Steve Malcomb's kid."

"The orange jersey," I said.

"Yeah," Coach nodded. "You saw him too, huh? Well, guess where he's going."

"Not the Eagles, I hope," I said. "They're already packed this year. I mean, they're not the Hawks, but they don't need anybody else. We do. And so do the Cardinals. And the Ravens lost just about—"

"He's going to the Hawks," said Coach.

"No way!" Donnie's voice cracked.

"Oh yeah," Coach said, keeping his eyes fixed on the field where a ten-year-old had bravely decided his foot was better at stopping ground balls than his glove.

"How can they do that?" I asked. "Don't the Hawks pick last? I mean, since they won it last year?"

"And the year before that," said Donnie, "and the year before *that!*"

"You'd think so, wouldn't you?" Coach was chuckling. Mr. Hornbuckle had a habit of laughing when other people thought he should be getting mad.

"Fact is, the boy is the Hawks' coach's nephew. We coaches have always agreed that if you're related to the boy, you should be able to have him on your team. Makes it more of a family league, you know."

Booger Clark, the Hawks' catcher, passed in front of us on his way to meet up with his team. Nobody seemed to know his real name. Everybody called him "Boog" because his hair was dirty blond like the Baltimore Orioles' slugger Boog Powell. We called him Booger. Sometimes to his face. He was a player; his batting average was about three times his fatty 140 pounds.

"Hey, losers," Booger mumbled through a humorless laugh.

"Come over here," I said loudly, "and we'll see who loses."

"Leave it be, Zack," Coach counseled.

I stayed locked in a stare with Booger. When he reached the area where the Hawks were gathered, he jumped his pitcher from behind and dragged him to the ground.

"What're you… get off me, Boog!"

Booger whined, mimicking the other boy. "Mommy, Mommy, the big bad boogeyman threw me down." He smirked at his teammate.

Bullying always seemed to light a fire under me. "Somebody's gotta straighten that kid out."

"Maybe so," Coach said quietly, "but it's not your job."

We were quiet for a while, contemplating many injustices. The coaches, scattered to various observation posts around and beside the field, watched as two other youngsters fielded ground balls.

"Coach," Donnie spoke up, "do you have any nephews who can hit?"

Mr. Hornbuckle tried to laugh and answer at the same time. "No, no, I don't have any of those."

I figured it was time to tell him and just let him decide if I was loony or brilliant. "Coach, I got to tell you this," I said, looking at my glove in my lap, "and I understand if you want to think I'm crazy or you just want to laugh or what have you. But… well… there's a kid here trying out who hits like he belongs in a higher league. A much higher league."

I paused a moment. For some reason my heart was pounding. *Just forget it. It's ridiculous. What are you thinking?*

"Well, son," said Coach, "you better point him out to me, and you better do it real fast, 'cause if you don't, Lonnie'll be penciling him on his roster."

The three of us watched the Hawks' coach, Mr. Lonnie Malcomb, handing the tall boy in the orange jersey a snow cone, patting him on the back.

"And buying him a cherry snow cone to boot," Coach said soberly.

"He's over there, sitting against that tree." I nodded in the direction of a barren, gray cottonwood on the perimeter of the school yard. Coach looked and saw Rafer sitting at the base of the tree.

"I'm not kidding," I said, my voice rising. "I'm telling you, that guy hits like... like Johnny Bench and Pete Rose *combined.* Line shots and deep shots."

"You wouldn't be pulling my chain, would you, son?"

"He's Babe Ruth and Ty Cobb, Coach! You ever seen him hit?"

"Can't say I have. But I ain't seen my grandma hit, neither. Don't have to."

I jumped down the bleacher steps to the ground.

"Where you going?" asked Donnie.

"I'm going to get him to bat," I said, walking away.

Donnie hustled up next to me and tried to talk in a whisper. "Zack, what are you doing? You can't let him hit in front of all the coaches and God and everybody. Remember what we said?"

"Yeah, yeah. I just don't feel right about it." I stopped and turned to my friend. "What about you? Doesn't it bother you that we're gonna try to sneak this guy onto our team? It's just wrong, Donnie."

"Yeah, it bothers me," he said. "Not enough to... to not do it, though," he said honestly.

I stopped and looked into my friend's eyes. "I'm surprised, Donnie," I said evenly. "Sometimes you really surprise me."

He just smiled a kind of silly, simple look. "I'm not an angel, Zack."

"I know, I know." I felt a little embarrassed, and it struck me that maybe he should be the one feeling funny, not me. But he looked perfectly at peace.

"I'm just like you," he said.

I wasn't sure what that was supposed to mean, but it was something Donnie said to me regularly.

"We're no different," said Donnie. "Except for the 'forgiven' thing."

He had said that same "'forgiven' thing" before too, more than once, on those days we loved to spend at the swimming hole.

"We both do bad stuff." He said it matter-of-factly, like he was giving a book report. "It's just that I get forgiven, and you don't."

"If that's true," I said, "then it's not fair."

"That's right. It's not fair." I didn't understand it, but Donnie sure did.

I started walking quickly again toward Rafer and his tree, and I used my best "cooler-than-you" voice on my friend. "Well, if it bothers you that we're trying to sneak him onto the team, then I'd think you'd want to help me make things right here." I thought I sounded more right than Donnie. Only I didn't feel more right.

"Lots of things bother me." Donnie scurried after me pleading. "Right now, mostly it bothers me that every year we beat everybody but the Hawks. I even prayed about it this year, Pardner. I prayed God would let us beat them, just once this year, before we're out of Little League."

"And you think God is answering your prayer with Rafer," I said. "Didn't you tell me God doesn't work that way? That he's not a candy store?"

"I was just telling you what my dad told me."

"So he *is* a candy store?" I stopped walking.

"I was hoping he might be, just this once." He smiled at me.

"All this God stuff . . . ," I paused. "It messes up my head."

"That happens to me too, Pardner. Going to church helps me clear things up. You oughta come with me."

"My parents never go."

"So that means you can't? Come on, Pard . . . whoa . . ."

I stopped so fast that Donnie bumped into me.

"What's the deal?"

Then he saw it too. A few yards away, Sawdust was sitting still, facing Rafer, who was patting the dog's head. Only it was not really like you'd pat a dog. It was more like just placing his hands repeatedly on Sawdust's head, just touching his head lightly, over and over.

"Well, look a yonder," Donnie said. "Looks like he's anointing him."

"I don't think he's annoying him. Appears to me, Sawdust likes it."

"I said *anointing*, not annoying," said Donnie. "It's like blessing him or something."

"Whatever." I called to Rafer, "It's time to hit, Rafer. Come on."

Donnie gave a final appeal. "You're sure about this? You're gonna let all them other coaches see him, Zack?"

"We are going to do this right," I said. "Rafer is going to try out, and the coaches are going to pick him if they want him."

"I was afraid you were going to say something like that." Donnie sighed. "It was a nice dream while it lasted."

Rafer picked up an ancient glove from the ground beside him and walked stiffly to us, Sawdust trailing him blissfully. "Rafer hit," he said.

"Okay. Let's go." We walked with him to the stack of bats. Rafer never looked at the different styles or lengths. To him, a bat was a bat. He dropped his glove and took a bat in hand.

Mr. Auld, the man running the tryouts, called me over. "Zachary, son, has this boy signed in yet? He's supposed to sign up for the tryout and get a number."

"I don't know that he can write real good, Mr. Auld. Can't you just give him a number, whatever the next one is?"

Mr. Auld looked up into the bleachers where coaches were listening and talking among themselves. Mr. McKenzie, the Eagles' coach, said "Go ahead and let him bat, Fred. Just give him a number."

I picked Rafer's glove off the ground and marveled. Long, brutal baseball wars were written all over it. Two fingers were gone entirely.

"All right." I heard Mr. Auld's voice. "Coaches, this is Rafer Forrester. He will be number twenty-eight."

I watched Rafer walk with deliberate, measured steps into the batter's box and stand there motionless. The pitcher, an assistant coach with the Falcons, went into his casual tryout windup and tossed the ball easily over the plate. Rafer only watched.

"All right, son," the pitcher said, catching the throw back from the catcher. "Here it comes, now. Ready?"

He threw the ball again, another good pitch to hit, the ball floating easily over the plate. No swing.

He stopped pitching, putting his hands on his hips. Looking into the bleachers at the other coaches, he called out, "What should we do, guys?"

I spoke up. "You have to throw the ball hard, mister."

"Don't tell him that," Donnie whispered beside me.

"You have to pitch it hard," I repeated.

"I don't think so, son." The pitcher had that look adults get when they're sorry but they have to correct you.

"No, really, you have to—" My voice was interrupted by a loud thunderclap.

"Everybody off the field!" Mr. Auld yelled. "Over to the snack bar!"

Coaches scrambled off the bleachers and ran toward the concession stand, a small snack bar with an overhanging roof. In only seconds, the rain fell in heavy sheets.

I ran up alongside Mr. Auld, who was frantically gathering scattered papers from a small table.

"What about Rafer?" I shouted over the rain.

"I don't know, Zachary." I caught some of the papers the wind was threatening to run off with and gave them to him. "Thank you, son. Come on now." He and I both ran to the snack bar and crowded against the wall with the others. Only then did I look back toward the field to try to spot Rafer. He was gone.

The thick rain was already forming ponds where the field dipped and sank in places.

"I think tryouts are over, son," said Mr. Auld.

"What about Rafer?" I asked again.

It was hard to hear, with the thunder, and with the rain pelting off the roof. But I thought I could make out the voices of some of the coaches.

"It doesn't matter to me."

"I'm fine with it. I can't see why, but if he wants him, he can have him."

"I think it's pretty big of Hornbuckle."

Mr. Malcomb, the Hawks' coach, crowded up next to Mr. Auld, on the other side of me. "Fred," he said, "if Hornbuckle wants the Forrester boy, he can have him. More power to him. I think we're through here, don't you?"

"That's fine." Mr. Auld nodded his head, and made a quick little mark on a crumpled sheet of paper.

I felt a hand on my shoulder and turned to see Coach Hornbuckle smiling at me, his face, cap, and shirt soaked with rain.

"We got him," said Coach. "But you know, Zack, he didn't look so good up there. I'm thinking he just swings at every third pitch. Is that it?"

Before I could answer, Donnie and Sawdust both took off running, out into the hard rain and onto the playing field. They ran back and forth together, crisscrossing the field, Donnie shrieking over the storm and Sawdust yelping like he had just treed a raccoon. I heard one of the coaches behind me, bellowing. "Who's that kid out there? Hey, get back in here outta that rain!"

"Ah, leave him be," said Mr. Auld.

"He's gettin' sopping wet. Crazy kid. Who is he?"

"That's Donnie White," I said. I heard my friend still howling over the sound of the downpour.

"I knew it!" Donnie's excited voice and Sawdust's raucous bark cut through the wind. "I knew you'd do it! Thank you! I knew it!"

"I'm with you, Ernie," said Coach Malcomb. "That kid better get over here. He could get hit, you know. By lightning."

"It's already happened," I said quietly.

CHAPTER 4

The 1971 Robins gathered for their first practice on the dried-out ball field behind the fire station. The older kids, veterans like me, were excited to be back to finish our time in Little League with the team that had launched our careers. Life has a sense of humor. On a Little League team, pimples mean you're one of the old guys.

The others, the rookies, were three very nervous ten-year-olds. The twelve-year-old rookie didn't seem nervous at all. He was different.

We loitered around home plate, joshing and jiving. BoDean's transistor radio, hanging on the backstop's wiring, was playing a song about wanting to change things, to even see the whole world changed. Only you don't know how to do that, so you decide you'll let someone else shoulder that burden. I wasn't sure what all that meant, but the song had an unforgettable guitar lick.

A few of the guys sat on their gloves with their backs against the backstop. April is a hot month in Alabama. I saw Coach at a distance, pulling baseball gear out of the back of his station wagon.

"Who's the creepy kid?" Our catcher, Duffey, was eyeballing Rafer, who was sitting under his tree. Duffey's massive girth fooled other teams into thinking he wasn't coordinated.

"His name's Rafer," I said. "He's not creepy."

"Oh, yes he is," Jimmy chimed in. "He's touched."

"Knock it off." I didn't like that word.

"Who touched him?"

I whirled, ready to light into somebody, and saw the question had come from a new kid, a really small guy with freckles and red hair the color of fire ants. His question was honest.

"Hi." I put my hand out. "My name's Zack. What's yours?"

"I know your name." He stuck his hand out so fast he forgot he had a glove on it. "Everybody knows your name, Zack," said the little guy, nervously taking his glove off his right hand to shake. His hand disappeared in mine.

"A lefty, huh? That's good. We need another lefty." I tapped him on the head with my gloved hand and he giggled. "Do you bat left too?"

"I don't know."

Only a Little League rookie would answer like that. "I don't know" means "I've never really played this game before."

"What'd you say your name was?" I asked.

"Oh," he blushed. "My name's Richard."

"Well, I'm pleased to meet you, Richard."

"Hey, Pardner!" Looking in the direction of Donnie's voice, I saw him chugging out of the woods just behind the left field fence. He tossed his glove over and then gripped the top of the chain-link fence and hauled himself over, plopping down on the other side. "Is he here yet?" He picked up his glove and jogged toward us.

"He's here. Where've you been?"

"Mom wanted me to empty the trash cans. I told her"—Donnie took a quick breath, downshifting to a fast-paced walk—"I told her that takes too long and we were having our first practice and all." He sidled up to the group. "That went over like World War III. You know moms. Where is he?"

"He's just sitting there at his tree. Yonder." I pointed.

"Oh, yeah. Hey, Rafer," Donnie called, "come on over." Rafer didn't move or even look up.

...ntington City Township
Public Library
255 West Park Drive
Huntington, IN 46750
www.huntingtonpub.lib.in.us

"Donnie, this is Richard," I said. "Richard already knew my name."

"Hey, Richard buddy, how's it going?" Donnie put out his hand, and Richard, who had put his glove back on his right hand, did his little act again, nervously extending his gloved hand, realizing his gaffe, and dropping his glove on the ground while he put his right hand out again.

"Kind of a nervous little fellow, aren't you?" Donnie grinned. "And a lefty. Well, we don't need any more lefties."

"You don't?" Richard was crushed.

"Donnie!" I said with some heat. "Why don't you just tell him to get lost?"

"Should I go home?" Richard was serious.

"Go home? What for?" Donnie rebounded. "Then we wouldn't have that left-handed hitter we've been looking for." He put a hand on the little fellow's head.

"But what if I don't field too good?"

"I'll teach you. I know everything there is to know about it."

"Gee, thanks." Richard beamed. "What did you say your name was?"

"Hey, Zack said you already knew *his* name." Donnie kidded in a tone serious and teasing at the same time. "If you know Zack, you gotta know me."

"Well, I guess... I guess I know Zack because he's a really great hitter."

There was a chorus of laughs and taunts directed at Donnie from the other kids. Donnie put his arm around Richard's shoulder. "Remember the name Donnie, my new little friend Richard. Hey... 'little friend Richard.' I like that. Little Richard. It's all right if we call you that, isn't it?"

"Sure." Richard smiled.

"Are you a singer, Little Richard?"

"No. I'm a kid," Richard replied. "But I like to sing Christmas songs and things like that. And I like 'America the Beautiful' and the national anthem."

There were a few snickers from the older kids.

Jimmy raised his head off the ground and propped it in his right hand, his elbow resting on the dirt around home plate. "You like to sing *what*?"

"The national anthem," Richard said again.

"What's wrong with you, boy?" said Jimmy.

"I think it's a cool song," he said. Then, in a softer voice, "My dad's in Vietnam."

Nobody said anything. Jimmy just shook his head.

"You gotta sing if you're Little Richard," Donnie said. "See, Zack is like Mickey Mantle, and I'm going to be Hank Aaron."

"And I'm Johnny Bench," said Coach Hornbuckle, dropping the equipment bag just behind the worn pitcher's mound. The kids sitting down sprang to their feet. Coach had a way about him. Some people, you can see they want to help you, they want to teach you. They don't *have* to, they want to. That was Coach. A few of us had already played two seasons for him. We would have run into a wall for him.

"I've got a piece of paper here, on this clipboard," he said, holding it up. "I need everybody to come and see if their name is on it, and if their phone number is right. Okay? Let's do that first thing. Everybody."

The returning veterans stormed the mound, and the rookies sauntered over at a more timid pace. It seemed a little silly to check my name and number, but I was glad I did when I saw it at the top. It's amazing how a little thing like that can make you feel you really are worth something. Little things. Your name on a piece of paper.

"Guys," said Coach, "we don't really have formal captains, but I think it'd be good for all of you to see who's a newcomer and who's back from last year's team. So, let's see, can I get Hank Aaron and Mickey Mantle and the rest of you sluggers over here?"

He pointed toward second base. "And everybody who's new, over by first base."

You would think that kind of lineup would take about thirty seconds. But with players running to get their gloves wherever they'd dropped them, and others deciding that now was a good time to take off the extra shirt their mom had made them wear and toss it over on the nice grass behind the backstop, it took us a good ten minutes to get in our little groups.

I saw Rafer hadn't moved from his tree. Donnie had hollered, but no one on the team had approached the strange boy. The guys were scared of him. Different is scary, to kids and adults. Especially adults.

"Coach, I guess I'll have to go over and get Rafer. I think he'll come over if I just talk to him real quick."

"That sounds good, Zack. Go ahead. No hurry."

I had brought an extra glove to give to Rafer. It was my old one, but it was way better than the antique he had brought to tryouts. I walked to his tree and stood there. He didn't look up at me, didn't acknowledge me in any way. It was awkward.

"Hey, Rafer, I'm glad you're here."

No answer.

"Ready to play some ball?"

Nothing.

I held up the extra glove. "I thought you might like to try this. It's not new or anything. But it's got all five fingers."

In a sudden move, he stood up. Dropping the ancient glove to the ground, he swiped my old glove from my hand and marched onto the field. I had to double-time to catch up with him.

"All right!" I said. "Time to play some ball." But just as I shuffled past Rafer onto the field, I saw him freeze in place, standing just foul of the third base line. I really didn't know what to do. Coach was placing everybody, doubling up old and new players at some positions like shortstop and first base. Donnie was lecturing Richard and some other new boy about something, hopefully baseball related. More likely, he was recounting his sixth grade exploits. If Rafer was going to get something out of this practice, it was likely going to be up to me. I wanted to show him stuff. I just wasn't sure how.

I stepped directly in front of him. "Hey Rafer, you wanna try to catch some balls? You wanna try the outfield? I think... I think you might like that."

"Third base."

Thank you God! He's talking today! But third base was out of the question. That was my position. "Rafer, buddy, you can try third base if you want, but, you know..."

"Third base dad."

"Oh, yeah, well, I think Coach is thinking of playing you in the outfield this season." I hadn't even talked to Coach about it, but that was my guess.

"Today," he said, still not looking at me. He seemed to be seeing other things, in other places.

"What's that?"

"Today," said Rafer. "Rafer third base."

"Well, okay, if that's the way you want it." I wasn't mad, just a little stumped. "But if you're going to play here," I said, moving to the right of the bag, "you gotta play *here*." I made an impatient X with my right toe, about four feet off the bag in fair territory. I turned back around, half expecting to have to carry him to the spot and set him down like a marble statue, but he was walking. He walked straight and still, like my Scoutmaster, Mr. Gabriel, told us Indians did. ("Not be-bopping down to the Piggly Wiggly like you guys.") Rafer stopped at the precise X spot, standing tall but facing left field.

"Hey, that's good, Rafer," I said, hurrying up alongside him.

"Rafer good," he said, and I thought maybe a smile was pushing to get out of him.

I noticed other players looking our way and trying not to laugh. At least most of them were trying. Jimmy was guffawing like a donkey, and Batman was doubled over, falling first to his knees, and then on his face. Batman didn't mean any harm. But Jimmy was growing up mean.

"Yeah, that's good. Only you have to face..." I circled around in front of him. "You have to face the other way, Rafer."

Looking into his face, I could tell he was listening. He grimaced, really reaching. There was a gap, a breach between my words and his mind. Later I wondered if I was really some distance behind him, not the other way around. Time shifts perspective; life's angles reverse. The weak become the strong, and the strong are worn to dust.

"You have to face the other way, Rafer," I said again, slower this time.

He dropped his head back and lifted his eyes straight overhead, like he was looking for answers in the sky. Then he started pivoting clockwise, very slowly in tiny turns. I heard Coach's powerful voice, "All eyes on me, right here, guys!" and I knew why I wasn't hearing the laughing anymore.

Rafer pivoted for thirty long seconds, until he faced home plate.

"That's it, right there, Rafer!" I said, my right palm up in a "stop" gesture. And he stopped, standing ramrod straight, facing the would-be batters.

"That's good, Rafer," I said. "Just like that."

"Rafer good."

"Yeah, that's right. Hey, how 'bout I hit you some grounders? You can try to throw to first, all right?" No answer. No eye contact. No gesture of understanding. But when I jogged over to where a bag of bats and balls slumped against the backstop, he talked again. In a quiet, solemn tone, he said the same word three times.

"Grounders... grounders... grounders."

Some chuckles came from the older guys. The new kids were quiet, but they were starting to stare at the mannequin manning third base. Coach paused in the middle of his lecture, giving me a quick, serious look. I guessed he was about to push me and my third base experiment off the field and start some infield drills.

Instead, he turned to the others and said, "Everybody hustle out to right field. We're going to learn the right way to catch fly balls. C'mon, everybody, pop-ups and fly balls."

They all started the feet-shuffle that kids think is running. "Except you, Harold." Coach pointed to Harold Valencourt, a thin guy who looked like a whippet hound, except his straight, dirty blond hair fell long over his eyes. Harold had no punch at the plate, but his reach was so long that he was invaluable playing first base.

"Harold, give Zack a hand. Get on first."

"Sure, Coach." Harold ran happily to the base. All Little Leaguers worry that someone else will take their position. It's not just a matter of losing playing time; it's more about losing your identity. Last season, Harold learned he was a first baseman, and now he prized that discovery, holding fast to it.

"Just rap him a few on the ground, Zack," Harold said, leaning over, his hands resting on his knees. "See if he can get 'em clear over to first with any zip."

"Okay, Rafer." With the bat in my right hand, I held up the ball in my left hand, ready to toss it up and stroke it in his direction. "You ready?"

Nothing. I really don't know why I asked.

Here goes nothing. I tapped a very easy roller to him, the ball moving just fast enough to not stop before reaching him. My mind shuffled several notions at once. *He's not going to move. This is a mistake. We gotta play him somewhere else.*

But I was wrong. When the ball reached Rafer, he dealt with it. Oh yeah. The very instant it came within reach, he picked it up quick and catlike, whirled toward right field, and hurled it hard, like it came out of a howitzer. I barely had time to holler.

"Look out, Mr. Hornbuckle!" Emergencies call for proper names. "Coach" is for the lighter moments.

Coach turned just in time to see the white projectile zeroing in on his head. They say the hardest ball to catch is one right between your eyes. Rafer's throw qualified. For an instant, I thought Coach might even snag it. But he was gloveless. He got enough of his left hand in front of his face, and enough of a duck started with his head. The ball ricocheted hard off the fat of his hand, rose about twenty feet into the air and fell with a lazy plop back to earth.

Coach was on one knee, rubbing his swelling hand. I hadn't moved from the batter's box. I was just staring big-eyed like everyone else. Nobody said anything for a solid stretch of seconds. Then Batman drawled.

"Holy cannonballs, Batfans. They's trying to kill our coach."

Mr. Hornbuckle stood up. He turned in my direction and called out in an easy, confident tone.

"Hey Zack, make sure he knows where first base is before you hit him another one, okay?" You knew it when you first met him. Coach was cool as grits. I miss him.

"Okay, Coach."

Rafer, who had turned smartly to launch the baseball, now turned back around to face me. I dropped the bat and walked up to him.

"Rafer, why did you throw the ball to right field?"

"Right field, no."

"Right field, yes!" I shook my head. "I mean, yes, you did. You threw the ball to right field."

"Right field, no," he said with no expression.

"Rafer, you almost killed Coach," I exaggerated.

"Coach, yes."

That was different. *Coach, yes?* I turned away from him, trying to pull my thoughts together. Harold was perched on first base looking skyward, balancing his glove on his head.

"Harold, get ready over there!" I said. "You got a death wish or something?"

"What's a death wish?" Harold asked, peering out from under his glove at me.

"Get the glove off your face and on your hand!"

"Whatever it is, I ain't got one," he said. But he got the glove on pretty fast, and I had to smile at how serious he was looking now. The lonely sentinel, at the farthest outpost, faithfully guarding first base.

"Listen, Rafer," I said to my new friend. "You said 'Coach, yes.' You mean you threw it to Coach?"

"Coach, yes."

I nodded slowly. Then I pointed dramatically, emphatically, at Harold. "That's Harold. Throw it to Harold. Okay?"

"Hair... Old. Yes."

I swallowed a chuckle. "It's really not... never mind. Throw it to Harold, okay?"

"Hair... Old. Yes."

I started back toward the batter's box, and stopped about halfway. Harold's eyes were big as dinner plates looking in Rafer's direction. I thought I had better say something.

"Rafer, you don't have to throw it so hard. Throw it like this." I called to Harold, "Hey, first base," and I made a straight, no-nonsense throw that Harold caught nervously. He started to throw it back to me. "No," I said. "Hold on to that ball. Just toss it to the side." I wanted the last vision in Rafer's head to be of a ball thrown easily to first base.

I picked up the bat and another ball off the ground behind home plate. *Here goes nothing.* My bat tapped the ball on the ground in Rafer's direction, a little more sharply this time. He still didn't look ready to field the ball, but when it reached him, he picked it up nimbly in his bare right hand and threw it to first with roughly the same velocity of my throw. Harold caught it, letting go a low, audible sigh of relief. "Thank you, God."

"Yeah, that's it!" I smiled big. "All right, Rafer."

I sent him about ten more grounders, progressively harder hit, with the same result. But when I started moving the ball to his left or right, even slightly, it got by him. He still had no idea how to play the position. He seemed to think I was doing something wrong when I hit it anywhere but straight at him.

Coach jogged in from the outfield.

"How's your hand, Coach?"

"It's a little swollen. How's he doing? Can he play infield, you think?"

"A little swollen! It's like a watermelon!"

Coach held up his injured hand, rubbing it gingerly. "Yeah, I guess it is a little big. Hurts like… hurts pretty bad too. He's got an arm and a half, Zack."

"Put him in the outfield."

"You think so?" said Coach. "He threw some nice ones to Harold."

"He throws good, but he can't field. Unless the ball is hit right at him. And I mean *right* at him."

Coach frowned. "Oh. Well, all right. We'll try him in right field. And Zack, that means we'll need you in center this year. Roger's gone, you know, and… well, we need someone who can move and catch out there. You'll probably have to cover some of Rafer's ground."

"Can I play third sometimes?" *I just found out who I was last year, Coach.*

"Oh, yeah. Sometimes. But we're going to need somebody reliable in center."

"Okay."

"Good man," said Coach. "This could be our year, ya know. Especially if he hits like you say."

"Coach, he belongs in a higher league. You'll see."

"So his bat is worth it?" He was really asking me. "It's worth your having to play center and babysit him in right field?"

"To have Rafer hit for us… even just to see Rafer hit, for us or anybody, I'd play the whole outfield."

He laughed. "I'm hopin' that won't be necessary. Skeeter's solid in left." Looking at Rafer still standing ramrod straight on the X I'd used to mark the third baseman's spot, Coach's eyes widened. "Let's see him hit, son. Bring him in."

Coach saw me as a necessary middleman to any communication with Rafer. And that's about the way it was. Donnie could get him to do some things too. But on the field, with anything concerning baseball, Rafer seemed to respond only to me. I didn't feel like it was a chore.

I called to Rafer as Coach walked back to right field. "We're doing batting practice now, Rafer. Coach wants to see you bat." I didn't say it, but everybody else wanted to see him bat too.

Rafer liked to hit. He grabbed a thick black bat, the same one I used, and stepped into the batter's box. I trotted out toward short center. "BoDean'll toss them in to you, Rafer."

"No, Zack. No. No." He stepped out of the box and dropped the bat to the ground.

I jogged slowly back toward him. "What's the matter, Rafer?"

"Zack pitch."

"Why?" What a stupid thing to ask. It was one of the last times I asked Rafer "why" about anything. He wasn't into explanations.

"Zack pitch."

"Rafer, BoDean can toss them in for you." I thought my smile might help. "I want to see if I can catch any of your hits. I don't think I can, buddy."

"Zack pitch. Zack pitch."

"Okay, okay. BoDean, is it all right if I pitch to him?" I knew it was; BoDean was mellow yellow.

"Go right ahead, y'all. I'll get the grounders," he said, drifting toward the shortstop position.

Coach hollered from his right field clinic with the younger kids. "Zack, how come I don't see Rafer hitting yet? Let's go, son."

"I got it, Coach." I waved to him to tell him I was on top of it. I grabbed four or five balls that were lying loose next to the backstop.

"Just leave 'em," said Skeeter from his post in left. "BoDean and I'll get the ball back to you. You don't need no more than two."

Skeeter was so innocent. I hustled onto the pitcher's mound and dropped all the balls but one to the ground at my side. "Ready, Rafer?"

"Zack pitch." He was set in his simple, straight up and down stance. He always looked too stiff to swing very smoothly. That just made it all the more magical.

"All right, y'all be looking now," I called over my shoulder at the fielders, all of whom I knew, in a few seconds, would be doing more looking than fielding.

"Just pitch it, why don't ya?" Skeeter socked his glove.

I wound up and threw the ball with considerable velocity. Rafer made a sound like he was chewing on something he really liked.

"Mmmmm."

He swung, a smooth flow of wrists and arms, and the bat cracked in the air like a .22 caliber. I heard Skeeter's "Wowwww," and saw him turn to chase and recover a ball that would not be coming down short of the wood line. I saw Coach abandon his right field fly-ball lessons and step briskly in our direction. A gaggle of kids floated behind him. Coach was whistling his unbelief at what his eyes told him. Everybody wanted to watch Rafer hit.

So did I. Winding up again, I let another fastball go, fueled by my happy adrenaline.

Rafer made another "Mmmmm" sound, enjoying his meal, and stroked this ball on a high line. It bounced once and hit the fence in the deepest part of center field.

"I'll get it," said three or four kids in Coach's group. They scrambled to beat each other to the ball. Balls off Rafer's bat were trophies.

After about ten or twelve more swings, Rafer had lost five balls in the woods behind the left field fence. Skeeter had gone in after them and it took him about ten minutes to locate four of them.

"There's one more ball, Skeeter," Donnie barked from his new position behind the left field fence, short of the woods. No balls fell there, though. When Rafer lofted them over the fence, they cleared Donnie's outstretched glove easily.

"I know it's in here, but I can't find it." We heard Skeeter's voice behind the tall timbers. "I heard it in the treetops over my head. Over *my* head, you guys!"

I walked up to Rafer. He still showed no emotion, no awareness of the impression he had just made.

"Rafer, I think God himself put you on our team," I said in jest. I did want to believe. Believing in miracles is the first step. Believing in a personal Miracle Maker is the real hurdle.

"This is going to be quite a ride," said Coach, coming up to pat Rafer on the shoulder. "That's amazing, son. Amazing."

"Rafer hit," said Rafer. He dropped the bat and walked up the third base line.

"Where you going, Rafer?" I asked.

He stopped and turned in his rigid pivot. "Rafer home." He rotated again and walked away from us.

"I guess he's through with practice," Coach laughed. "Can he hit like that in real games?"

"He can do it," I said. "I know he can, Coach." Imitating my new friend, I droned, "'Rafer lose balls.'"

Donnie ran up, out of breath from running all the way from outside the left field fence. "Hey, Pardner, we'll win it all this year, over the Hawks and Eagles and everybody!" He was wild with anticipation. "You need to come to church with me Sunday."

He said it with confidence, like he thought it made sense. I looked at him like he had two heads.

"You have to, man!" he said, with passion, maybe anticipating something else. "Everything's cooking now, with God giving us Rafer and all."

"You can't honestly believe God cares about us beating the Hawks this year."

"God cares about everything! That's what makes him God!"

CHAPTER 5

We sat in the front pew as a team at Silas Baptist Church that Sunday. It was pretty near all of us. Except for Rafer and Coach. Coach had "other plans," and I hadn't even tried to hunt down Rafer to ask him.

But the rest of us Robins were in God's house. We probably looked pitiful or endearing or pitifully endearing, depending on who was looking. I was wearing an oversized shirt; I had to borrow one of Dad's. Batman's tie had, well, Batman on it. Duffey's shirt was way too short. And he'd managed, I don't know how, to button the top button, making him a serious threat to pass out before the service ended.

Donnie did his best to demystify the service for me and the others.

"You don't have to put anything in, guys," he said when the offering plate came at us like a saucer floating through nimble hands.

Little Richard, who seemed completely comfortable, leaned across Jimmy to ask me, "Are we coming next Sunday, too?"

Jimmy said, "Don't even think about it," and Batman said, a little too loudly, "Once is plenty for God."

"Let's just get through today first," I said.

Little Richard nodded and sat back to enjoy the proceedings.

I heard BoDean say to Duffey, "I kinda like it. Do you like it?"

"I'm having trouble breathing."

"Duffey, man, unbutton that top button."

I looked in time to see Duffey glare at him. "We're in church, BoDean. You're not supposed to be comfortable."

Across the aisle, I spotted a classmate, Rebecca Carson. Her eyes always worked on me something powerful. She saw me too, and waved discreetly.

"Oh yeah," Donnie whispered. "I forgot you liked Rebecca."

"I don't like her."

He just eyed me, didn't say anything.

"Okay, I like her," I whispered.

Batman broke in, "You sure we don't have to put something in the money plate?"

"They're so glad to see y'all in here visiting," Donnie said, "they'd probably pay you to come back."

"Really?" Batman's eyes gleamed. "Maybe we can work something out."

The sermon was a big letdown. I don't think Pastor White said *hell* even once. He did talk about heaven, though, which I thought was a pretty strong sign he believed in hell. Mostly he talked about Jesus. He said Jesus loved me.

"I'm wondering if there's anyone here this morning that needs to be forgiven." Pastor White's voice was gentle and strong, like the man himself.

Duffey leaned toward Donnie, "Somebody in trouble with the church?"

"We all need to be forgiven," Donnie answered. "Me too."

"A nice guy like you?" Jimmy wasn't believing it. "What did you do?"

"It's not about being nice, you bozo," said Donnie.

"I guess it ain't, you bozo," Jimmy fired back.

Batman leaned toward us. "Y'all wanna hold it down? Preacher's talkin'."

Pastor White picked up a book from the pulpit. "Let's sing 'Victory in Jesus' together. It's number 199 in your hymnal."

We were flummoxed by the hymnals, rummaging through them like doves scattering at a shotgun blast.

When the song ended, Pastor White said, "Please know, my door, and God's door, are open. I would love to pray with you anytime. All rise for the benediction."

We rose.

"The grace of our Lord be with you," Pastor White said warmly.

"And also with you!" The congregation's enthusiastic response startled us a little. I thought Duffey might actually keel over, but he steadied himself.

The organ went into a fast tune. The people milled about, shaking hands.

Duffey came over to Donnie. "Everybody chimes in at the end there, huh?"

"Yeah. Sometimes Dad even says, 'Greet all the brethren with a holy kiss.'"

"Don't jive with me like that, man."

"It's in the Bible!" Donnie chortled.

Behind us we heard an immense voice that turned us all around. "Good to see y'all!" A giant of a man was shaking all our hands.

"So good to have you boys here this morning! I'm Robert Earl Carson. You might know my daughter, Rebecca." Rebecca, slightly behind her dad, gave a little wave to us. "You know these boys, don't ya, honey?"

"Daaaaad..." A little embarrassed, she recovered quickly. "Hey guys," she said.

We all murmured, "Hey."

She looked at me. "Hi, Zack."

"Hi, Rebecca."

Her dad's hand swallowed mine in a handshake. I was impressed. "Your hand is massive," I said.

He laughed. "Well, I needed that to grab running backs and throw 'em around."

"Dad was a linebacker," Rebecca said. "For the Chicago Bears."

She might as well have said, "Dad owns Disneyland." Robins crowded around him like he was Santa Claus.

"Was you any good?" Jimmy asked.

"Don't ask him that!" Donnie frowned.

Mr. Carson just laughed hard and said, "I was so good, they had to let me go after five years so I wouldn't overshadow Butkus."

"You played with Dick Butkus?" I asked. This was unbelievable.

"I showed Butkus how the game is played." His eyes danced, and we thought the man was serious. "I had to cover Butkus's mistakes."

"Daaaaad!" Rebecca slapped his big right arm. "Don't fib like that in church!"

While everybody laughed, Mr. Carson stuck a finger out at me, pointing.

"I know who you are. You're Del Ross's boy."

"Yes, sir."

"I work with Del at the plant," he said. "He's a good man. I'll have to tell him we missed him here this morning."

"I'm guessing... that might not be such a good idea, Mr. Carson." I didn't know exactly why, but I couldn't see dad enjoying that conversation.

"You never know, Zack," Rebecca's dad said, smiling. "Might be a great idea for me to talk with him."

I thought my going to church might tell me why Mom and Dad never went. I was curious about that. Something told me it was not just a matter of keeping their Sunday mornings free. That night was one of the few times we ever talked about church in our house, when Mom asked me how it had gone.

"It was pretty cool," I said. "I kinda liked it."

"Donnie's a good boy," Mom said.

"Yeah," Dad nodded.

"And his dad seems like a really nice man, Del."

Dad took a long breath, which means he wasn't sure if he should say what he wanted to. "They all seem nice until they're in the pulpit, Paulette."

"Now, Del..."

"Then all of a sudden we're all devils..."

"Del..."

"... headed for—"

"Del!" Mom looked so hard at Dad that I thought she might reach across the table and, I don't know, straighten him out.

There was a tense, pregnant pause around the table. This was really the first time I was aware that Mom and Dad seemed to have different ideas about God, church, and the whole salvation thing. My head was down. I thought it might be a good idea to lose myself in the mashed potatoes on my plate. But what we all thought was going to be a dark family episode suddenly turned funny. I started to giggle.

"What's so funny, young man?" Mom wasn't sure if she should sound strict or warm. My giggle turned into an outright chuckle, and I looked up at Mom. Her countenance, in spite of her best efforts, broke in the direction of a smile.

"Donnie says..." I laughed again. "Donnie said his dad told him he's tired of talking about hell. But he can't stop."

Now Mom started giggling, and Dad snorted his amusement into his iced tea and set down the glass, coughing.

"He says he can't stop talking about hell," I laughed, "because Jesus didn't stop talking about it."

At this, the three of us erupted in laughs. I'm not sure why. Something about seeing Donnie's dad, Pastor White, shaking his head and raising his hands in exasperation over having to talk about hell struck us as hilarious. Some would say the serious issue of hell caught our sensibilities off guard, that comedy and tragedy are bound together. We laugh because the truth is grim. Life is serious stuff.

"Well, if he doesn't want to talk about hell," said Dad, "why does he? He must know we don't want to hear it."

"He must really believe it," I said.

Dad shoveled a lump of meatloaf into his mouth, swallowed it, and said, "How's that?"

"Well, I mean, if he doesn't want to talk about it, and he's smart enough to know people don't want to hear it, the only reason to talk about it is that it's true. Can I have another biscuit, Mom?"

"You sure can." Mom handed me the basket of biscuits, and I noticed her general mood toward me had brightened considerably. "I think that makes a lot of sense, Zack," she said, smiling at Dad. "Don't you, Del?"

Dad wasn't laughing anymore. "It is a good point, Zack. I'm glad to see you thinking that way. I'm starting to worry a little bit that you're smarter than me."

Mom made a short, odd sound, and I thought the potatoes might have gone down the wrong way.

"In fact, you probably are smarter than me," Dad said, looking hard at Mom. "And I'm glad about that, son." He turned to me. "Every dad worth his salt wants his boy to be smarter than him. I'm glad, son," he said again.

"Thank you," I said through a mouthful of biscuit. I felt like I should say something else.

"But listen, Zack. I still got a little smarts on you while you're twelve and I'm thirty-two."

"Thirty-four," Mom said quietly, just before hiding behind her tipped iced tea glass.

"Thirty-four then," said Dad. "And you got a little fly in the buttermilk... I mean, what you just said is not totally right."

"It's not?"

"No it's not, smarty-pants."

"Del, he's only twelve."

"Paulette, this is between my son and me now. Yeah, he's twelve. That means real soon, sooner than any of us realizes, he's gonna start wrestling with what it means to be a man. Just let me talk to my son, Paulette."

Mom said, "Okay," and all of a sudden I wanted to finish supper real fast and go watch *Charlie the Lonesome Cougar* on Disney.

"You say that the stuff Donnie's dad doesn't want to talk about, all the stuff about hell, must be true. Because he doesn't want to talk about it, and people don't want to hear it, but he makes himself talk about it, it must be true. That's what you said, right?"

"I could be wrong." I didn't want to duel with Dad, ever.

Dad softened. "I'm not attacking you, son. I just want you to see something. You're smart enough to see it, and I want you to see it, okay?"

"Okay." I wanted to see it. Dad and I were a lot alike that way. We wanted the truth. Some people don't.

"Donnie's dad talking about hell, even when it's not popular to do that, only means"—here Dad slowed down for emphasis—"that Donnie's dad *thinks* the hell stuff must be true. Do you get it? It doesn't mean that the hell stuff *is* true. It just means he's convinced that it is. Does that make sense?"

"Yeah." It did.

"People can believe all kinds of different things, Zack."

"I get it."

"And just because one person believes something," said Dad, "doesn't make it the truth, right?"

"Right."

Dad seemed satisfied with our exchange, and Mom seemed a little miffed with Dad, so the table was quiet for a few moments. I maybe should have kept quiet. I never know when to do that. But I wanted to say something else.

"But it seems like..." I paused, and Dad's meatloaf shovel stopped in midair. "It seems like one person believing something doesn't make it wrong, either."

"What are you saying?" Dad's voice suggested he really didn't see the need for any more father/son talk.

"I mean, Donnie's dad could be right, couldn't he? He doesn't have to be wrong. What you said, Dad, is really just that he *could* be wrong, not that he *is* wrong. I mean, we don't know if he's wrong or right about hell, do we?"

"I got a pretty strong idea, son." Dad wasn't happy.

"But you don't *know*, Dad. It seems like what you were saying is that nobody can know, right? I mean, nobody can know that he is right *or* wrong. Right?"

Mom couldn't resist. "He's right, Del," she said in her brightest voice.

"Paulette, please! This is between my son and me."

"Okay," she said, her voice still light. She was happy.

Dad looked straight at me. Again I thought how nice it would be to be watching Tinker Bell buzz out of the Disney castle and start the show with her magic wand.

"Son, a pastor is going to talk about hell because it's his job to talk about hell."

That concerned me. "Even if he doesn't believe in it?" I asked.

"Even if he doesn't believe in it." Dad's voice was level.

I felt like he had me. I'm sure he felt he did too. "That's pretty bad," I said.

"Yeah, tell me about it, son," he said with the hollow triumph of the skeptic.

I found one more card to play. It felt like someone put the card in my hand. "Well, I guess I need to go back then, pretty soon."

Dad just looked at me like I'd said I wanted to go to the dentist. "Why?" he asked in a dim tone.

"'Cause I need to see if he believes it or if he's just pretending. Mom, may I be excused?" That's how they taught me to say I wanted to leave the table.

"Are you finished eating?"

I always thought that was a funny question, but Mom liked certain protocol, and who was I to challenge it?

"Yeah. It was good, Mom."

I got up to go, picking up my plate to take it into the kitchen. Dad pushed himself away from the table. I could tell he was going to say something else.

"You still won't know if it's true, Zack," he said. "You'll just know that *he* believes it's true."

"Yeah, I know, Dad. But that'll help me know, won't it? I mean, that'll help me know if I believe it's true."

"You know I don't believe it, son."

"I know, Dad."

"You're going to believe some preacher over your own dad?" He tried to look like he was hurt, but I knew him well enough to see he really just wanted to see how I'd answer him.

Without thinking about it, I put my hands in my jeans' back pockets, just like I'd seen Dad do a thousand times.

"It just seems like it's pretty important," I said. "Heaven and hell, and all that."

"But it's only important if it's real, if it's true. Right?"

"That's what I mean. If it's true, it means everything. If it's not true, it don't mean nothin'. So I want to know."

"All right." I was pretty sure he wasn't really mad about it. He just looked a little disappointed. "You go to church again with your friend." He pushed himself away from the table and got up.

"Don't you want to know, Dad?" I asked.

He sidled up next to me and patted me on the back. "You go back to church some time with your friend, son."

"You might want to check it out too, Dad," I said. "You might want to—"

"You don't know what I want!" he thundered, glowering at me. I had never seen him that angry. About anything.

I'm not sure Mom had seen him like that either.

"Del?" she said in almost a whisper.

He towered over me, and thinking back, I should have cried. I was only twelve. But I didn't feel afraid of him. I felt sorry for him.

After a few more white-hot seconds of tension, Mom made a suggestion. "We could all go together. It'd be a family thing and—"

"No!" Dad and I both said it at the same time. I said no because, after Dad's outburst, I was thinking there wasn't enough casual, free air in that church for Dad's questions and my own mind to roam around for answers together. I'd check it out by myself.

"Okay, okay..." she retreated. "No need to get all worked up about it."

That night, I culled through all the "God stuff" winding like muddy rivers through my mind. How do you find God? Can it be done?

Maybe God finds us.

I hoped that was true. Even before I knew him, I had a lot more confidence in his power to rescue me than I did in my ability to track him down.

"Here I am, God," I said aloud, before drifting to sleep.

CHAPTER 6

Beginnings are deceptive. We welcome the deceit, the sweet trap of the promise that we can watch something grow. More often we are watching things end. That's the way it is down here. We have to look beyond this place to see things that always grow.

Opening Day in Little League is brilliant with promise. The jumble of fun and accomplishment, the sort of mix a kid can't find in school or at home, is on the baseball field. Games will be hotly contested, won and lost, celebrated and lamented with snow cones. Heroes emerge from behind nerdy eyeglasses. Last year, it was some other kid who seized the day and the season. This year, it'll be you. That older kid in your neighborhood who plays Pony League ball, he's schooled you in his back yard after supper. You're better in all phases of the game.

At least that's the way it had felt last year, and the year before that. This year would be different. The difference between ages eleven and twelve is more than time.

This year, I wasn't thinking about my goals, about my Little League star. My nova had flared red last year when I snuck up on the league. Now I was *supposed* to be good. They wouldn't notice my star now unless it burned out. It wasn't a sad thing for me. It was just the way it was. At twelve, change isn't the enemy. It's not a friend, either. It's just change.

This year, I was anxious to see a new nova. I sauntered into the dugout and sat next to Coach. He was filling out the lineup card.

"I think you should bat Rafer fourth."

He looked up from his clipboard and eyed me seriously. I don't know whether he really listened to our suggestions or not, but he sure acted like he did. For us, that appearance of attention and respect was as good as the real thing. "What makes you say that?"

"You saw him, Coach," I said plainly. "He's got a truckload of pop in his bat."

"In practice. And I hope he carries it into the game with him. But Zack, you know things change in a real game. We saw it with Jimmy last year. Remember?"

"Yeah, I know. But I can't see it happening with Rafer. He doesn't..." I wasn't sure how to say it. "He doesn't seem to worry like the rest of us. I can't see him getting nervous about the game situation and all."

"Is that right?" Coach lifted his cap, looking out onto the field and rubbing his head with his free hand. "You might have something there, Zack. Maybe." He smiled and looked at me. "Just the same, I'm going to bat him sixth."

"Sixth?" I didn't get that at all. Rafer was going to separate the ball from its cover, or he was going to take three strikes. None of that in-between, sixth-in-the-order stuff.

"I'm just breaking him in." He put his hand on my shoulder. "Don't sweat it. We're solid even without Rafer. BoDean's one. Then we got Donnie. Batman's third. You're fourth. Duffey's fifth. And we'll slip Rafer in sixth. How's that sound?"

It sounded daffy. "Okay, Coach." I trotted toward where the other guys were throwing, warming up their arms.

"And Zack," he called to me, and I stopped. "You're wrong about Rafer not worrying like the rest of us. He just worries about different things. Probably bigger things."

I nodded quickly, and ran to the warm-up lines. I stopped

behind Rafer, waited for him to catch a toss from Donnie, and then stepped in front of him.

"Rafer, how ya feeling today? Ready to play ball?"

He set his glove and ball on the ground, pulled something out of his pocket, and extended his hand.

I put my hand out, and he pressed it into my palm.

"Hey, pretty cool," I said, looking at the quarter-sized gray rock, turning it over. "What's this? I mean, what's it for?"

Rafer had already picked up his glove and was throwing the ball to Donnie.

"Well, thanks anyway." I shoved it in my pocket.

The game should have been ours from the get-go. Even without Rafer, we should've eaten the Cardinals for lunch. It didn't happen. It was like we were sleeping through the game.

In the top of the fifth, the game even at five runs apiece, Duffey led off for us and poked a hot grounder just inside the third base line. He should've slid into second for an easy double. But Duffey liked to stroll through life and baseball games. He only ran as hard as a situation demanded. He went into the bag standing up, safe by a cat's tail.

"Where's my slide, Duffey?" Coach barked across the diamond from the first base coach's box. "A little more hustle!"

"I'm safe, ain't I?" he grinned back.

Donnie and I were perched at the end of the bench, our backs leaning on the chain-link fence that wove behind, in front, and over the top of the little bench that was our dugout. Sawdust dozed peacefully at my feet.

"If the world was fair," Coach bellowed, "you'd be out!"

Rafer was up. We were all anxious to see him tomahawk the ball, but he'd been taking pitches all day. He did it again now, taking a belt-high strike one.

"I don't get it." Donnie shook his head. He and Batman leaned against the chain-link fence, peering out at the pitcher and the rest of the Cardinals. "As slow as this guy's throwing, Rafer should rocket the ball out of here."

Rafer watched the next pitch go by too, a ball just off the plate. He showed no inclination to swing at anything.

With Skeeter on deck, I felt like we really needed Rafer to clobber the ball. Skeeter was always a gamer, giving his all, but his batting "all" wasn't close to what I'd seen of Rafer's.

Rafer took another pitch for strike two. He hadn't moved in the box. After the next pitch crossed the plate at Rafer's eye level, the umpire announced, "That's a ball. Two balls, two strikes."

I jumped off the bench, hollering to Coach at the same time. "Call time, Coach! Call time!"

"Time out, Blue!" Coach hollered to the umpire.

I hustled out toward home plate, waving for Coach to follow me. I saw Mom and Dad in the bleachers, shrugging and muttering, unsure of my intentions. I pulled Rafer to the side for a tight, private conference with me and Coach.

"Pretend like we're talking here," I whispered.

"We *are* talking here," Coach whispered back. "Whaddya doing, Zack?"

I slapped Rafer on the back and started walking away, breaking up our little conference. Coach gave the ump an uneasy smile and walked after me.

My voice was loud enough for everybody to hear. "'Too slow,' he says. I thought that was it." To my teammates on the bench who were looking at me like I was one huge question mark, I yelled, "He's throwing too slow! What can you do?"

The tall Cardinal pitcher flushed red. "Gimme the ball, Randy!" He took the throw back from his catcher.

The ump said, "Play ball," and Rafer stepped into the box.

"Too slow, huh?" the pitcher glowered at him. "Pray I don't hit you, chump!"

He wound up with ferocious focus and fired.

Rafer's bat came around, fluid like stream water over rocks. It's not in the arms. It's the wrists, and the velocity of the ball out of the pitcher's hand. Rafer's swing birthed a sweet *crack* and a chorus of cheers and ooohhhs and aaahhhs from parents on both teams' bleachers. It's what we liked to call a moon shot, clearing the left field fence easily.

Our bench was a circus of cheers, stomps, and back slaps. In the bleachers, Mom hugged Dad *and* the fellow on the other side of her. Dad let it pass in the rush of celebration.

"Amazing!" Jimmy gripped and shook the chain-link in celebration. "Absolutely amazing!" Donnie's hug lifted Richard off the ground.

I ran up to Coach. "Whaddya think of that!"

"That'll take us to the promised land!" We both had fists high in the air. Rushing toward home, I almost tripped over Sawdust, who clearly knew something wonderful had happened and didn't want to miss the party. Boys, dog, and man collided many times, slapping Duffey and catching Rafer at the plate when he came tearing in from his race around the bases. Apparently he didn't know what a home run trot was.

I heard a bright, clear voice, a girl's voice. "You really clobbered that one, Rafer!" said Rebecca Carson, smiling through the chain-link fence.

"Clobber Rafer one," Rafer answered flatly, setting off another chorus of laughs and cheers.

I found Coach in the happy melee. "I told ya he'd come through for us."

Donnie yelled, "Rafer's our ticket! We can go all the way!"

Robins 7, Cardinals 5. I had that calm feeling you get when you sense things are blowing your way so much it'd take a hurricane to turn the air current against you.

We hustled happily back to our side of the field. Rebecca was standing just off the bleachers, on the other side of the fence. She was close enough that I could stand at our bench and she could still hear me say hello.

"Hello," I said.

"Hi," she said, moving close enough that we could now share a conversation. "You guys are doin' good." She smiled. "Y'all got a good team."

"Thanks." Skeeter walked past me into the dugout. I didn't see him get out. Rebecca was better looking.

"Of course," she said, "Batman's playing a little too far in the hole at short."

"Yeah, we—whaddya mean 'too far'?"

"Seems like he's a little too deep." She shrugged. "Cuts down on his range up the middle."

That was interesting. I didn't know what to say.

"Not a lot," she continued. "Batman's two, maybe three feet too far toward third." She wasn't through. "And I guess you know the Cardinals' pitcher is bringing his curve every fifth pitch."

"Every fifth pitch?"

"Like clockwork. Four fastballs, then the curve. It's coming right now." Jimmy must have struck out. Coach was encouraging Harold. "You're ready now, son. Catch up to that fastball."

Harold swung early and tapped it weakly back to the pitcher for the third out.

Coach called to him, "Ohhh! He's tricky with that curve. Snuck it in on you. Tough break, Harold."

Turning to go, Rebecca said, "Maybe I'll see ya after the game."

"Yeah." I nodded. "After the game."

When we trotted back out to the field, I paused at the shortstop position to talk to Batman. "You playin' too far in the hole?"

"I don't think so." Batman shook his head. "You think so?"

"Just a couple feet," I jogged past him toward center. "Maybe three feet," I said over my shoulder.

The first Cardinal batter hit a grass cutter up the middle, just out of Batman's reach, for a single. While the next batter settled himself in the box, I watched Batman take three steps closer to second base. I smiled when the Cardinal hit another ball near the same spot his teammate had. I smiled bigger when Batman fielded the ball deftly and turned a double play.

"You were right, Zack-man!" he hollered to me, grinning.

In the sixth and final inning, BoDean struck out, but I stroked a double, scoring Donnie and Batman ahead of me. We were up 9–5.

After Duffey popped out, Rafer stepped in. The game was over, barring some miraculous comeback by the Cardinals in their last at-bat. And I didn't believe in miracles. Not yet.

I was pumped to see Rafer launch another missile. It was like swatting slow flies for him.

I clapped my hands. "Let's go, Rafer!"

Another voice roared over mine. "C'mon Rafer, show 'em what you're made of!"

I looked toward the bleachers but couldn't tell who had spoken. The loud voice came again, "Show 'em what you can do, son!"

Then I saw him—Rafer's dad leaning against the side of the bleachers, not sitting on them with the other parents. As soon as I saw him, I knew he was teasing his son. It's funny, I didn't know he was being sarcastic and mean until I saw him. People are so good at being cruel.

"That's a strike." The umpire said simply, after Rafer took the first pitch.

"Okay, now you're ready." Mr. Forrester clapped his hands together, mocking. "Do what you do best."

I saw Sawdust had walked to the end of our bench, where the chain-link fence separated players from fans and parents. He growled at Rafer's dad.

The second pitch was identical. The pitcher was on automatic, grooving the pitch.

"That's another strike," the umpire said.

"Strike two!" bellowed Rafer's dad. "You know what you're doing, boy. Give it your best shot now!"

I was hoping he was not sober. But I was afraid he was completely himself.

For the second time that week, I said something to God out loud. A whisper of a prayer. "God, make him swing. Let his dad see it. Open his eyes, God."

The pitcher cocked his arm and let go a third pitch. A third strike. Rafer never moved.

"That's three strikes. You're out," the umpire announced flatly. I think he felt bad for Rafer. Normally this guy, a local sheriff's deputy named Felton Yates, called third strikes with dramatic flourish. I started walking toward the bench.

Mr. Forrester cheered, throwing his arms into the air, his eyes on fire with… something. "All right, boy! You did it, just like I knew you could. Way to go!" He started clapping.

Sawdust growled again, louder this time.

Mr. Forrester looked over at my dog. "Y'all gonna shut that mutt up, or am I?"

Sawdust barked at him, loud enough to make me worry that a man versus dog row might be coming.

"Donnie!" I called to my friend. "Get a hold of Sawdust."

Donnie put his arm around the dog's neck, petting him. "Easy boy," he said. Sawdust looked at him. "Just gotta let some things go," said Donnie.

While Rafer walked back to the bench to get his glove, Coach walked briskly toward Mr. Forrester. *This'll be good. Give it to him, Coach.*

"It's good to see you, Mr. Forrester." Coach's smile was real.

Rafer's dad was stumped, confounded by Coach's genuine grace.

"I want to thank you," said Coach, "for letting your boy play with us this year. It's been fun getting to know him."

Mr. Forrester's scowl contorted his face. "You want him?"

"What's that, Mr. Forrester?" Coach said evenly.

"I said, 'Do you want him?' because you can have him. It's me who's thanking you."

"How's that, sir?"

"Don't give me that 'sir' trash neither. I'm just as good as you."

Everybody was listening. All the parents, and the children sitting in the bleachers and on the ground, looked at the two men.

"I'm just thanking you, Mr. Forrester, for letting Rafer play for us this year. He's a fine young man." He waited for a response. The other man looked at him like Coach had called him something foul.

"A fine young man," Coach repeated. "I'm sure you know that better than I do."

"I know... I know what he is," Rafer's dad said slowly, drawing out words like knives. I had stopped halfway between first base and our bench to listen. I was riveted; I'd never seen such hatred and such pain at the same time. I wonder now if it's the same thing.

"Last inning!" Umpire Yates said in his loudest voice of the day. "Play ball, guys!"

"I just wanted to thank you, sir... Mr. Forrester, for Rafer, for letting him play. He's a special young man." Coach backed away, raising his hand in a little friendly wave to the angry man. "Gotta go. Gotta coach one more inning." He called to us, motioning us onto the field. "Take the field, guys." We started jogging toward our positions.

"Hey!" Mr. Forrester called after Coach, "Hey! You can keep him, Mr. Candy Stripes. I don't want him!" He spat on the ground. "You hear me?"

On my way out to center field, I heard a small voice say, "I hear you," and I glanced in the direction of the comment. A smiling older woman, all five feet of her, stood behind Mr. Forrester. Just for a second, a folded lawn chair was silhouetted against the sky, before the woman brought it around sharply, striking Forrester square on the jaw.

"Ka-boom!" Her voice carried over the field.

Rafer's dad staggered a couple of steps, clutching the side of his face, his eyes wide with surprise. "Who *are* you?" he managed to ask.

"I'm Batman's grandmama." She stepped in closer and clubbed him again with the chair, this time on the top of his head.

"Holy lawn chairs!" she roared.

Mr. Forrester went down, clutching his head, then came to his feet pretty fast, primed to strike back. I saw Mom say something sharp to Dad, and Dad started to move down the steps of the bleachers. He stopped, though, when a large man, dark and muscular, jumped off the bleachers, landing between Forrester and Batman's grandmother. For such a big guy, he moved awfully fast.

"If you want to stay on your feet," the big guy looked Rafer's dad in the eye, "you better use them to walk away."

He did. He walked slowly toward the parking lot, cursing low and rubbing his head.

I'd seen Duffey's dad lots of times, but I always marveled at his size, the biggest guy I'd ever seen.

"Duffey," Batman called out. "Your pa don't take no guff from anyone, does he?"

"Nope, that's my pappy." Duffey grinned.

We heard his dad, in as fine and pleasant a tone as you can imagine, say to Batman's grandma, "Would ya do me the honor of sitting next to me on the bleachers?"

"It would be a pleasure, kind sir."

Batman laughed. "His pa's half Cherokee. Just don't use the word *half* around him."

"I won't." I smiled.

The Cardinals went down easy in the bottom half of the inning. Rafer caught the last out in right field, his first catch of a fly ball. Only he didn't use his glove. He took a few steps to get in the line of the ball's flight, and snagged it with his bare hand. He was starting to understand you have to go after the ball. It's not coming after you. Baseballs—and life—are like that.

I looked for Mr. Forrester after Rafer's catch, hoping maybe he hadn't really left. I wished he had decided to stay so Rafer'd show him what he could do. Coach said once that the world would change if people would just show what they could do. I hoped Rafer would get another chance to do that. When you're twelve years old, you hope and wish so many things.

Mom and Dad caught my eye and waved. "See ya back home, son," Dad called. They knew Donnie and I always liked walking the short way home through the woods.

"See ya." I waved.

The Cardinals and Robins lined up at the pitcher's mound and shook hands. Rafer walked the line, but didn't shake.

We were all pumped up by our victory. Donnie said again we could win it all, and Duffey agreed. "We can rock and roll with Rafer!"

Rebecca walked in among us, standing beside me.

"You gotta keep his dad away, Zack," she said.

"Maybe... maybe we can get Rafer to forget who's watching."

She shook her head. "I don't think Rafer forgets anything. He's smarter than people think he is."

"Rafer?" Duffey was incredulous. "The guy don't even talk good."

"And you do?" Donnie laughed.

"Who cares how he talks?" said Batman. "The guy is Babe Ruth! It's our year!"

We all walked toward Rafer now. He was still standing by the pitcher's mound where we'd shaken the Cardinals' hands. Batman put his arm on Rafer's shoulder. "Rafer buddy," he said, "how 'bout some ice cream?"

"Creamy ice," said Rafer.

Batman, Rafer, and Jimmy marched together in the direction of the snack bar. I thought that was a really good sign.

Donnie, Rebecca, and I walked over to the Robins' bench, where Coach loaded up the equipment bag.

"Hey, Coach," I said, "did you know their pitcher was bringing his curve every fifth pitch? I told the guys to watch for it."

"Really?" He looked at me. "I didn't see that. Good for you, Zack! That's the kind of thing that'll make a difference for us!"

I smiled at Rebecca, who was teasing me by pretending she was unaware and uninterested in what Coach and I were discussing.

"Coach, this is Rebecca Carson," I gestured. "She noticed the fastball counts, and the curveball counts. She knew when the breaker was coming. Not me."

They shook hands.

Coach was direct. "I'm looking for someone to keep stats." He handed her his clipboard.

"I know how to keep stats," she said.

"Would you be willing to do that for us?"

"Does it mean I have to hang out with this guy every game?" She nodded her head in my direction.

"I have to hang out with him every game." Coach grinned. "Why should you get a pass? And would you please clue us in on any stuff like what you told Zack?"

She nodded. I pushed her playfully with my gloved hand, and she laughed.

"Now let's all go get some ice cream," Coach said.

As we walked toward the snack bar, Pastor White came alongside us.

"Did you see Rafer knock the cover off the ball?" Donnie asked his dad.

"Till his pa showed up," said Rebecca. "It's sad. Rafer's a bit different and all, but he's really nice."

"Well, his dad is *not*," I said with emphasis. "And Rafer freezing up like that... something's not right." I had an idea that I hoped wasn't crazy. "Pastor, sir, do you think you and I could stop by Rafer's place sometime? Just kind of drop in on his dad and him. You know, see them together?"

"That's a crackerjack idea!" Pastor White beamed. "If it's okay with your parents, you and I can go see Rafer and his dad after the game next week and—"

Raucous laughs from the direction of the snack bar interrupted the pastor. We could see Batman and Jimmy pointing at

Rafer, who was holding a large glob of ice cream in the palm of his hand. He was eating it, apparently oblivious to their laughter. I ran toward the scene, faintly hearing Pastor White say to Coach, "Wait—let's watch how Zack handles it."

"Shut up!" I got in Jimmy's face.

"Oh my gosh, look at—" Batman was still pointing.

"Both of you!" I glared at Batman.

"We're just funnin', Zack," said Jimmy.

"It's not funny if Rafer's not in on it," I shot back. "He's not a freak show." Rebecca and Donnie had raced up to Rafer.

"You played so good today, Rafer," Rebecca said, patting him on the back. He was still eating the ice cream out of his hand.

"That looks like some good ice cream," said Donnie.

"Creamy ice," said Rafer. "Magically delicious."

I can't be positive, but I'd guess he learned that from the Lucky Charms TV commercial.

Then I saw Duffey. He was off to the side, eating happily from a glob of ice cream in his own hand.

"Ain't a bad way to eat it," he mumbled. "What?" he said, when he noticed we were all staring at him.

"This ..." I said smiling, my hand on Duffey's shoulder, "... is a freak show."

CHAPTER 7

After school let out on Tuesday, the afternoon was still young, and I hustled back to the house so I could tell Mom that Donnie and I had something fun planned for Rafer. I was hoping I'd be telling Mom and not asking her.

Donnie and Rafer waited outside, romping with Sawdust. At least Donnie was romping. Rafer was watching. I noticed Rafer pushing a little rock into Donnie's hand and Donnie shrugging while he put it in the pocket of his cutoffs.

I bolted into the house through the side screen door, nearly colliding with Mom and the laundry she was carrying.

"Where's the fire?"

"Mom, I was—"

"Did you sweep out the garage? You remember I asked you to."

I felt my plans shriveling. "Yeah, I'll do it later. I promise." Nothing to do but go for it. "Donnie and me are taking Rafer swimming. You know, at the creek, with the swing?"

"Is that right?"

"I know, I know." I put my head down. "I can't go."

"Did I say that?"

I tried to look pitiful. It wasn't hard.

"It's a weekday," she said. "But... you've been pretty responsible lately..."

I looked up at her, thinking I saw a little light.

She continued, "I think Sandy swimming hole is a wonderful idea. But you have to promise to be back in time to do your homework..."

"I don't have any homework," I said, too fast. It sounded like I was just not going to do it. But the truth was, I didn't have any.

"... and sweep out the garage."

"I promise, I promise, Mom."

"Then have a good time—but be back *before* the sun goes down, Zack."

"I will, I promise, Mom." I hugged her and the laundry basket she was carrying. "You're the best mom in the world!"

She hugged me back. "Flattery will get you... a lot, young man."

I ran out the door and joined up with my partners in chaos: my dog, my best friend, and my new friend. Donnie had his bike, and Rafer doubled up with me on mine. I let him do the pedaling because he seemed to want to. On the level streets, I stood up on the back of the seat and held onto the top of Rafer's head. Sawdust barked his approval; he was at least as much a risk-taker as I was. I waved at Mrs. Thacker, an older woman who was a permanent fixture on her front porch.

"You're gonna get killed, Zachary Ross!" she greeted me.

As we reached the end of the street and the start of the path, Rafer stopped, braking hard. I went flying over the handlebars, landing in Mrs. Thacker's neighbor's yard.

"Are you all right, Zack?" Mrs. Thacker called to me.

Miraculously, I was. It's amazing what twelve-year-old boys survive. I bounced up, waving to her.

"You get out of Thelma's yard!" she chided me. "I'm calling your mama right now, Zachary Ross." She didn't get up from her seat.

I scrambled back onto the bike, and this time Rafer was *my* passenger. We caught up with Sawdust and Donnie, who'd already snaked his bike partway through the narrow path that would take us deep into the woods and to the swimming hole.

After a few minutes, we had to dismount and walk our bikes. Sawdust knew precisely where we were headed. It was one of his favorite places too.

"Rafer," Donnie looked at him seriously, "you can't tell nobody. Cross your heart and hope to die. Nobody knows this place but us and Sawdust."

Sawdust barked gleefully at the sound of his name.

I wasn't sure Donnie knew what he was talking about. If my mom knew about this creek and the swimming hole, there had to be scads of people who knew. Maybe it was one of those urban legends each generation pretends to own exclusively.

"I don't think Rafer's going to tell anyone anything," I said. "He's not much for talking."

"Just the same, he needs to know this is a secret we're letting him in on." In our world, the world of kids, that was important.

"And this is just the sort of thing that might get a guy to start talking, if he wasn't before," Donnie maintained. "You know what I mean?"

"I guess so."

We rounded a corner and there it was. A muddy creek with a center body of water big enough to play around in.

"Water," said Rafer.

"I told you he was going to talk about it," Donnie moaned.

"Lighten up," I said. "He just said 'water.'"

Sawdust took off running along the bank, and we chased after him. A rough old wooden pier some kids and their dads had put up stretched over the water, and Sawdust ran up and down it, barking his head off.

"You're ready, aren't you boy," I called.

Donnie and I shed our T-shirts and shoes, leaving us with just our cutoffs on. I scaled a tree that had wood blocks nailed to it for easier climbing.

Donnie poked Rafer affectionately. "Get a load of this."

Reaching the level branch that served as our launch pad, I took hold of a rope tied to a higher limb, leaned back, and jumped off.

"Rockin' Robins rock and roll!" I shouted as loud as twelve-year-old lungs can shout.

As the rope carried me out over the water, Sawdust tracked me along the pier, running off the edge when I let go of the rope. For a second or two, boy and dog were in the air at the same time before plunging into the cool water for a happy, wet time together. The water felt great. Aprils are mostly hot in Alabama, and today was hotter than most. Sawdust and I swam back to the bank and scrambled out.

Donnie had scurried up the tree, and I ran the rope back and tossed it up to him. He leaned back and jumped off, the rope carrying him far out over the creek.

"Geronimo!" he hollered. "Robins rock and roll!"

He splashed down. Sawdust didn't jump in with him. He was running between Rafer and the tree, barking.

"It's your turn, Rafer," I said.

It didn't surprise me when Rafer didn't move right away. Sawdust sat down in front of him, and Rafer put both his hands on the dog's head like I'd seen him do a number of times before. Then Rafer walked to the tree and climbed to the takeoff limb. Sawdust ran onto the pier again.

"Sawdust will only jump in with Zack," said Donnie, throwing the rope up to Rafer.

Rafer took a strong hold on the rope and raised his feet off the limb. Swinging out over the water, he spoke in what was a loud voice for him.

"Geronimo . . . was a rock and a Robin."

Sawdust ran along the pier, jumped off into the air, and splashed down into the water with Rafer.

Donnie was astonished. "Well, roll me in the mud. Looky there."

They frolicked in the water—well, at least Sawdust was frolicking. Rafer was more like bobbing up and down. He was breathing fine, though. I could tell he'd been in water before.

They climbed out together onto terra firma.

We got the afternoon's worth out of the rope and the creek. Donnie did some unintentional belly flops, which Rafer started announcing as "flop bellies." And Rafer came up with a new victory slogan when he let go of the rope, "Roll the rock over Geronimo." It was a slogan for him, not a victory shout. He never shouted. Except for the one time near the end.

I tied Donnie's and my shirts together in a bundle and threw it into the water. Sawdust retrieved it, taking it to Rafer. Rafer tugged on one end, while Sawdust held the other in his mouth. Then it ripped in half.

"Hey!" Donnie objected. "I need that shirt!"

"For what?" I said. "As hot as it is."

"Good point," he said, and I knew he felt like I did. When you're having that kind of fun, a T-shirt lost is a small price to pay.

We got tuckered out and lay for a while on the bank, lounging in the sun.

"Superman or Batman?" Donnie asked.

"Superman," I answered.

"Spaghetti or pizza?"

"Pizza."

"Swimming in the summer or cow-tipping in winter?"

"I guess ... swimming in summer."

Donnie smiled. "So, if we can get pizza out here, and then go swimming, we'd be in heaven. I'm thinking we already got Superman." He shifted his eyes in Rafer's direction, and pulled the rock out of his pocket.

"Rafer gave me this. In your front yard, while we were waiting for you today."

"Yeah." I looked at it. "He gave me one of those too."

"Whaddya think it is?" he asked in almost a hushed tone, like we were talking about state secrets.

"A rock."

He elbowed me, a jab that poked my chest hard enough to make me cry out and laugh at the same time. "Ahhhhh! Hey, don't do that."

"I *know* it's a rock," he yelped. "Why's he giving it to me? What's it for?"

"It's just a Rafer thing. Why does Rafer do anything?" I sighed. "I got to be getting home soon, I guess."

"One more," said my old friend, returning the stone to his front pocket. "Baseball or football?"

"Baseball," I said. "Baseball's like when you let the rope go, and you hang there for a couple seconds over the water. I think... flying feels like that."

I made it home before the sun set, in time to sweep the garage while Mom heated up my supper. It was what I called a perfect day. I don't know how much Rafer took away from it. A lot, maybe. Such days, hours, and even minutes of peace and joy mean more than we know. They carry us, powerfully, through years of conflict and loss.

It took me a while to fall asleep that night. On the bed next to me, Sawdust was pretending hard, but he was awake too. I'd left my radio playing low. The song made me imagine somebody singing to me across a wide span of time, of space. They were promising to travel millions of miles and cry millions of tears to get to me.

My window was open. The night air pushed the little curtains.

I decided to say something to God.

"I just wanna thank you. If you can hear me, I wanna thank you for Rafer. Thanks for bringing him."

Moonlight passed through the leaves on the trees outside my room, casting shadows over my body and bed. On the radio somebody was promising to cross an ocean, to travel the roughest terrain, even to the mountain's peak, just so I could be near them.

"Maybe we can win it now," I said. "So, if you're listening... thanks."

He didn't say anything back to me, but I slept real good.

CHAPTER 8

So you honestly think Batman could take Superman?" I challenged Donnie.

"Absolutely." He didn't look so absolutely sure.

"You're outta your gourd." I shook my head.

"Well..." He shuffled his feet. "I mean, yeah, I don't know, so long as they don't gotta do no flyin' while they fight."

Kids were streaming through McInerney Elementary School's doors next to us. We'd just gotten off our bus, which was almost always the last bus to get there. A group of kids huddled around a smaller bus at the far end of the parking lot. I recognized Mrs. Armistead, a Special Needs teacher, leading some students on a walk to a side entrance to the school.

"There's Rafer." I pointed at him standing alone near the front of the parked bus, by the front passenger wheel.

"Hey buddy," Donnie hollered.

Then we saw trouble. Three Hawks. Booger Clark, Pepper Jasper, and the redheaded guy from tryouts approached our friend.

I started running toward them, Donnie not far behind. I could make out Pepper's words. "We thought you'd like a new cap to wear."

"Heeyyy!" I roared.

Pepper put a cap on Rafer's head. I saw something red and yellow streaming from the cap down into Rafer's face. The Hawks were laughing, only it wasn't real laughing; it was the fake, mean kind.

"Ya get free ketchup and mustard with the cap," Pepper crowed.

Just as Rafer told Pepper "thank you," I ran hard into the massive Booger from behind.

"Oooommfff," Booger exhaled, hitting the ground.

My crash into Booger took me down too, but only for an instant. I jumped up and raised my fists in time to give Pepper second thoughts, as he'd started to come at me. Now he just put up his fists and darted his eyes back and forth, trying to see me and his buddies and the approaching Donnie all at the same time.

Donnie came alongside me, giving the redhead reason to keep his distance for the time being. And Rebecca Carson went up several notches in my book by coming out of nowhere to be at Rafer's side. Pepper, Donnie, Red, and I were circling, moving like mad, hungry dogs.

Booger got back to his feet, and I was never so glad to see Duffey in all my young life. He appeared out of the pack of kids who are always drawn like magnets to a school fight and positioned himself so he and Booger were eyeball to eyeball. The two of them blocked out the early morning sun.

Nobody said anything except Rebecca. "Rafer, I'm always so glad to see you." She had taken his cap off and was wiping his face with tissues. Girls always have tissues for such times.

Rafer thanked her in the same flat tone he'd used to thank Pepper.

I heard Mrs. Armistead hustling up from behind, pushing her way through the gaggle of kids.

"We are not fighting!" she said as loud as she could.

No, not yet, but in just a few more seconds...

"Zachary Ross, put your fists down! Zachary!"

It occurred to me that Pepper's fists were just as "up" as mine, but she wasn't addressing him. I swear teachers purposely pick out the justified warriors at such times and ignore the guys who started the whole fracas.

I put my hands down, knowing I could put 'em up again if need be. Pepper leered at me, but I saw the fear in his eyes.

Mrs. Armistead was valiantly trying to seize this peace accord before it vaporized in the simmering tensions.

"Everybody to class!" she said in her most authoritative manner. "Go on!"

Some kid, who, judging by the high pitch of his voice, had to be pretty young, said, "Ain't Zack gonna hit him?"

"No, Zack is not," she said. "Zack is definitely not going to hit this young man. Right, Zack?"

Who's a young man? That's what I thought. But what I said was, "I reckon not."

But then he went and said it. Pepper muttered to Rafer, loud enough for lots of us to hear, "Have fun with the other retards."

I socked Pepper Jasper square on the nose, and he went down.

Rafer said, "thank you," for the third time this morning; this time to me.

Pepper jumped back up and the melee was on. We were punching away, hitting and missing. I saw enough of Booger and Duffey's donnybrook to know they ended up wrestling on the ground like two hungry bears. Red took a swing at Donnie, but Donnie ducked and the Hawk's fist hit the Special Needs bus. That took a lot of the fight out of Red.

About five or ten minutes later (it's hard to keep track of time when you're going toe-to-toe and trying to survive), the six of us combatants were sitting in Principal Stoneham's office. Three Robins in chairs against one wall, and three Hawks across the room against a different wall.

"You said you weren't going to hit him," Mrs. Armistead said. It sure sounded like her main beef about the whole incident was that it didn't go down in accordance with her plan. Justice and injustice weren't on her map.

"I changed my mind," I said. Duffey giggled, and Mr. Stoneham cleared his throat.

"I fail to see the humor, mister," Mrs. Armistead said to Duffey, who recovered nicely. She glanced in Mr. Stoneham's direction, and then tried to look right through me. "You cannot act like gestapo. We are very fortunate that Rafer Forrester did not get hurt out there."

"He *did* get hurt out there." Now I was looking through her.

"What's gestapo?" Donnie asked.

"You saw what they did to the guy," I continued. "You don't think he knows what they're about? You don't think he knows when people are respecting and liking him, and when they're abusing him?"

"You can watch your tone with me, young man." She had never liked me. That's just the way it was.

"Rafer knows," I said.

"They didn't hit him," she said. "They didn't knock him to the ground."

"That would've taken more courage than they got," I said, looking right at the Hawks, who were sitting peaceably now, as if they were victims of the Robins' wanton aggression.

"All right—" Mr. Stoneham broke in. "Here's the deal. We *are* lucky that Rafer didn't get hurt, and we're fortunate no one else did either."

There was a soft whimper from Red, who was still rubbing the fist that had missed Donnie's head and found the bus.

"Well," Mr. Stoneham continued, "not seriously." He stepped away from his desk, closer to all of us. "I'm sending you all home today. Your parents are coming to pick you up."

"They won't come for me," Booger said without expression. "Not my ma or my pa."

"I know. I'll be driving you home, son," Mr. Stoneham said.

That was the only clue I ever had about what might have made Booger such a hard case. You never know what someone's going through on the home front that makes them the way they are.

"Zack," the principal said, "I'd like for you and Donnie and Francis to step outside into the hall with me, if you would."

I figured "Francis" must be Duffey, but that was news to Donnie and me. As we stepped out into the hall with Mr. Stoneham and Mrs. Armistead, I gave the Hawks one last look. Only Booger returned my glare. The other two were idly eyeing the floor.

In the hall, the principal put a hand on my shoulder.

"Zack, I know you were just defending the Forrester boy," he said. "The other boys"—he pointed back toward his office—"were wrong. And I'm going to talk with them."

He paused to look at Mrs. Armistead, who was entirely disengaged from the conversation.

"You've got compassion, Zack," he said. "You've got a big heart. But I want you to try to think of ways that you can show that compassion without using your fists. I don't think fighting solves anything, really."

I didn't know what to say to that. Fighting seemed to settle all kinds of things, in the world and in the school yard. I was old enough, and I'd seen enough, to know that fighting wasn't a good thing, but it was the way it was. Imagining there were no bad guys was just that… imagining. Somebody had to pay the freight and defend the defenseless.

"Do you understand what I'm saying, son?" Mr. Stoneham looked at me with evident sincerity. But you can be sincerely wrong, too.

"I'm trying to get what you're saying," I said softly. Mr. Stoneham was good. But not everyone is. I couldn't just stand there and tell him he was mistaken. He'd have to learn that.

He patted me on the back then. "You do have a big heart, and big hearts change the world, Zack." He straightened up, looking at Donnie and Duffey too. "Now y'all go on with Mrs. Armistead. She'll take you to your rendezvous with your parents."

Rendezvous sounded kind of sophisticated for what was really happening. What was really happening was a one-day suspension.

The four of us walked down the hall, Mrs. Armistead keeping far enough ahead of us that no one could accuse her of being "with us." Our Robin camaraderie had gotten tighter by the morning's events. We were tied by cords of conflict now.

"Did he call you 'Francis'?" Donnie smiled up at Duffey.

The big guy, walking in the middle, put his arms on our shoulders.

"That's my real name." He rolled his eyes. "Can you imagine? What were they thinking?"

"Duffey's better than Francis," said Donnie.

"It sure is," he said. "It'd be cool if y'all can keep that Francis thing to yourselves."

"We won't say nothin' to nobody," I said.

"Much obliged," said Duffey. "Hey, I guess we get the day off, huh?" He was grinning.

"Donnie," I said, "you think your parents are going to understand what happened?"

"Nope."

"You worried about that?" Duffey looked concerned now.

"Nope."

"Why's that?" I asked.

"'Cause what's done is done," he said with finality. "And what's gonna happen is gonna happen. Worrying about it… it doesn't make a lot of sense."

"I ain't worried about it either," Duffey chortled. "Dad don't like me getting in a fight, less'n it's protecting somebody else. And that's just what happened. So things'll be fine at my house."

"What about you, Zack?" Donnie looked at me.

"I can't rightly say." Dad might understand, but Mom was going to be a tougher sell.

"They gonna give you a time-out?" Donnie asked seriously.

"What's a time-out?" Duffey and I both said it at the same time.

"You know," Donnie nodded, "when you have to go to your room and you gotta stay there and can't go anywhere and stuff."

I looked at Duffey and he was just as baffled as I was.

"Is that," Duffey ventured, "supposed to be some kind of punishment?"

"Of course!" Donnie laughed. "Y'all don't ever get time-outs?"

Duffey said, "Nope. I've had Dad's belt on my backside hard enough to make me set still in my room for a spell. Taking my own time-out, I guess."

"I been there, Francis," I said.

CHAPTER 9

That Saturday, we played one of those outrageous games in which your team can do no wrong and the other team can find no hope. The Ravens were pretty bad. All their decent players had moved up to Pony League and their coach was building for the future, filling the roster with ten-year-olds. Next year, they'd give you a good game. Two years from now, they might be championship material. But this year they were Charlie Browns.

By the fourth inning, the score was 22–3. Little League had no "slaughter rule" or "mercy rule" back then. No kid wanted one. Even if your team was getting smoked, you played all six innings.

By the top of the sixth, Donnie and I were sitting kind of sprawled out on the bench.

"What did your dad say about the fight?" I asked him.

He smiled. "Dad surprised me. He was pretty cool. Almost like he thought it was a good thing it happened."

"Your mom?"

"She was all right too. After she heard the whole deal, the whole story as it happened."

I shrugged. "Yeah, well, I didn't get that far."

Donnie giggled. "Mom just said, 'If it happens again, let Zack and Duffey go at the boys, and you stay out of it.'"

I wasn't real keen on that advice. "She said that?"

"She said y'all can take care of yourselves. She said it's not worth missing a day of school." He looked at me. "What about your parents?"

"Well..." I thought about how to put it. "Dad shook my hand and Mom shook all of me. Hard."

"Haaaaa!" Donnie howled. "Now *that's* funny."

"I'm glad you think so." I tried not to smile.

Donnie changed the subject. "I'd liked to have seen Rafer hit this guy's pitching."

Rafer's dad came and got him before the game started. Said he didn't want his boy to embarrass himself. It wasn't a serious blow to the team; the Ravens were clueless.

"Yeah," I agreed. "I'd liked to have seen that too."

"He woulda socked the ball like Paul Bunyan today."

"Like who?" asked Batman.

"Paul Bunyan," Donnie said again. "You know. The big guy that chops down trees and dug the Grand Canyon and... you know..."

"My Aunt Ethel has some," Jimmy said from his spot on the bench.

"Some what?" asked Donnie.

"Some a' them bunions. Around her big toe," he said, pulling a Chick-O-Stick candy from his pocket. "Says they hurt like..."

"Never mind, Jimmy," I said. "Never mind."

Jimmy started peeling the wrapper off his candy. I noticed Sawdust's eyes open wide. Richard, in his friendly tone, said to Jimmy, "I never had one of those. Are they any good?"

"Oh, these are dynamite, little man." Jimmy put the candy stick in his mouth like it was a long cigar. "Only the coolest guys eat these."

I suddenly noticed that Sawdust was not reclining at my feet. Sometimes he just disappeared.

Richard left the bench and took a spot against the fence between Donnie and Batman. "I like those stories about Paul Bunyan. They're myths, ya know. They're really deep. Lots of double meanings."

"Are we talking about the same guy?" Donnie gave Richard a blank look.

"Sure. Paul Bunyan, the big lumberjack. He was a giant, really. It's the myth of a giant. He's got a mule named Bluebird, I think."

Jimmy took his candy cigar out of his mouth and glared at the little guy. "Did this fellow play baseball?"

I spotted Sawdust, sitting directly behind Jimmy. He was still as pond water, except his tongue was licking Jimmy's Chick-O-Stick quietly and repeatedly.

"No," said Richard softly. "I don't think he played baseball."

"Then why are we talking about him?" Jimmy scowled, brandishing his candy like a baton.

"I wouldn't put that back in your mouth," I said.

Jimmy looked down in time to see Sawdust reach for the Chick-O-Stick again.

"Hey!" He jumped up to a chorus of hoots from his teammates, and jerked the candy away from the would-be thief. Sawdust darted away, wagging his tail to beat all, enjoying this marvelous game he was teaching his friend Jimmy. Jimmy looked with dramatic disgust at his candy stick.

"I can't eat this now."

"Might as well give it to him then," I said. Jimmy looked at Sawdust, who looked back at him from his new seat on the grass about thirty feet away.

"Oh no," said Jimmy. "He's not getting this. I'll throw it away later." He rewrapped it and put it back in his pocket.

The Raven on first base called out to our bench. "It was Baby Blue. The mule's name. Not Bluebird. I saw it on Walt Disney."

Coach turned to me and Batman. "What'd he say?"

Batman took the wad of gum out and answered. "He said the mule's name was Baby Blue." He stuck it back in.

"That's what I thought he said." Coach scratched his head.

A loud voice behind us, a carefree male voice, quaked the

whole dugout. "You boys taking a vacation today, or what?" It was Donnie's dad, the preacher. He came late to some games, after working at the church.

"My gawd, Dad, you scared me," Donnie said, clutching at his heart.

"Don't say that, son."

"Aww... I didn't mean to say 'God,' but you scared me, Dad."

I was a little puzzled. "Why don't you want to say 'God'?" I asked seriously.

"It's takin' the Lord's name in vain," Donnie said.

I turned to his dad. "What's that mean?"

"Well, it means—"

"It means saying the word *God*," Donnie interrupted, "but you're not really talking *to* God or talking *about* God."

"Hey, that's pretty good, son," Pastor White said.

Donnie whipped off his cap, bowed his head, and said simply, "Sorry, God."

The little guy sitting next to him snickered.

"You think that's funny, Tigger?" Donnie thumped him over the head with the cap in his hand.

Tigger's real name was Timmy Hargrove, and he was every bit as little as Richard. Donnie had started calling him Tigger, and the rest of us were making the name stick. When Tigger wanted to run straight ahead, he started to bounce a lot. He got excited, and he couldn't seem to keep his feet on the ground long enough to get traction. It was pretty hilarious.

Donnie's reprimand seemed to encourage Tigger to laugh again, harder. "Yeah, I think that's funny." He giggled, putting his hands over his head to defend himself from further attack.

"Donnie, let it go," Pastor White chastised his son. A lot of times parents think their kid is mistreating another kid when he's really just bonding with him. The pastor unfolded a lawn chair. "Let's enjoy the game a while." He sat down.

I glanced toward the bleachers and saw Mom looking my way

and nodding her head to something Dad said. I was surprised to see Dad step down from the bleachers and amble over to where Pastor White sat.

"Hello, Reverend." Dad smiled. Sometimes I think Dad just wanted me to see that he could be just as civil, just as nice, as the pastor, without embracing all that "salvation" stuff. Which means Dad missed the point.

"Well, hey there, Del." The pastor stood up.

Dad patted him on the shoulder. "Keep your seat, Nathan."

They shook hands and Donnie's dad sat back down.

Dad's smile scanned the whole lot of us up and down the bench. "You boys are playing a whale of a game."

"It's goin' great, Mr. Ross," said Richard.

"We're killing 'em," Duffey boomed, his voice as big as he was. "I had a double off the fence."

"Do you know the score, Dad?" Donnie asked. Before the pastor could answer, his son said, "It's twenty-two to three, and the game ain't over yet. Even Tigger's getting in the game." He put his arm around Timmy's shoulder.

"Says who?" Tigger was not convinced.

"Timmy Hargrove," Coach said from his spot in the first base coach's box. "You're on deck."

We Robins took up a makeshift chant.

"Tigger! Tigger! Tigger's gonna bat! Tigger's gonna run!"

"Oh by gosh." Tigger bounced off the bench and began fretfully picking through the batting helmets. "Coach," he yelled. "Coach, these helmets are too big!"

"Where's the little one, Timmy?" Coach asked calmly. "I know I brought it."

I looked at the rookie who was currently at the plate for us. "Clay's got it, Coach," I said.

"I'll get it from him when he's done," Tigger said as he edged out into the on-deck circle.

"Put something on your head while you're waiting for Clay's

helmet, Timmy," Coach called out sharply. "Even one of those oversized ones. We want to be safe."

Tigger grabbed a large helmet and plopped it on his head, effectively masking more than half his face.

"I can't see, Coach," he said, nervously taking several little bounces inside the on-deck circle.

Pastor White encouraged him. "It's all right. It'll protect you."

"Do I look stupid?"

I'm not kidding. He really asked that. But before any of the guys on the bench could holler out the obvious answer, Pastor White dispensed mercy.

"You're looking fine, Timmy," he called to the wiggling helmet.

I turned to Donnie's dad, grinning. "You wouldn't be bending the truth a little, would you, Pastor?"

"At a time like this, I am counting on God seeing my heart is in the right place." He gave all of us a big smile. "Have you had a good game, Zack?"

"It's been all right. I got a double, and then Coach took me out. We're letting the rookies play today. These innings don't mean nothing, anyway."

"Anything," he said.

"Anything what?" Donnie asked in earnest.

"I'm sure Zack meant to say, 'They don't mean *anything*,' not 'nothing.'"

I said seriously to Donnie, "Your dad agrees with me."

Skeeter chimed in. "I told you, BoDean. Preacher man says it don't mean nothin', and he ought to know. He talks to God."

"Okay, okay." BoDean threw up his hands. "If God told him, then I take it back. Maybe this game don't mean nothin'."

"Boys," Dad chuckled softly, "the Reverend was really just making a little grammar comment."

We didn't know what a "grammar comment" was. It didn't sound interesting.

Little Richard decided to speak his mind. "Pastor, I honestly think every inning is significant. I think the really good teams play hard all the time, no matter who their opponent is."

"That's a good point, son." Donnie's dad smiled. "Is that something you came up with on your own?" He waited expectantly, as if he really wanted to know.

"My dad told me."

We all got serious right away. Everybody knew Little Richard's dad was flying combat missions in Vietnam.

"He likes sports a lot." The boy didn't seem overly concerned about his dad, and he wasn't the kind to pretend everything felt okay to him if it didn't. He was too smart and too honest.

"He's coming to see us play," he said in a matter-of-fact tone. "I mean, if he makes it back all right." The little guy was way past the rest of us in understanding the vagaries of life and loss.

Heavy silence. I was sure Pastor White was going to say "He'll make it back, son."

He didn't. Instead he said, "I tell you what, Richard. If your dad makes it back, we'll have a big picnic behind the church after he watches you guys whup whoever you play that day." Then, to all of us, "What do you think of that, boys?"

We erupted in a chorus of "yeah mans," and "all rights." Pastor White always knew what to say. It was like somebody was feeding him lines.

Clay struck out and gave Tigger his helmet. When the first pitch arrived, Tigger swung and got a little bit of the ball, dribbling it fair down the third base line. He ran toward first, a kind of spring-loaded scurrying that beat the throw.

"Safe!" I put a fist in the air.

"Stay on the bag." Coach was counseling from the first base coach's box. "You've got to stay on the bag, Timmy."

Tigger was actually on the bag most of the time. He just loved being airborne, I guess.

"I got a hit, Coach," Tigger shrieked excitedly.

Coach was trying not to laugh at the little guy. "I know, son, but you need to settle down and get ready to run to second base."

"Okay, Coach."

I thought maybe I should stop the guys from laughing so hard and pointing. But some things are just too funny.

"This is the last inning isn't it, Zack?" my dad asked.

"Yes, sir. Coach is playing everybody. 'Cept Rafer, of course."

"Why not Rafer?" asked Pastor White. Scanning the bench and dugout area quickly, he answered his own question. "Rafer's not here."

"No." I shook my head. "His dad took him away. He thinks Rafer's embarrassing himself, playing ball with us."

"That man's got some deep problems," Pastor White said softly. "Sometimes, I wonder... It's going to take a dramatic move of God to see him change." Then, he seemed to catch himself. "I shouldn't say that, boys. God can take any man, woman, or child and grab them, and love them, and pull them into his family."

Bold words, but coming from the pastor they sounded reasonable. Authentic believers say authentic things.

I thought the pastor wouldn't mind an honest question, so I took a stab. "How come, Pastor, only some people believe in God?"

His eyes glistened. "I really like that question."

I looked quickly at my dad, but his eyes were focused on the game. Harold had just struck out and the team was running out to the field for the bottom of the inning.

"You do?" I said simply.

"Yeah, I do. Usually when I get a question like that, it's, 'How come some people *don't* believe in God?' But you asked me, 'How come some people *do* believe?'"

Donnie looked confused. "It ain't the same question?"

His dad smiled. "I don't think so. What about you, Zack? Do you believe the gospel? I know you've heard it. It was good seeing you in church that Sunday."

"Yeah, well... I liked church. I didn't think I would, but I did."

He smiled again. "So do you believe the gospel, Zack?"

"You're worse than Donnie," I said, playfully shoving my friend.

Pastor White didn't say anything more; he just kept smiling at me, waiting.

"I'm thinking about it, sir." I was, too. A lot. I expected that spring would be completely dominated by visions of a Little League championship. Those visions were there, but they floated on the waters alongside other visions. I wanted to believe, but I wasn't going to swallow every authority figure's words. I wasn't eight years old anymore. I sometimes felt like I wanted to take that leap, but I honestly felt I couldn't. Still, honesty is fertile soil.

"That's good," Pastor White said softly. "You know, everybody thinks about it. More than you know."

"Maybe you're right," I answered, glancing quickly at Dad again. But it looked like he was still studying the game on the field, instead of the one beside him.

It's funny how I hoped my dad believed the gospel, even before I believed it myself. Very strange. Unless, of course, I was already moving toward the light. Wanting my dad to come along with me, or even ahead of me, made sense.

"I know..." I struggled for the right words, "I know we all want to be decent, to do the right thing."

"I wish that were always the case, Zack," the pastor said. "But people can be decent, really decent, in ways that a lot of people respect... and that can be their biggest obstacle to faith."

That was way over my head at the time.

The game finally ended and Pastor White stood up slowly, dusted off his trousers and shirt, and folded his chair. "Zack, you 'bout ready to do this thing?"

"Sure." I wasn't really ready, but who is?

My dad looked at me. "Do what thing?"

"'Member I told you, we were going by Rafer's trailer? Just to meet his pa and all."

Dad looked relieved. "Oh, yeah. I think that's good."

"You're welcome to come with us, Del," Pastor White offered.

"No, no. I'd just be in the way, I'm sure. Y'all go on." Dad shook the pastor's hand again and then tousled my hair affectionately. "I think it's great, son. Helping Rafer out, and all. It's the right thing to do."

"I wish I could come," Donnie said, and he meant it. "I got a truckload of homework."

"It's Saturday." I was a little confused. "You got all day Sunday."

"Yeah, but that scrapbook on America's due Monday."

"We've had a month to work on that!" I said.

"I'm a little behind. Let me know how it goes." He sounded disappointed. "Oh yeah, I guess Dad will."

Walking toward the car, Pastor White said, "Your dad's proud of you, Zack. He loves you very much."

"I know."

He changed the subject. "I've never seen a boy hit a ball as hard as Rafer. He even chokes up on the bat."

"I think that choking up really helps him. Keeps the knob from messing with his swing. That's his trick, if he's got one. He just meets the ball."

"And says good-bye!" Pastor White laughed.

"Yes, sir. I hope it was all right, Pastor, for me to talk to you about his dad."

"Sure it's all right, son."

"I'm just worried is all."

"I understand," he said. "We don't know yet what's happening. We just want the best for both of them. For the man and his son." He smiled at me. "So let's just see what's up."

I felt like we were going on a dangerous mission together. Those were some of the first moments when I saw the pastor as something of a hero. I started to think that maybe I might want to be like him.

CHAPTER 10

This is something I don't recall being covered in any seminary course," Pastor White announced as we pulled onto the pebbly dirt that served as the Forresters' driveway. "But then, why should this be any different than pretty much all my other days in the ministry?"

We climbed out of the pastor's Impala and heard a man shout something inside the trailer. Then a blunt sound, like a two-by-four hitting a thick rug.

I moved quick with the pastor up to the cinder blocks that were the trailer's front steps. The voice inside roared again, words I couldn't make out. Then the blunt, slapping sound… and something else. A low sound, like you make when a toothache won't leave.

Pastor White pushed the door and we hustled in.

We were in a cramped combination kitchen–living room, empty of furniture, save one massive old stereo record player against the wall to our right. I don't think it played records anymore; it was stacked with dirty dishes.

"Who's there?"

The quiet question came through the wall to our left. It was not the loud voice we'd heard outside. It was a low, empty monotone.

"It's Nathan White, Cecil. And Rafer's friend Zack," the pastor announced.

No answer.

"I wonder if we could talk with you."

Nothing.

"For just a few minutes maybe."

"You're that preacher man, right?" The voice came through the wall flat, almost resigned.

"Yes ... that's right. Cecil, is Rafer home?"

"A man of God?" It was a question.

The pastor took a few steps toward a tiny hallway that looked like it might lead to the room housing Cecil's voice. Suddenly Rafer's dad was in the passageway, not four steps from the pastor. He had a baseball bat in his left hand.

"Hello, Cecil." The pastor took some cautious steps backward. He made himself smile. I just looked on. If I'd had any brains, I would have been terrified.

"Cecil, you probably don't remember me, but I shook your hand in the market the other day. I remembered seeing you at the boys' Little League game last week." He paused. "My boy Donnie plays ball with your boy. With Rafer."

I spoke up. "I play baseball with Rafer too, sir." I remembered too late that he didn't like being called "sir."

"You a man of God?" he asked Donnie's dad again.

"Yes, I am. Can I do something for you today, Cecil?"

"I dunno. Can ya?"

"I'm here." The pastor's voice was calm.

With his free right hand, Rafer's dad motioned for us to follow him.

We walked the tight hallway. The walls beside us had massive holes in them. The hall ended, opening into a room where the wallboard was beaten in, with much of it cracked or gone.

Rafer sat in the far corner. He raised a hand toward me when he saw me. He wasn't smiling, but he didn't seem upset either. He had a big dark spot on his right cheekbone. The pastor moved to him quickly, kneeled, and gently rubbed the dark spot. It was dirt.

"Rafer, son, how are you?"

Mr. Forrester came alongside the pastor. "I drink too much, Preacher. But I don't hit my boy. Ever."

Pastor White breathed deep. "Is it okay if I just rest here a minute, Cecil?" Without waiting for an answer, he sat down on the floor next to Rafer and leaned against the wall.

I walked over to them and sat down on the other side of Rafer, letting my shoulder touch his.

"How's it going, Rafer?" I asked.

"Zack." Rafer said evenly.

"He's been saying your name a lot lately." I was heartened by Mr. Forrester's smile. "He says 'Zack,' and he says 'Jesus' a lot. And 'sawdust,' whatever that's supposed to mean.

"You don't look so good, Preacher," Forrester continued. "Can I get you a glass of water or anything?"

"I'm fine, really I'm fine." For a few moments, the four of us were quiet. Pastor White, Rafer, and I sat on the floor, resting our heads against the mostly intact wall behind us. Rafer's dad stood awkwardly a few steps from us, the ball bat still in his hand. I was thinking about the sounds we'd heard outside. Pastor White must've been recalling those too.

"Cecil... what are you doing with the baseball bat?"

He took a few slow steps toward us, and for a couple seconds I thought we might have to defend ourselves. But he just sat down on the floor cross-legged, opposite Rafer, close to us.

"I like to hit things, Preacher."

"Call me Nathan."

"Okay, Nathan. I like to hit things. Not people, just things."

"Why do you think you do that, Cecil?"

Rafer, whose face had evidenced no emotion thus far, started to turn his head slightly, following the conversation.

"I don't have to think about it. I *know* why I hit things." His eyes misted. "I hit things because my boy is the way he is. I hit things because Felicia's not coming back. But you gotta believe me, Preacher—"

"Nathan."

"You gotta believe me, Nathan, that I ain't never hit my boy. No sir. I never will. I yell at him a lot, and I know I shouldn't, but sometimes I feel like if I don't open my mouth and yell something, I'm gonna keel over dead. Maybe that wouldn't be so bad."

"That would be very bad." It looked like Pastor White was readying himself to say something more, but it was Rafer who spoke next.

"Rafer dad… alive," the boy said, raising his right hand up to touch the side of his dad's face. "Rafer dad… alive," he said again.

Cecil's eyes brightened then. Something close to a smile raided his grim countenance. "He's been talking a lot more lately. More than ever. I don't really know why. Nothing's changed."

"Are you sure?" the pastor asked.

"Oh yeah. He never used to talk at all. I mean never. 'Cept one word now and again. Maybe once a week, if that."

"I mean… are you sure that nothing's changed? Are you sure there isn't something happening that might explain him talking more?"

Mr. Forrester breathed in and out heavily, as if rearranging the oxygen inside would rearrange his thoughts, too.

"'Course he's playing ball with the other kids. That's somethin' new, but I can't see how that would change anything. That just reminds him, and reminds me, of how different he is."

"Different?"

"He's touched, Preacher," Mr. Forrester said.

Rafer repeated the word. "Touched."

"That's right, son," Mr. Forrester's tone lightened. I noticed he addressed his son directly only rarely. Too rarely, I thought. "The boy's touched. No use in pretending he ain't. It's why Felicia left."

Now it was the pastor's turn to take a long breath before he spoke. "Your boy *is* different, Cecil, but God makes all kinds, and he loves them all."

Mr. Forrester grunted, his eyes cast down at the floor.

Pastor White decided to shift his counsel from the dad to the son. "Rafer?" He turned to face him and put a hand on the boy's shoulder.

"Rafer, do you think you're different?"

"That's no good, Preacher. He don't understand that kind of question."

"I think he does, Cecil." Pastor White looked in the boy's eyes. "Rafer, do you think you're different from other boys?"

For a few moments, I worried that Rafer's dad might be right. Rafer's expression gave no sign that he could tender an answer. But then, in an abrupt tone that demonstrated he understood quite a bit of the conversation, he said, "Rafer different."

Encouraged, Pastor White ventured further. "Are you okay with that, son? How do you feel about being different?"

"Rafer different," he repeated. Then, in the same clear tone, he announced, "Rafer same."

For the first time since we'd come into their home, Rafer's dad was looking into Rafer's face and eyes. "Son," he said seriously, "you are not the same—"

"Cecil, I don't think it helps to say—"

He held a hand up. "This is my boy, Preacher. My boy." Turning back to Rafer, he said again, "You are different, son, and you will always be different. It ain't nobody's fault. And it can't be helped, you being touched. You understand me?"

Rafer did not seem fazed by his dad's words, his dad's correction. I thought of how many times the boy had probably heard the same words from his dad's lips, the same truth that was not really the whole truth.

"Cecil—" the pastor started to say something, but Mr. Forrester interrupted again.

"I know what's best for my boy, Preacher. And for me."

Something snapped inside me. I stood up.

"Mr. Forrester, sir, I don't believe you do know what's best for Rafer. Or for yourself."

"Zack?" Pastor White looked at me.

"You better come down off that high horse…" Mr. Forrester stood up.

"What are you going to do, sir?" I said calmly.

"Zack, I don't know what you're doing." Pastor White stood up too.

Mr. Forrester backed up and raised the bat. "Don't come near me, y'all." He seemed to be addressing both the pastor and me. I didn't know if he meant business or not. It didn't matter to me. Rafer mattered.

After a few seconds with the three of us standing still as stones and Rafer just watching from his seat, the pastor said, "Let's all calm down. Cecil, remember you said you don't like to hit people."

Rafer stood up then. He stepped to his dad. Touching the baseball bat, he took a good hold of it. Cecil let go. "Hit baseball," Rafer said. He walked then to the center of the room and cocked the bat in a hitter's stance.

"Don't hit anything," said his dad.

"Oh, come on, Mr. Forrester!" I heard my voice crack. "Why not? Don't you *want* to see him hit something? Don't you want to see him take aim at something, swing the bat, and knock the bejeepers out of what he's aiming at?"

Mr. Forrester looked hard at me. Weighing me, I know now.

I wasn't through. "You got any eggs, Mr. Forrester?"

"Eggs?"

"Eggs," I said again, blunt. "You got any?"

"Well, yeah, but…"

"Follow me. All of you." I ran down the hallway, back to where I'd seen the fridge near the front door. I opened it and saw a carton of a dozen near the back and four eggs nestled in the door, in those little holes designed for loose eggs. I grabbed the carton in one hand and three of the loose eggs from the holes in the other. Pastor White and Rafer's dad looked at me blankly. Rafer stood behind them in the hallway, still holding the bat.

"Outside. Let's go." For whatever reason, they listened. I positioned Rafer in front of the trailer, walked twelve feet back from my friend, and went into a pitcher's stance. Rafer's eyes glistened, anticipating.

"Stand back," I said.

"You gotta be kiddin' me, boy," Mr. Forrester said to me. Then to the pastor, "Preacher, you gotta help me here."

"Just watch," Pastor White said, folding his arms and staring first at Mr. Forrester and then at me and Rafer. "Let's see how different Rafer really is."

"But he won't even swing. I've tried," said Mr. Forrester, exasperated. "He used to, when he was younger, and Felicia was still around. We used to have a blast when he was really little and I was teaching him to play."

"You played ball, did ya?" Pastor White grinned.

"Yeah, and boy howdy I was good. I used to dream about Rafer playin' the game. He was a little package of baseball dynamite when he was a sprout. But he hasn't liked playin' now for nigh on two, three years. He won't swing."

That intrigued me. "Have you pitched to him lately?"

"I lobbed a lot of balls in to him, and he just looks at me," Mr. Forrester said.

"Do you ever pitch to him like you mean it?" I asked.

"Like I mean what?"

"Like you were trying to strike him out."

Rafer's dad was shaking his head now, probably imagining trying to convince people that the Silas Baptist preacher told him to watch while a crazy kid threw eggs at his touched boy.

I wound up slow and let go an egg with some speed on the throw, but not near to what I could hurl. Rafer watched the egg as it tailed down and away from him and cracked into the trailer behind him, the yoke cascading down, dull yellow streaks on the siding.

"That's it, son. I don't know what's eatin' you…" Mr. Forrester stepped toward me.

I wound up again and launched a second egg, as hard as I could bring it.

Rafer swung the bat with what seemed impossible quickness, shattering the egg into multiple fragments of shell and gooey yolk.

"Did you see that?" Pastor White cried out. "Did you see how fast his bat is?"

Mr. Forrester's voice was almost a whisper. "Throw another one."

I heaved a third egg with all the speed I could generate. The pitch was lower, further outside. Rafer stepped toward the wide pitch, moving his legs, hips, and arms with the speed and agility of a panther. He struck the egg full on the heart of the bat.

"Nice one, Rafer," the pastor beamed, glancing at Mr. Forrester. "Did you see that one… ?" he began, and then started tripping over himself laughing.

Cecil Forrester's face and chest were covered with egg-shot. His mouth was open, his eyes riveted on his boy.

"I can't believe it," he said. "I can't believe he's that quick, that…" He wrestled for words. "That coordinated."

"That's not just *coordinated*, Cecil," Pastor White said cheerily, "that's *gifted*. Your boy has a gift."

"Zack pitch," Rafer broke in. "I hit."

"You want another one, Rafer?" I said, drunk with joy.

"I hit."

A fourth egg met the doom of Rafer's bat. The yard was ruins now, egg ruins. The rubbish and remains of what a father believed to be his son's intractable handicap. Pastor White picked up the egg carton and walked to Mr. Forrester.

"Cecil, we'd love to stay here all day and play egg-ball with you and your boy. But tomorrow's Sunday. It's kind of a big work day for me. I'm sure you understand. Why don't you toss him a few?"

Rafer's dad took the eggs. "Oh, yeah. I understand. I can toss him a few." He walked toward my spot, stopped, and then ran inside.

"Where's he going now, you think?" I asked.

The pastor shrugged.

We heard him through the open door. "I think we got some tomaters in here." Running back outside, arms cradling tomatoes, he said, "If he can swat those itty-bitty eggs, imagine how he'll tomahawk these."

"Yeah," Pastor White called out coolly, "I imagine he'll feast on those. Well, don't let us stop your game here. We've got to be going."

"See y'all later," Rafer's dad said.

"See ya," we both answered. We started walking to the car.

"Thanks for coming, Preacher. And thank you, Sawdust."

"You're welcome," I said. "It's Zack."

"Thanks, Zack."

I thought Pastor White would invite him to church in the morning. He didn't. I guessed maybe such an invitation felt out of sync with the rest of the afternoon's events.

We heard a "splat" like the one Wile E. Coyote makes when he slams into a wall just before he can grab the Roadrunner. Then a man's voice echoing through the Alabama dusk. "Whoooaaaa... that was a good one, son! I can't believe you pulled that pitch! That was way outside!"

Pastor White backed carefully out of the driveway and onto the road toward our homes. We were quiet for a few minutes before both of us, at the same time, looked at each other and snickered, then chuckled, and finally laughed so hard I know it was tricky driving.

"That was absolutely"—he struggled to get the words out, laughing and crying at the same time—"absolutely ridiculous!"

"I . . . I don't know what came over me, Pastor." I was laughing so hard my stomach hurt. "Saying and doing . . . what I did. I got more sense than that."

"I know *you* do, son!" He pulled off to the side of the road and stopped the car. He rolled down his window and stuck his head out.

"God," he hollered, "you must be crazy!"

The two of us sat there a while, just laughing at God, laughing with God.

It occurred to me that if God was crazy, then the pastor was crazy to be serving him, obeying him. I shared what I was thinking.

"I reckon that's so, Zack." I didn't expect him to agree.

He pulled back out on the country road. "Remember when you and the other boys came to church? You remember what I preached about?"

"Not really. Just pieces here and there. Sorry." My honesty got me in trouble sometimes. Not this time.

"Don't sweat it. You *saw* a better sermon today."

I sat still then, still feeling the glow, the burn, from God's touch back at Rafer's.

Pastor White recited then, his voice light as dew on grass, "Where is the wise? Where is the scribe? Where is the disputer of this world? Hath not God made foolish the wisdom of this world? Because the foolishness of God is wiser than men; and the weakness of God is stronger than men."

Those words hung around our hearts and heads while he drove me home.

CHAPTER 11

That night, I asked Mom to drive me to church in the morning.

"Sure," she said. "I'll take you."

"You can come in too, if you want." I didn't want her to think something silly like I didn't want to be seen with her.

"No..." She was a little nervous. "Not tomorrow. But I do want to go some time."

At the time, I was disappointed. Now I know her reluctance was actually respect for a faith she was beginning to see as the truth. When unbelievers are nervous about going to church, it often means they see it as something formidable. That can be a good sign. They may be recognizing God as a real Power, and a gathering of his people as significant.

I hadn't told Donnie or his dad I was coming, so Donnie was nigh ecstatic to see me.

"Did your dad tell you what happened at Rafer's trailer?" I asked.

"He couldn't stop talking about it." Donnie grinned. "He said it was crazy, but it was just like God."

That still sounded a little odd to me, to hear a pastor talk about God like he's kind of "off the wall." On the other hand, I figured God had to be a little crazy to make kids like me, Donnie, Duffey, and Tigger. And Rafer.

I sat with Donnie and his mom near the front, in the second

row. It wasn't until near the end of the service that I noticed Rafer and his dad sitting alone in one of the back pews. I only caught sight of them because I was trying to get a quick look at the clock on the back wall.

It seemed they were paying a lot of attention to Pastor White. Even Rafer seemed intent on listening. In fact, he looked to be paying more attention than me.

"You are all sinners, every one of you." Pastor White's voice was very soft. "I am a sinner too, every bit as bad a sinner, or worse, than anyone in this sanctuary this morning."

I knew that wasn't true. Maybe he hadn't seen Mr. Forrester in that back pew.

"I can see every single one of you from this vantage point up here," he said clearly. That was a little unsettling. I tried not to dwell on it. "There is no one in this room who is less worthy of redemption, of salvation, than me," said the preacher.

That made no sense. My idea of salvation, of being a good person, rattled in my head like so much junkyard debris.

"I know this because God's Word is clear. 'For there is no difference; for all have sinned and fall short of the glory of God.' 'There is none righteous, no, not one; there is none who understands; there is none who seeks after God.... There is none who does good, no, not one.'"

He spoke deliberately, clearly, with no rancor. He did not try to convince us. He was simply making a statement.

"So you understand, don't you my friends," he said, eyes gleaming. "You understand that it is not about all the bad things you do, and all the good things you do. It's not about which outweighs the other."

I sensed everyone was focused, listening close. I know I was.

"It's about how God is entirely good, altogether good, righteous, perfect," he said. "And it's about how we are entirely, utterly lost. We are without hope. Not only do our good deeds not save us, they deceive us into thinking that we're okay. You don't like hearing that, I know. I don't blame you. I don't like hearing it, either. But here it is, in the Word of God. 'There is none who does good.'" He paused, letting the weight of God's truth settle on God's people. "'No ... not ... one.' 'Not one' means nobody. Not Gandhi. Not Billy Graham. Not your sainted grandmother."

I heard a few nervous chuckles behind me. But the clear sense in the people around me was agreement. Across the aisle from me, I saw Mr. Carson, Rebecca's dad, nodding his head, concurring.

"I would like to give you an invitation this morning," said Donnie's dad. I thought that sounded neighborly.

"I'm going to ask you to do the easiest and the hardest thing you'll ever do," said Pastor White. "I'm going to ask you to get up out of your seat and walk down this aisle, and say to the Lord, 'I belong to you, God. I want my sins forgiven. I want to be saved by the blood of your son, Jesus Christ.'"

I recognized his words. He had said them the last time I had come to church. Only I didn't feel like I was watching a rerun. He was totally sincere this morning, wholly serious, and loving. And his words were just as genuine and heartfelt the last time I'd heard them. I was old enough to smell a phony, and this invitation was Alabama-pine clean.

I felt kind of bad for him. Nobody had come forward the other morning, and I expected the same today. But I was mistaken.

I heard a slight rustling behind me and looked back. Mr. Forrester was walking the aisle to my left. When he passed our pew, I saw Rebecca grip her dad's wrist hard, like she was unsure if what she was seeing was something to fear or something to celebrate. Mr. Carson was beaming.

When he reached the front, Mr. Forrester just stood in place, his hands folded in front of him, his head only slightly bowed. He was not crying.

Pastor White just nodded in Mr. Forrester's direction, like it was the most common thing in the world to see the town's darkest sheep come forward to be born again.

"Is there anyone else?" he asked.

Isn't he enough? I thought, turning my head around to look.

"Anyone else this morning who'd like to give their lives to the Lord?"

Seeing no one, the pastor put his arm around Mr. Forrester's shoulders and the two of them whispered to each other.

"Mr. Cecil Forrester wants to give his life to the One who sent his son to die on the cross for his sins. He has come forward, in front of God's people this morning, to make his decision public."

Here Pastor White bowed his head. Everyone else did too, except me. I wanted to keep watching Rafer's dad.

"Thank you, Lord, for saving souls. All of us here this morning, who know you as our Father and your Son Jesus as Lord and Savior, thank you for giving us what we do not deserve... everlasting life."

The organ played muted notes, a melody familiar even to someone as unchurched as I was. "Amazing Grace" filled the sanctuary. Every head was still bowed, except mine. I half expected to see some circle over Mr. Forrester's head, or some bright light emanating from him. But he looked the same, only very still and quiet. I remembered Rafer and turned to see how he was taking all this. He sat motionless, his face placid and somewhat detached, as always. He did look, though, like he was watching everything. It was the first time that I felt Rafer and I were perhaps on the exact same page. I sensed he was, like me, not ready to walk any aisles. I respected him in that moment maybe more than I ever had. Rafer was not a pretender. Nor was I.

But I also had to admit to my head and my heart that Mr. Forrester was not acting in pretense either. I respected his going forward, and I respected Rafer's decision to stay seated. Even a twelve-year-old boy knows real things come from real decisions, and fake things come from deciding to just go along with other people's decisions.

When I got home, I told Mom and Dad about it. Dad surprised me.

"I think that's great, son."

"You do?" Mom and I said at the same time.

"Sure I do. That's the kind of thing that'll make Forrester's life better."

"Oh," said Mom, sounding a little disappointed.

"It's gonna make Rafer's life better, too. I'm happy for both of them," he said sincerely.

Mom stepped out of the room. I think she was shaking her head.

The morning's events stayed with me through the afternoon and into the evening. I was relieved that no one pressured me to go forward. But I felt disappointed too. I wondered whether Mr. Forrester might have found something precious, something truer than anything I or Rafer or my dad had. Would I be asked again? Could someone other than a pastor ask me? Do they ask every Sunday? I really didn't know how it was done.

CHAPTER 12

Everything cruised. We had been winning by wide margins: 30–3, 8–0, 21–9. Today we'd beaten the Blue Jays 15–4. But the Hawks had been winning too.

"If the Eagles can't hit him, we can't either." Donnie said aloud what Duffey and I thought.

The three of us were on the bleachers, watching Pepper Jasper mow down the Eagles, who were not dry grass. The Eagles could hit most anybody, but Pepper was having his way with them.

I noticed Umpire Yates laid aside his customary flourish when announcing third strikes. He either felt bad for the grossly overmatched batters, or he didn't want to stroke Pepper's ego. Maybe a little of both.

"That's strike three, son," Umpire Yates said evenly. "You're out."

"Zack can hit him," Duffey offered. "I think."

"Yeah, Zack can hit him," said Donnie.

"Rafer'll take him downtown," I said.

"Yeah," Duffey drawled, "Rafer takes him downtown and you take him partway there, and the rest of us, *he* takes down. In flames."

"Kinda like Snoopy," Donnie said with a little light in his voice. "When the Red Baron shoots down his flying dog house."

Duffey looked at him like he was headless.

"I always thought that was kind of cool, y'all." Donnie was trying to recover.

"It ain't gonna be so cool when we're on the dog house," said Duffey, "and it's our butts gettin' burned."

Pepper fired another pitch and the batter whiffed.

"How come I never see Pepper in any classes?" I said. "You guys got him for anything?"

"I do," Duffey said. "He's in art class with me. And he'll be in Mr. Wilson's P.E. class with you and me, Zack. Coming up this week."

"What are we doing in there, anyway?" I asked.

"Some kind of gymnastics stuff," Duffey answered. "That horse thing and junk."

"You ever talk to him?" Donnie asked.

"Oh yeah," Duffey snorted. "We have great conversations. Mostly about how we can help each other with homework. And where we go to church. Stuff like that."

"You're being sarcastic, aren't ya?" said Donnie.

Duffey took his cap off and whacked him over the head three or four times.

"Cut it out, cut it out!" Donnie pleaded.

"So, you've never talked to him at all?" I asked.

"Once. He thinks he's God."

"Well, so does Sawdust, but I still talk to him a lot," I said.

The umpire said it again. "Strike three, son. I'm sorry."

"Out there"—Donnie nodded to the ball field—"he *is* God."

Duffey put his feet up on the empty bleacher step in front of him. "He calls me Earth Mover."

"Why?" Donnie asked.

I chuckled, soft enough to be polite. Duffey stared at me, and I stopped. Then Duffey, God love him, laughed too.

"Don't matter none," he said. "I thought it was funny too, the first time he said it."

Pepper pitched again, and we caught the rare sight of the bat hitting the ball. A pop-up back to Pepper on the mound.

"Well," I said, "unless a truck falls on him between now and Saturday, I think we got a good chance of losing to the Hawks. Just like last year."

"A truck?" said Donnie.

"You know," I said, "like when the coyote thinks he's finally got the roadrunner. And then a truck or something falls on him. Pancakes him."

"That always cracks me up," Donnie laughed.

"Not me," said Duffey. "I kinda feel for the guy. I'd like to see him fry that roadrunner up one day." Duffey got a weird look on his face then. "You said we need a truck to fall on ol' Pepper, Zack?"

"What? Oh, yeah. It's just an expression. Fat chance."

"Yeah . . ." Duffey got awful quiet. "Fat chance," he said real low.

Two days later, Duffey and I and a whole clan of boys, including Pepper and Booger, listened to Mr. Wilson explain a gymnastics maneuver he wanted us to try. We'd be learning gymnastics until school let out in three weeks for the summer. The school thought we should have at least a minimal exposure to the sport. Some guys loved it, and some despised it. It really wasn't too different from lots of other classes in that regard, except there were no girls.

"It's simple guys," said Mr. Wilson confidently. "You run as fast as you can toward the horse. Then you jump on the springboard. It will bounce you into the air and over the horse. Open your legs and push the horse underneath you as you clear it. Then you land on your feet on the other side."

He might as well have told us how to orbit the moon without an Apollo spacecraft. I wasn't sure at all that I could do it, and I was one of the more athletic kids in the class.

He demonstrated for us. Mr. Wilson ran down the lane to the springboard, jumped, soared, straddled, and landed perfectly.

He turned to face us, wearing a big smile. "Nothing to it, guys.

When you're done, I need you to help me spot the next guy so that everybody lands safely. We can catch you if you start to fall. Okay? Go ahead and start us off, Greg."

Greg Smethurst was the first kid in line. Duffey was fifth and I was right behind him.

Greg turned to his buddy Stuart and said, "Tell Mary Thornton I love her."

"Mary Thornton? Really?"

"Just tell her," Greg said.

"Let's go, Greg!" Mr. Wilson bellowed.

Greg leaned forward, then ran, jumped, and cleared the horse, landing just in front of Mr. Wilson, who reached out to steady him.

"All right!" said our teacher. "Ya see? It's not that bad. Stuart, you're up."

Stuart, heartened by his friend's success, ran and leaped over the horse. He landed on one foot instead of the perfect two and took a couple hops, but he caught himself and kept from keeling over.

Pepper was now first in line, and Duffey, third, was whispering to the boy who was second. Duffey slid in front of him, behind Pepper.

"Okay, Pepper," Mr. Wilson called. "This is a milk run for you."

Pepper called back to us mortals behind him. "Y'all boys watch how a man does it."

I have to say, his arrogance was matched by his execution. His athletic run, jump, flight through the air, and landing were flawless. Wilson backslapped Pepper congratulations. Now Pepper was helping spot for the next guy… my buddy Duffey.

The intercom crackled and buzzed and we heard the school secretary's voice. "Mr. Wilson, your wife is on the phone."

"I'm on my way," he said. "Hey, Freddy!"

He was calling Booger by his real name. Some of the boys giggled and Booger turned and stared at them. "That's Boog to all y'all," he glowered.

"Fill in for me, Freddy. We need a big, strong guy helping Pepper spot here."

Booger hustled over behind the horse and Wilson left the gym.

Duffey was sporting an odd smile. "A two-for-one deal," I heard him say.

"Okay, Earth Mover," Pepper crowed. "Try not to fall on your fat butt."

Duffey's wicked smile turned to serious focus. He treaded heavily down the path, jumped onto the springboard, and bounded high into the air, completely out of control. I caught sight of Pepper's and Booger's eyes, wide at Duffey's ponderous descent. They would have been much better off if neither had tried to catch him. It's like trying to catch the Hindenburg. You just get out of the way. They didn't.

Duffey came down hard on Pepper's outstretched arms. Booger also took a serious hit, since he slipped on the floor and was directly underneath the descending Duffey.

"Oww!" Pepper jerked his pitching arm out from under the prone Duffey, probably doing it more damage. "Man, that hurt!"

"Sorry about that, guys." Duffey took his time getting to his feet.

Booger was the last one getting up. "How much do you *weigh*?"

"Uh, I dunno," Duffey said. "'Bout the same as you."

Nothing was broken, just severely sprained. The injuries were bad enough to keep Pepper off the mound for ten days and Booger out of the lineup for a week.

I asked Duffey if he planned the whole deal.

"Well, Zack," he drawled, "it's not like I meant to hurt nobody."

"You fell on top of them, Duffey," I said. "You had to know that was going to cause some damage."

"Yeah, I guess so," he said quietly, "but I'll be denying that if you tell anybody."

"Don't worry." I laughed. "I don't think anyone would believe something like that could be planned and executed with that kind of success."

"It did work out pretty good." He nodded. "I kinda figure the Lord was with me."

"What?" I wasn't buying that. "I don't think God approves of that kind of foul play."

"Foul play?" He looked hurt. "They just stood there thinking they could handle what was coming. I can't be held accountable for them being that cocky."

I laughed again. "I'm just glad you're on my side."

"Always, Zack. Always."

That's the way he was. A sinner, just like me, in need of grace.

CHAPTER 13

At the first big game of the season, we had a special assistant coach show up to help us. Rafer's dad, hands in his pockets, stood smiling beside Coach.

"Mr. Forrester here is gonna help us out. He knows baseball. I can tell he was quite a player in his day. He'll coach at third and give y'all lots of pointers."

Coach nodded to the man. "Do you want to say anything to the boys?"

"Just that I'm happy to be here. And I'll do whatever I can to help you boys, and... well, the whole team. That's all."

His face morphed into an odd smile, like he was still learning how that smile thing worked. He was gentle; he didn't seem to be the same man.

Coach focused on us. "Guys, today we play the Hawks. We can beat this team, but we'll have to work for it. Our wins have been coming too easy. We're not gonna win it all unless we learn how to win." It was a pregame reality check.

"But we *are* winning, Coach." Duffey wasn't the sharpest knife in the drawer. "We're going to be the champs this year. Everybody's talking about it. Even Marty—you know, the Falcons' catcher?—Marty says that—"

"I don't think Marty's got any crystal balls, does he?" said Coach, writing on his clipboard.

"No, I don't think so. He wears a cup just like me, Coach." Duffey was serious.

I tried not to laugh, at least not in front of Duffey; I didn't want him to think I was making fun of him. Turning away quickly, I called to BoDean who was chaining his bike to the bike rack beside the parking lot. "Let's go BoDean... time to warm up."

Coach was trying hard too. "Listen guys..." He tried to swallow a laugh, and it surfaced as a strange sounding chuckle. "Listen guys," he started again, and stopped. "Oh, Duffey..." Another short laugh. "Duffey, you're going to kill me."

"What'd I say?" Duffey asked. "What'd I say?" He was jazzed that he'd said something funny. He just didn't know what it was. We all want to be funny and entertaining when we're kids. When we're adults, we want to be wise and serious. Along the way, we decide humor and wisdom are poles apart. That's a mistake.

"Just start throwing with somebody, Duffey," I said.

"Guys." Coach had recovered his composure. "Guys, we need to learn how to win when it's close... when the other team is just as good. Or when, that day, they're playing as good as we are."

Coach liked to walk around us and talk while we threw balls back and forth to warm up our arms. We all listened because it was Coach and he was cool. But I'm not sure how much difference it made, the things he said to us. Most kids play ball because it's fun. And they play to win because that's more fun than losing. Adults want you to play to your potential, be the best you can be. If you *should* win because you're a better team, then the adults are upset if you lose, because you didn't play as well as you could have. But kids? Most just want to play. Donnie and me were different that year. We had the "win" fixation real bad.

"Coach, I don't think anybody's as good as we are," Richard, of all people, said in a thin, shrill voice. "I think we're the best in the league this year."

There were murmurs of agreement, especially from the rookies. All they'd ever known was winning.

"You may be right," said Mr. Forrester. "Y'all are a special team."

"But we haven't been tested yet," Coach interjected. "And today's the day."

"We have a test today?" Batman turned his head away from his partner's throw, and the ball plunked him in the chest. "Oowww... Jimmy! That hurt, you chump!"

"It's not my fault! You're supposed to be looking when I throw the ball," Jimmy pleaded.

"Holy warm-ups," Skeeter snickered softly. "Batman's hurt."

"Shut up, Skeeter," Batman warned, his voice loud enough to tell me he was okay.

"You all right, Batman?" Coach asked.

"He's all right," I said.

"I guess so," Batman said, rubbing his chest hard and frowning at me. He didn't think I was sharing his pain like I should.

Coach tried to reclaim center stage. "Listen up, guys. Everybody sit down."

We sat. Even Rafer, who lots of times would do the exact opposite of what he was told. But today he sat down, looking at Coach, just like the rest of us.

"This is a big test today," Coach said again.

"Tests and me, we don't swim in the same water, y'all," said BoDean.

"Nobody's taking any tests, guys!" Coach belted out in a voice we didn't hear often. He took off his cap, rubbed his head, and took a long breath. "These are the Hawks. We play every team two times, so we're gonna play these guys again this season. The good news is we lucked out big time today, and twice." Coach was clearly excited.

"First, Pepper Jasper can't pitch for them. He's got some kind of sprain, or something happened at school I think. Y'all know he just two-hit the Eagles. And we got another gimme, because their cleanup hitter, Boog Clark..."

"Booooo," Duffey droned.

"... Boog Clark is out. He can't play; he had some kind of fall at school too, I guess."

Duffey whispered to me, "Some kind of fall—he fell on his brain when I fell on him."

"Something you want to share with us, Duffey?" Coach asked.

"No, sir."

"He's been sharing enough this week with lots of people," Donnie said smoothly.

"All I'm saying, guys," Coach continued, "is we got a real shot here, but we need to be ready. These Hawks are topflight. Hey..." Coach stopped and smiled. "'Topflight Hawks.' That's pretty good, huh guys?"

Nobody answered, so I said, "Pretty good, Coach."

"Thank you, Zack."

"Coach pretty good." Everyone turned to look at Rafer. Most of them had only heard "I hit" or "I run" come out of Rafer's mouth. Donnie reached across me and patted Rafer on the back.

"That's right, Rafer." Jimmy chuckled. "Coach pretty good, huh?"

"Coach pretty good. Yeah."

There were giggles all around, and Coach said through a big smile, "Well boys, I'm starting to get a good feeling about this game." He looked into our eyes, all of us sitting around him in a semicircle. With a quick movement, he gestured with his hands at the ball field behind him, and shouted the words we were waiting for: "Let's go play ball!"

We yelled our game cry, "Rockin' Robins!" On our feet now, we jogged as a team toward the field.

I had a good feeling like Coach. I thought we could win.

BoDean trotted up between me and Donnie, looking slightly puzzled.

"Y'all ain't gonna believe this... I just dreamed that Rafer said something about Coach."

"Really?" Donnie's face was stone serious. "What'd he say, BoDean? I mean, in your dream."

"Well, I think he said Coach was a pretty good guy. Or a pretty good coach."

I got in on it. "It's hard to imagine Rafer talking. That's a pretty good dream, BoDean."

"Yeah, it was." He looked proud. "And you guys are always trying to keep me from sleeping. I'm telling you, my uncle has it right. People don't sleep enough."

Donnie eased his leg in front of BoDean's trot, and our starting pitcher went tumbling onto the grass. "Hey! What's the big deal?"

I laughed and kept jogging, but Donnie's heart got the better of him. He circled back to BoDean and helped him up. I heard the sleepy fellow say in a hurt voice, "What in the Sam Hill was that for?"

"BoDean," said Donnie in his warmest tone, "I'm glad you're on my team. You make things a whole lot more fun."

BoDean didn't answer, and I thought he might be pouting. But when I looked over my shoulder, he and Donnie were hitting each other over the head with their caps.

I was confident. We were going to win.

But we didn't start well at all. It was like we were sleeping, or at least trying to get the sleep out of our eyes and heads.

I struck out twice. In my first at-bat, I took a called third strike for the first time in two years. Two years! I struck out a few times every season, but I always went down swinging. Not this time.

"What was that?" Coach was more baffled than angry.

"I don't know." I decided to be honest. "I guess I was thinking about something else."

"Like what?"

"I was thinking about a Zero candy bar."

My second time up, I struck out swinging at a pitch in the dirt. Walking back to the dugout, I looked up at Mom and Dad in their spot on the bleachers. Mom's chin was resting in her cupped hands, her fingers almost covering her eyes, like she was afraid to look anymore. Dad cocked his head, looking at me quizzically. I put my head down.

I heard some other adults in the bleachers, parents I didn't recognize, saying, "This game is over."

"It's only the third inning, honey. And that quiet boy hits real good."

"He's not quiet, Marge, he's retarded. If we have to rely on him to beat the Hawks, the game's over."

"He's already got a homer. I've never seen a harder hit ball than that one."

"Game's over, Marge. I'm going to get a Coke. Want anything?"

I would have gone with the man if I could've. A Coke sounded like a great way to drown my troubles.

—

Little League games last six innings. Sometimes that's fairly short and sometimes it's an eternity. When the Robins played the Hawks that spring of 1971, the sixth inning was the hinge of fate.

I consciously revisit certain moments in my past. Large moments, larger than this life.

Looking back, I honestly believe that this inning I started to see life as open range instead of four walls. If you could see the snowcaps and the lakes, you could get there and back again. You can see anything and go anywhere. Or you can live within the small space of your own self-imposed limitations.

In the bottom of the inning, our whole team seemed to be waiting to lose. Except for Donnie and Richard. The two of them paced back and forth in the dugout, telling all of us we could still win.

"I know we're better than this team, you guys." Richard was almost pleading. "Let's go. We can take them."

"Fellas," said Donnie, "I'm not leaving here losing to the Hawks. They're good, all right, but this is our year, guys. Ain't that right, Rafer?" he said, patting Rafer on the back.

The score was Hawks 11, Robins 7, in the bottom of the sixth and last inning. Most of us were thinking about what color to paint the walls that held our lives in hopeless check. Something to make life a little less drab. Third place wasn't so bad. Safe. Tame.

But after Skeeter whiffed for the first out, we started a slow ascent up the walls. Harold walked. BoDean hit a hard grounder deep in the hole at short. The Hawks' shortstop, Eddie Glass, dove and snagged the ball, but couldn't put enough fire on a throw from his knees to get Harold at second. I was in the on-deck circle when Batman laid down a beautiful bunt up the first base line. The pitcher, Tony Graham, and the first baseman collided while scrambling to the ball. Tony didn't even make a throw.

The bases were loaded. *Maybe God is a candy store*, I thought.

On my way to the plate, I heard Dad's voice. He had stepped down off the bleachers and was pressed against the fence near the batter's box.

"Keep your head down," he said low. "You're pulling your head."

I nodded. I knew what he meant. It was an old habit I thought I'd broken entirely, but one that came back to haunt me when I was overanxious. A lot of hitters pull their head away from the pitched ball when they swing too hard. Their eyes follow their head's turn and they miss the pitch.

Tony had got me swinging the last time. He knew he was a gifted athlete, and he wanted you to know it like he did. I was surprised to see him walk Harold, and I made myself take a couple of pitches that were close. I thought they were in the identical spot, but the umpire didn't agree. One ball, one strike. The third pitch split the plate knee-high—or it would have. Instead, I kept my head down and drilled the ball to dead center. The center fielder had shaded me to pull the ball toward left, and he hadn't taken more than a step in the direction of the ball before it caromed off the chain-link with a satisfying clang.

All three of my teammates scored, and when I saw the center fielder plucking the ball from the base of the fence as I rounded second, I knew I had third base standing up. I did a little pop-up slide, just for good measure, and came up clapping my hands like a madman.

"Nice hit, Ross," said my friend Eddie Glass. He was a peer in sports. Good at everything. Almost as good a hitter as I was.

"One out," I said, breathing a little heavy. "I can tie the game on a ground ball or deep fly from Duffey or Rafer."

"If I were you, I'd have braked at second," Eddie said, strolling back to his position.

"Yeah, well, you're just lucky I didn't score."

I remembered to look in Mom's direction. The sight of her jumping and shouting in the bleachers, her fists in the air, stays with me to this day. Thirty-six years later. I remember Dad, too, still beside the fence by the plate, smiling and nodding. Kids remember stuff like that.

I talked to myself, quiet but out loud, about the game situation. "You're the tying run. Tag up on a fly. Freeze on a line drive. On the ground, don't run unless you're sure you can make it."

The massive Francis Duffey was at the plate.

Coach clapped his hands. "Tied up, Duffey. Just a base hit. Choke up a little, now. We need it, son."

Duffey wasn't about to choke up. He took a big, roundhouse swing at the first pitch, missed most of it, and popped up weakly to the pitcher. Coach shook his head.

"Nice one, Francis," the Hawk pitcher said, loud enough for Duffey to hear, but low enough to not get in any trouble with the ump for saying the batter's name.

I heard Duffey talking as he walked back to our bench. "I just missed that one, you guys. I coulda socked that pitch to the moon."

Rafer was in the batter's box in an instant. His zest for hitting had only grown more pronounced throughout the season. I don't know how much he understood the game situation; but I did know he always wanted to hit, and I was real glad about that now. Very few people, kids or adults, really want to be *the man*—the guy at the plate when the team's down to its last out. Everyone likes to hope, but not everyone wants to be in the situation where that hope is *you*. Only fools and champions want to hit under those circumstances. I never thought Rafer was a fool.

Tony Graham was mad at himself for letting me connect. That's the way some guys see it. It's about them. It's never that the other guy made a good play. It's that they didn't. You didn't succeed; they failed. They carry that with them, sadly, into adult life. It's impossible to find peace when everything's about you.

Stock-still in the box, Rafer waited for Tony's fastball.

He didn't get it. Tony was ticked, but he had enough presence of mind to *pitch* to Rafer and not just try to fog his fastball by him. The first pitch was a kind of changeup, a very slow pitch. Nobody really throws a changeup in Little League. Except Tony Graham when he's pitching to Rafer Forrester in a big game. Somebody had had a serious talk with Tony about Rafer.

Rafer took the slow pitch—of course.

"That's a strike," the ump said bluntly.

Donnie hollered from the dugout. "Swing the bat, Rafer-man." Then he shouted to me on third, "Tell him to swing, Zack."

"You got it, Rafer," I called to my friend, clapping my hands.

Rafer actually glanced at me, a rare maneuver when he was focused at the plate. I felt sure he would swing. He still seriously preferred the speedballs, but we'd seen him swing at medium-fast pitches the last few games. He was learning to stop waiting for the fun to come to him. I hoped this was one of those times when he would just reach out and smack that ball regardless. "Just reach out and smack that ball," I said in a plain voice. He didn't acknowledge me, but he did something that buoyed my hopes considerably. He smacked the plate with the bat. Hard. He must have seen Donnie and Duffey do something similar, when they would tap the plate with the bat to get their bearings up there. Only Rafer didn't tap the plate a couple of times; he tomahawked it three times. Very hard.

Booger mumbled something I couldn't hear, and the ump said, "Don't break the bat, son." Rafer didn't respond. He just readied himself for the next pitch. I leaned over, ready to take off from third.

Tony crossed us a second time, throwing a big, slow, roundhouse curve. Seeing the pitch coming in high and tight, Rafer ducked, dropping to his knees to avoid being hit in the head. The ball swooped like a seagull, angling lazily across the heart of the plate.

"That's strike two!" The ump was getting a little more animated, and some cheers erupted like little firecrackers from the Hawks' dugout and their supporters in the bleachers.

I spotted Donnie in the dugout, raising his hands skyward, and giving me that "What can we do?" look. I took my hands off my hips, raising them in like manner as if to say, "We can't do anything, my friend."

As Rafer got off his knees and back into his simple "ready" batting stance, Tony started his windup again, a look of conquest in his eyes.

Another slow curve swooped toward the plate, breaking huge again like it was turning a street corner.

Rafer didn't duck this time, or go to his knees. He waited for the ball to break over the plate, and then brought his bat around hard, like a young Lincoln splitting a rail. The ball was off his bat like a bullet, coming straight at my face. I fell, an instinctual collapse that preserved my eyes, nose, and teeth. I remember *hearing* the ball, a low murmur, the sound my granddaddy used to make when he was blowing on hot coffee in his saucer.

Scrambling to my feet, I looked over my shoulder to see where the ball had come down. It hadn't. I watched in hushed awe, along with the rest of the spectators, as Rafer's six-foot-high liner held its altitude all the way to the left field pole, banging off the metallic cap and dropping into the field of play.

"That's a fair ball!" the umpire yelled.

I trotted home, looking at Rafer all the way. Rafer was fast when he wanted to be, but he still struggled to grasp the concept of keeping stride through the bases. Most times he stopped, or at least stutter-stepped, at each base, before continuing on. It was the only reason he had no triples to go with his truckload of doubles, homers, and some of the longest singles I'd ever see.

This time, Rafer surprised us all by not stopping at second base. Instead, he did his odd little "stop and step" maneuver before lurching on toward third. Not a great idea with the ball out in left field. Fortunately, he had hit it so hard that the ball had a little backspin on it when it struck the left field pole. It rolled away from the left fielder, spinning like crazy. By the time the third baseman took the throw, Rafer was standing on the base with his arms folded across his chest. You'd think he'd be played out and breathing heavy after his run, but Rafer wasn't normal. I had never seen him winded. He looked like he was watching the game instead of playing in it. In a way, he was.

With the score now tied, Donnie was our last chance to avoid extra innings. He was choking up on the bat, but even so, there's no way he should've gotten good wood on Tony Graham's fastball. He just wasn't quick enough. Unless he got some outside help.

C'mon God, let him be a hero, I prayed silently. *He's a good kid. I know you're with him.*

Something happened in the heavenlies, I guess, because Donnie White lined the first pitch cleanly to center field, Rafer ran home, and we had beaten the Hawks, 12–11!

We all ran out to Donnie, who'd stepped on first and then turned to grab us running into him with our back slaps and hugs. Rafer got a little confused when we all took off toward first base. I think he thought we were all going to run the bases as a team. I grabbed him and told him to go slap Donnie on the back. He did—too hard, knocking Donnie down. But Donnie didn't care. We were still undefeated!

CHAPTER 14

That Wednesday, after school, Dad and I stood on top of Richard's house. It was a strange but cool feeling, eyeing roofs to our right and left and the tops of houses across the street on Patricia Drive.

"It won't be so cool or strange if you fall off," Dad drawled. "Lots of roofers do. Come away from the edge."

"I'm not gonna fall."

"Get your butt over here."

I got my butt over there, close to where he kneeled, away from the roof's edge.

"Is it a bad hole?" I asked.

He peeled back a rotted shingle, clawing it with the back of the hammer. "It's a leak, not a hole."

"That's good."

"No, that's bad," he said. "Rain gets under the shingles and soaks the wood. If it was a hole, you'd see it quicker and fix it sooner. Less rot." He bent closer to the damage. "Leaks are sneaky."

"We got enough shingles to fix it?" I hoped so. The bundle of shingles was a bear to haul up the ladder. Dad hollered down for me to bring them up. I heard him snickering when I tried them under one arm before setting them back down, sizing up the task.

"Put them on your back."

I did, and stepped onto a ladder rung careful-like.

"Come up slow. If you feel anything start to slip, let the shingles go."

I took it slow and got it done, Dad relieving me of the load at the top. It was a scenario no mom would have tolerated, me negotiating ladder rungs with close to fifty pounds on my twelve-year-old back. But dads and sons do this sort of thing.

"We have plenty of shingles. Here, throw these to the ground." Dad pushed remnants of worn shingles at me. "But first peek over the edge to be sure you're not tossing them on somebody's head."

I crept close to the edge, but not close enough to see over it, and dropped the spent shingles.

"That was pretty close," a kid's voice said simply. I peered over and saw Richard's round face.

"Hey!" he beamed. "What's it like up there?"

"It's really cool. You should check it out."

Richard grabbed the ladder rungs and pulled himself toward the roof.

A screen door slammed. "Richard Powell, you come down that ladder this instant," Mrs. Powell called up from the ground. "You hear me?"

"I can see it some other time," he said real casual, shootin' the breeze with his baseball buddy.

He stepped down one, two, three rungs, quick.

"Slower, Richard," his mom admonished.

Sure that her boy would make it down safe, Mrs. Powell called up to me.

"Zack, would you and your dad like some lemonade?"

"Yes, ma'am."

Behind me Dad said, "We'll come down and get it in about ten minutes."

"We'll be down in about ten minutes," I echoed. "Thank you, ma'am."

"You're very welcome. Thank you both for the work."

Mrs. Powell disappeared into the house. I heard her telling Richard he could forget any foolish notion of him taking a tray of lemonade up the ladder to me and Dad.

"Scoot over here," Dad said. "Here's what you need to see if you're gonna learn something up here."

"I didn't come up here to learn anything," I teased.

"Too bad." He pointed to water stains in the exposed wood. "The point of overlapping shingles is to keep the water sliding off. A roof can take a lot of storms if the shingles are properly laid, so they work together. Reinforce each other."

"What if they're not properly laid?"

He shrugged. "Then the storm waters find places to cut in between shingles."

My gaze shifted to the many houses, the many people-less roofs. The air was so still, it was like we were floating. "It's kinda lonely up here. It's like we're not supposed to be up here or something."

His eyes caught mine. "Do you see how the shingles work together?"

"I see it, I got it." My mind was elsewhere.

Dad set down his hammer and leaned into a sitting position next to me. "You think it's lonely up here?" he asked.

"Don't you?" I looked at the cloud-covered sun, sliding into setting. "I mean, it's just us and the roof and... nobody."

"I kinda like the nobody part," he said. "People are tolerable tiresome."

"What does tolerable mean?"

"Tolerable? It means..." He thought about it. "It means something might, kind of, gradually be wearing you down."

"I think hauling shingles onto roofs like this would wear me down."

He chuckled at that. "I wouldn't want to do it for a living. Then again, you don't have to deal with anybody. You don't have to make small talk with people all day, like with some jobs."

"What do you mean, 'small talk'?" I knew what he meant; I just wanted to hear his answer.

"Small talk? It's just, you know... 'Hey, how's it going? I'm fine, how are you?'... You know, small talk."

"You mean," I said, "words that don't mean anything?"

He thought that was funny too. "Yeah, I guess that's right."

"What would big talk be, then?" I smiled, ready to answer my own question. "Talking about things that mean something, like living and dying, heaven and hell and stuff?"

"Now what made you say that?" He looked serious.

"Say what?" I asked, innocent.

"Heaven and hell," he said slow, distinct.

"I don't know. I guess we're talking about big things, things that matter a lot to people. Everybody wants to go to heaven. Don't they?" He wasn't answering. "Nobody wants to go to hell. Right?"

"When you die, you die. It's just over."

I didn't say anything. I just looked at him, waiting.

"Robert Earl, Rebecca Carson's dad, came up to me at the plant the other day. Said he met you at his church." He gave me a soft smile.

"Oh yeah." I tried to sound only slightly interested, but I was anxious to hear his next words.

"He's a good man. Honest. Hard to believe that..." He paused, shifting gears. "You and Rebecca are kind of sparkin' a little."

"Dad," I blushed. "We're twelve." Now I shifted gears. "You like Mr. Carson?"

"What's not to like? He's decent. Genuine. You know I never knew my dad."

"I know."

"Mom raised your Uncle Travis and me. She did a great job, worked her butt off. Until... I was about your age, maybe a year older. Travis was ten or so. Mom got real sick. Cancer. Couldn't nothin' be done. Everybody said so. Except the church."

"Y'all went to church?"

"We started going when Mom got sick. They'd come and pick

up Uncle Travis and me. The church folks came round every other day to pray for Mom. To lay hands on her. She got better."

"She got better?"

"It's called remission. For a time, the cancer subsides and the person gets better. People were dropping by the house to see the miracle. Mom walking around and laughing. Hugging and kissing me and Travis."

He stopped talking. I waited. Kids learn when to wait for someone to start talking again.

"It was a great few months. We all agreed God had healed her, especially Mom. 'I'm a walking testimony,' she said."

"What happened?"

"It came back and took her quick. I was in the hospital room her last day. She was so weak, so little. People kept coming in the room. Church folks. Whispering things to Mom that Travis and me couldn't hear."

He looked back at me. "I can't forget those minutes. All my life, I hear her voice, her words. 'I guess God must be upset with me about something,' she said. She was crying. 'But I don't know what it is. I can't think of nothing.'"

"Oh no," I said. "That's not it."

"That's right. That's *not* it." He spat the words. "You and I know that's rot. But that was her last thought, Zack."

He took a deep breath. "I'm not mad at God. That'd be like holding a grudge against someone who's dead. They're not there. It's a waste of good anger. But I do hold some powerful things against people who say they know a God who loves, a God who heals. They made Mom's last days, and her last minutes, miserable."

He dropped his stare, stood up, and stepped carefully toward the ladder. "Let's go get some lemonade. We'll come back up and knock this job out. Shouldn't take us more than a half hour, now that I got the rotted shingles stripped off."

I followed after him, to the roof's edge. "I won't go to church if you don't think I should, Dad."

"I never said that," he said. "That's the sort of thing everybody decides on their own. I just don't want you getting hurt. Does that make sense?"

"Yeah." From his perspective, it made a lot of sad sense.

"Wait till I'm off the ladder," he said. "Then I can hold it for you at the bottom."

I watched him descend. He stepped off the ladder and held it secure, looking up at me.

"Okay," said Dad. "Come on down. Slow."

I turned around, my hands flat on the roof, feeling for the ladder with my foot but not finding it. I turned back around, a little scared.

"It's hard to take that first step," I called to him. "You can't really see what you're doing."

"Tell me about it," he muttered, but I heard him. "You'll be fine," he said louder. "Just take it slow. And trust the ladder. You know where the ladder is."

I tried again, trusting Dad's counsel and my own coordination. In twenty seconds, I was back on the ground.

Mrs. Powell stuck her head out the front door. "Ready for some refreshment?"

"That sounds great, Jackie." Dad smiled.

Richard poked his head out from behind his mom. "Mom says I can't go up on the roof until Dad's with me and I'm Zack's age."

"You listen to your mom," said Dad. "She loves you."

"I told her I'll never be Zack's age, 'cause Zack'll always be two years older than me. That's right, isn't it?"

I chuckled at Richard's big smile. "How do you think of stuff like that?" I asked.

Richard's mom hugged her little man. "He's too smart for his own good."

"What's that supposed to mean?" Richard wondered aloud.

Over the next few minutes we washed down oatmeal cookies with lemonade and made small talk.

"How are you and Paulette doing, Del?" Mrs. Powell's voice was pleasant, kind.

"We're fine. How're things with y'all? Hear anything from your husband?"

"Same story. He's either bored or flying a quick mission. Seems a strange way to live, when you're over there."

"I'm sure it is."

I wondered how Dad made such small talk, right after he and I'd talked about the biggest things. I don't wonder anymore. Small talk is a seeming safe harbor. For a time.

CHAPTER 15

I ate supper at Richard's house the next night. It started out so fun. They ate, not in a dining room, but at a tiny table in the kitchen. And they were laughing from the get-go.

Richard talked about how much power Rafer had.

"You had to see it, Mom! I don't even know if Dad could hit one that far."

"Now you're telling a big one, young man. Your dad played college ball." She pointed at Richard's plate. "Eat your broccoli. Zack's eating his."

"I like it," I said.

"You see?" she smiled with mischief. "And you know your dad likes broccoli."

Richard frowned. "But Zack and dad are old."

Mrs. Powell and I laughed pretty hard. "You think I'm old?" I looked at Richard.

"You're in sixth grade!" he said, as if that settled the matter.

"I'm only two years ahead of you," I giggled.

"That's what I'm saying," he insisted. "Two years is forever!"

His mom recovered from laughing enough to make a point. "You know, from his perspective," she said to me, "I guess you are old. There's a vast difference between ten and twelve years old. Now when you're thirty-two and he's thirty..."

"Oh man," said Richard, "we might as well be dead!"

Mrs. Powell roared with laughter. "Ooohhhh! I'll be sure to tell your dad you said that! Eat your broccoli. It's one of your dad's favorites."

"Broccoli is old fogies' food," he mumbled. "Old fogies eat different."

"So now we're old fogies!" she challenged him.

"Not you, Mom. Just Dad."

The phone rang. Mrs. Powell rubbed her son's head, messing up his hair. "I love you."

"I know," said Richard sincerely.

The phone rang again and Mrs. Powell picked it up.

"Hello? Yes, I am Mrs. Powell."

Her face darkened. She put a hand over the mouthpiece.

"Richard, honey, you and Zack go play outside."

"You mean it? I don't have to eat it?"

She waved a hand at him. "Just go, honey, please."

Richard bolted in the direction of the front door, and I followed him. He stopped, turning back to his mom. "Is everything okay, Mom?"

"Richard, please." Her face was stiff, her eyes darting, like she was trying to see what had hit her.

We walked out the front door and sat down on the front steps. We could still hear his mom's faltering voice.

"Was this today?... But that's two days... I understand, I know it's possible... Please, as soon as you know anything. Thank you, Major."

We heard his mom hang up the phone. And we heard her say, "Please God." Then she was dialing.

"Maybe I should just go on home," I said to Richard.

"How? You gotta call someone to pick you up."

I'd forgotten about that. We didn't live close to each other.

We heard his mom again. "Hi, is this Patty?"

The only Patty I knew was Donnie's mom.

"Patty, this is Jackie. Jackie Powell." Her voice sounded calm now. "Donnie plays baseball with Richard... Yes, that's right... Oh, I'm fine—no, I'm not." Now it started to give way. "It's Rich, Richard's dad. He's... missing... shot down... No, they don't know yet... Two days, they said... Yes, please, Patty... Oh, God, yes... please, God."

She hung up. I didn't know what to do, where I should be. It was at least a minute before the screen door opened.

"Mom?"

Mrs. Powell sat next to Richard and put her arm around him. We could see she'd cried, but her eyes were wiped dry now.

"I can call my mom or dad to come get me," I said.

"That's fine Zack." She gave a brave smile.

I started to squeeze by her back inside to the phone.

"Wait a minute, Zack." She put a hand on my arm. "Richard looks up to you so much. I think you should know this. You can help him. Would you sit down?"

"Yes, ma'am." It was dusk, and nobody else was out. The street in front of us was quiet, still.

"Richard, honey," she said. "That was a call from somebody who works with your dad."

"In Vietnam?"

"That's right. He flies with your dad."

"Cool," he said quietly.

She took a long breath. "He said that..." she broke a little. "He said that Dad's plane went down."

"Was Dad in it?"

"They don't know that yet." She swallowed. "He could have gotten out before it went down."

"Yeah." Richard nodded. "He could have ejected. Dad would do that before ... you know."

"They haven't been able to get to the plane... where it went down." She stroked her son's hair. "And they haven't heard anything from him on his radio."

"Maybe the radio doesn't work," Richard offered.

"That's right." She nodded, glancing at me. I nodded too. "So they're out looking for him. They've got real good men looking for your daddy, Richard."

"Are they gonna find him?" His face wrinkled up, but he didn't cry.

I said, "Lots of times they find guys." His mom nodded to me. "They can find him, Richard." I didn't know if they could, but I wanted to believe it.

"Well, Zack is going to encourage you, Richard," Mrs. Powell said. "He's going to see you at school and he'll be somebody you can go to if you need something."

"That's right," I said. I was surprised how much I really wanted to be there for Richard.

"Maybe you should go in now and call your mom, Zack."

"Yes, ma'am."

I stood, walked into their house and over to the kitchen phone. I could still hear Mrs. Powell's voice.

"They're really good men, looking for your dad…" she said again. "Real good men."

CHAPTER 16

The next day, Friday, Donnie and I filed through the cafeteria lunch line.

"Hey Zack." He sounded a little nervous. "I was going to ask you if you want to come to church with me on Sunday."

"Again?"

"Yeah. Again. I thought you liked it."

"Well, yeah, I did." I grabbed a tiny milk carton out of a pit of crushed ice. "But I guess I didn't think… I mean, I don't think I need to go back. At least not right now."

"It's not like getting a shot or something." He smiled, picking up his own milk. "You don't go once or twice and say, 'I'm glad that's done, I got what I need, but I ain't goin' back again.'"

"I just thought I pretty much heard what I needed to hear."

"I don't know if you did or not." His tone was sober now. "Anyways, I just wanted to invite you back."

I wasn't sure what to say. I guessed he still wanted to say something else, maybe something serious. My guess was right and wrong.

"Well, to be honest with you, this Sunday's 'Friendship Sunday,'" Donnie said.

"What's that mean?" I didn't like the sound of it.

"It means…" he said, opening his brown lunch sack and

looking down into it like there was something awfully important he needed to check there, "it means that if you come, I'll get a hundred points added to my Sunday school tally."

"You're kidding me," I said a little too loud. "Don't you think that's kind of fake? Kind of wrong?"

He looked up at me and defended himself. "They're just trying to get us to bring people to church. What's wrong with that?"

"I don't know. Maybe nothing's wrong with it." I thought I was angry, but it was more like disappointed. "It just seems kind of… corny, don't you think?"

"You don't have to come," he said quickly. "Forget I said it. Forget I said anything."

"Okay I will," I said just as quickly. It was one of those moments when preteen friends pretend to be a little angry, a little tough with each other. "Friendship Sunday," I said under my breath, loud enough for Donnie to hear my righteous, indignant tone.

We looked for a table, and spotted Rafer and Rebecca alone at one. Two tables past them, Booger Clark and a few other kids sat facing away from us, making ugly giggling sounds.

Walking toward Rafer and Rebecca, I could make out Booger's words. "That must be the retard table."

"I could never eat all this." Rebecca was showing Rafer something. "Want some of these chips?"

I handed Donnie my lunch and passed them in a blur.

"I didn't know Rebecca was a retard," said Booger, "but I guess… heeeyyy!"

I grabbed Booger's shirt collar hard, spinning him halfway out of his seat. I let him twist free, hoping he'd start punching. He didn't. We were face to face for several awkward seconds. He was gauging me. I heard somebody yell out "Fight!"

I felt a gentle pressure on my shoulder, from behind. Rebecca's hand.

"Zack… can you and Donnie sit with Rafer and me?"

More seconds passed as Booger and I waited for the short fuse to hit the powder keg.

"C'mon, Zack," Rebecca said, soft as eiderdown.

I let her little grip start moving me. To Booger I said, "Nobody's a retard here."

Like that, it was over. Rebecca and I walked back to Rafer's table. He'd kept his seat through the whole deal.

"Don't let Booger get to you," Donnie said.

"You don't think I can take him?"

"I didn't say that."

The three of us sat down. Rafer was balancing a fork on top of the fingers of his palm-down right hand.

"Boog just doesn't understand some things," said Rebecca.

That made absolutely no sense to me. "He understands all right. He's just mean."

"So y'all beat each other up." She put those blue eyes on me. "Then what?"

"Then I'll feel a whole lot better! Aren't you glad I stood up for you? And for Rafer?"

"Yes. I am, Zack. You want to protect Rafer and, well… me. You have a big heart. And you're brave. But…"

"But what?"

"But Jesus would not punch out Boog!"

I didn't know how to answer that; didn't want to. Donnie did.

"You sure about that?" Donnie leaned across the table toward her, talking pretty fast. "'Cause I'd like to see Jesus or Zack or *somebody* clean Booger's clock. I know Jesus said for us to love our enemies. But it's tricky. I think we oughta defend people that can't defend themselves. Maybe the question is, what's inside us? Are we defending people who need our help, or do we just want to kick butt?"

"Kick butt," Rafer said flatly. Head down, he arranged potato chips in a line on the tabletop.

Rebecca and Donnie laughed, and I was glad to laugh with them. We pulled our lunches from brown bags.

Donnie wanted to know what kind of sandwiches we had. Rebecca, already munching, said, "PB and J." Donnie asked if she liked it, and she mumbled through her sandwich, "Who doesn't... like PB and J?"

"I like it," I said, too quickly.

She smiled at me. I decided I really liked chestnut hair pulled back in white ribbons.

"What've you got?" She leaned slightly in my direction, apparently fascinated with my brown sack lunch food.

I said I had a bologna sandwich, "toasted," because I liked that "extra little crunch." Donnie seemed to think that was hilarious, but Rebecca was sympathetic.

"Cool. I'm gonna get Mom to toast mine, too."

I had a strange peace. I was eating lunch in the cafeteria of McInerney Elementary School and I couldn't imagine wanting to be anywhere else, doing anything else. I saw Mrs. Hunt step through the cafeteria doors, her fourth graders following sharply on her heels, in line. She taught Little Richard. He saw the four of us and stopped to wave, causing a slight traffic jam. Students behind him bumped together awkwardly.

Donnie and I gave little waves back. Rebecca raised her hand, swallowed a lump of peanut butter, and called out, "Hi!"

The boy behind Richard pleaded with his teacher. "Mrs. Hunt, can I pass Richard in line, 'cause he stopped and waved to some of the big kids and..."

"Stay in your line," said Mrs. Hunt. "Move along, Richard."

"Did y'all hear about his dad?" Donnie asked us.

"He's a pilot in Vietnam," I said.

"Ohhh..." Rebecca's tone was sympathetic.

"He was shot down," Donnie continued. "His mom called our house and told us. He's MIA."

Rebecca looked at me. "What does that mean, Zack?"

"Missing in action," I said.

"I'm so sorry..." She meant it, her voice trailing off. "That's pretty bad, isn't it?"

"Yeah, well..." I felt like maybe we shouldn't talk about it. Like it was bad luck or something.

"We should pray for him," she said, her voice now very clear, strong.

"Yeah," said Donnie. "For him and the whole family."

"Let's pray right now," said Rebecca.

I seemed to be praying a fair amount lately. Before that season, the only time I remembered praying was when I fell out of the oak in Donnie's back yard and knocked the wind out of my lungs. I prayed then because I was sure I was dying. *Dear God, this is Zack. I can't breathe. I got no air inside me. So I'm coming up there to where you are now. I'm looking forward to meeting you. I hope you feel the same.* When my air came back, I told myself I ought to talk to God more often. But I didn't.

"It doesn't have to be a long prayer," Rebecca said softly. "I'll do it." And she started in.

Donnie bowed his head. There was nothing to do except close my eyes and bow my head.

"Dear God, it's about Richard's dad. He's going through some really hard stuff right now. We don't know where he is, or what he's doing. But you know. Help him God. Right now, this minute, help him. He's got a family, God..." Her voice cracked just a little, and I opened my eyes to see if she was crying. But she wasn't. She looked strong and peaceful. Rafer's head was up, and he was looking at Rebecca. Listening, too.

"He's got a family, God," she said again, "that's waiting for him to come home. So, we're asking you to bring him home safe, to his loved ones. In Jesus' name, amen."

"Amen," I muttered, and then Donnie in a clear voice after me, "Amen, God."

The five-minute bell rang. "Oh my gosh, it's 11:45!" Rebecca shot up out of her chair, stuffing half-eaten food back into her lunch bag. "I have to talk to Susie about last night's homework."

"But you didn't finish your lunch." I wanted her to stay longer.

"Oh, I'm all right," she called over her shoulder. "I can never finish it anyway."

I watched her take two or three quick steps away. But she spun around sharply and darted back, kind of out of breath.

"I forgot." She looked at me. "This Sunday is Friendship Sunday at church. If you come with me, I get a hundred points on my Sunday school tally sheet. Will you come?"

"Uhhh, well... okay."

"Great! I know where your house is. We'll pick you up about 9:15. Okay?"

"But I thought church didn't start until 11:00 o'clock."

"But you have to come to Sunday school!" Her mouth broke into a wide smile. "I get a hundred points!" I felt myself smile back.

"Nine-fifteen," I said. "I'll be ready."

"I'll be ready," said Rafer.

Hey, why not? "Can Rafer come?" I called after her. "He's gotta be points too, right?"

"Two hundred points!" She put a little fist in the air in triumph. "Can we get your mom and dad to come, too?"

"I can ask 'em," I said. "But I wouldn't count on any more miracles than just getting me and Rafer there."

She thought that was funny, and she laughed while she hustled over to where Susie Yates, the umpire's daughter, was wolfing down a piece of bread and poring over some pages in her math book. Rebecca sat down next to her and said something. Susie looked in our direction. I put my eyes back on my toasted bologna sandwich.

"So..." Donnie had that wise half-smile on his face that meant he was going to say something he considered extremely intelligent.

"So, anyway," Donnie said, eyes shining, "I was wondering if you wanted to come to church with me this Sunday. On account of it's Friendship Sunday."

I should have felt embarrassed, maybe even ashamed. I didn't. The Carpenters' song "Close to You" steamed like a sleek freight train through my mind. Everybody just wants to be close to the one whose eyes are blue starlight.

"It's Friendship Sunday," Donnie droned on. "Some might say it sounds kind of corny and fake and everything, but if you come with me, I'll get a hundred points on my Sunday school tally."

I smiled at my best friend. "Am I gonna get this the rest of the day?"

"Oh, I think this is good for more than a day, don't you?"

"Donnie..."

"I mean, I'm only your best *friend*, and it's only *Friend*ship Sunday and all..."

The second bell rang. Lunch was over and we were supposed to get a move on back to Mrs. Massengale's classroom.

In the hallway, we passed Rebecca and Susie on the way to their own class and teacher. I was really hoping she might not say anything. Maybe Donnie would let it go too, and I'd have some peace. But when she did speak, it sounded real good.

"I'll see you Sunday, Zack."

"Okeydokey."

Donnie looked at me with pity-filled eyes.

"What?" I said a little too loudly. "What's the matter?"

"Okeydokey?"

I shrugged.

"Hopeless." He shook his head. "You're hopeless."

I jumped him, wrestling. After a few takedowns in the hallway, we scrambled into our classroom.

"You're both late," Mrs. Massengale said, trying to frown. "Do you two have an excuse for getting back late from lunch?"

"No, ma'am," I said.

"Does him being a traitor count?" Donnie's smile always melted Mrs. Massengale's heart.

"Sit down, you two."

CHAPTER 17

Some of the stranger moments in a twelve-year-old boy's life are when he sits next to a twelve-year-old girl who likes him, in the back seat of a car driven by the girl's dad.

When the boy's newfound friend, a kid with mystical baseball powers who doesn't talk unless some odd spirit moves him, is also sitting in the back seat next to him, the episode is even more bizarre.

If the group is headed to church, well, those wondrous moments are not forgotten for long years to come. Maybe never.

"You're Paulette's boy, aren't you?" Rebecca's mom smiled at me from the front seat.

"Yes, ma'am." I considered saying I was Del's boy too, but thought better of it.

"And you don't have any brothers or sisters either, do you?"

"No, ma'am."

"So, you and Rebecca have something in common, then," Mrs. Carson said politely. "I like your tie."

"I like it too," said Rebecca. "Red's my favorite color."

Mr. Carson chimed in. "I thought your favorite color was blue."

Mrs. Carson gave him a look with very sharp edges, and he spoke up again. "'Course that was a while back, when Rebecca said her favorite color was blue."

"Yes it was," Mrs. Carson said, her eyes still riveted on her husband.

I told them how it really wasn't my tie; it was Dad's. And how Mom got it out of their closet for me, and I'd never seen Dad wear it, but he must have.

"It looks very nice on you," said Mrs. Carson.

Rebecca leaned slightly toward me and whispered, "You don't really have to wear a tie."

"I don't?"

"No."

"Well, I just wanted to make sure you got your Sunday school points and everything."

She giggled and I chuckled softly. Her mom looked at us. "What's so funny back there, you two?"

"Nothing, Mom."

Mr. Carson ventured to speak again. "Get that laughing out of your system, kids. There's no laughing in church, you know."

"Don't tell the boy that, Robert Earl." His wife punched his arm.

"Owww," Rebecca's dad moaned.

"Owwww," said Rafer. "Owwww."

Rebecca patted Rafer's knee. "Dad's just kidding, Rafer," she said.

"Owwww," Rafer said again.

"Dad's just kidding," Rebecca said to me, now.

"I thought he probably was." But I really didn't know. Just like church, *church people* were another world to me.

Mr. Carson glanced from the road to his wife and back again. "Do you know that hurts when you do that?"

"Oh, stop being such a baby," she chided.

The suggestion that Robert Earl Carson, former Chicago Bears linebacker, was ever remotely like a baby was very funny to me. I tried to kill it, but a laugh came out anyway. I was relieved when everybody laughed with me. They were really happy, a fun family. I thought I was lucky to be going anywhere with them.

"Hey Zack, I heard about y'all beatin' the Eagles, you catching that long fly yesterday for the last out." Mr. Carson sounded genuinely excited. "You want to stop over at our house after the service? We could get some lunch, and throw the ball around. Some of the neighborhood kids come over then, you know."

"Sure!" I said, just about jumping from the back seat into the front with excitement.

"Rafer, honey," Mrs. Carson tapped his knee, "you can eat with us too." He didn't respond.

Rebecca looked at me. "Do you think his dad will let him eat with us, Zack? Maybe even let him play some ball with us?"

"I'm pretty sure his dad would be okay with that."

"All right Rafer!" Rebecca put her arm around Rafer's shoulder. "I bet you're as good at football as you are at baseball!"

"Football?" I found Mr. Carson's face in the rearview mirror. "Are we gonna throw the football, sir?"

"That all right with you?" he asked.

"That would be great!" If it turned out I knew any of these "neighborhood kids" who played football with Robert Earl Carson, they were gonna get an earful from me for not letting me in on it.

"Can I be on your team, sir?" I asked.

"Oh, you don't want to be on his team," Rebecca laughed. "He's terrible."

"I am not!" Mr. Carson was indignant.

Mrs. Carson interjected. "He always wants to be quarterback. And he throws like a girl."

"That's not true!"

"Yes it is, big shot," his wife insisted. "You always want to be quarterback."

"I do *not* throw like a girl." He sounded pretty serious to me, and I thought maybe his wife and daughter ought to change the subject. Not on your life.

"Yes, you do, Dad." Rebecca had grabbed the top of the front seat and pulled herself close to her dad's face. "It's okay, though. You were a great linebacker. Nobody expects a linebacker to be able to throw the ball."

That was true. I was impressed that Rebecca seemed to know a lot about such things. More like thrilled than impressed. But I was definitely gonna do whatever it took to get on Mr. Carson's team. I would've paid good allowance money just to get to watch Robert Earl Carson play a pickup game. Now he was gonna let me play with him. After he fed me lunch!

Rebecca looked at Rafer. "Rafer, did you know that my dad played for the Chicago Bears?"

"Bears in the woods," said Rafer.

Rebecca and I laughed pretty hard at that. Her mom looked concerned.

"It's cool, Mom," Rebecca said, patting Rafer's knee again. "Rafer's funny." From the miniature purse she held on her lap, she pulled out a little rock.

"Thanks again, Rafer, for this really cool stone you gave me." Rebecca smiled at Rafer. "I like the blue streaks on it."

"What kinda streaks?" I asked. "Lemme see."

"Put your hand out," she said playfully, her blue eyes dancing.

I hesitated.

"I'm not gonna hurt you," she laughed.

I put my hand out.

She cocked her head. "You goof! Turn your hand, so your palm's open."

I did. She dropped it, and I caught it. It was smaller than mine, but had thin blue lines crossing it, almost like the work of a paintbrush. Only it wasn't. Not a paintbrush held by a human, anyway.

Mrs. Carson ooohed and aaahed from the front seat. "Where did you find that, Rafer?"

"Yes," he answered, sort of. "Found."

I gave it back to Rebecca. "That's really swell looking." She put it back in her tiny purse and clicked it shut. She looked me in the eye, her smile so big I thought my world would stop and start again.

As we pulled into the church parking lot, I asked God a silent, serious question. *What have I done to make you so happy that you would fix me up with a family like this?*

We piled out of the car. Except for Rafer. I held the door for him, but he didn't move.

"Rafer," I said. "We're here, Rafer. We're at the church now."

I looked at the Carsons standing there, waiting patiently. Rebecca stepped back to the car, poked her head in it, and said something real quiet to him. He bolted out of the car and walked at a fast clip ahead of all of us. I hustled and caught up, giving Rebecca a questioning look.

"I told him there's free ice cream inside," she said with a straight face.

"Get out."

She laughed. "I told him … I told him Jesus was inside."

The church service went roughly the way it had the last time I was there. That surprised me a little. For some reason, I expected church services to change a lot from week to week. Of course, Donnie's dad's talk was different. But it had the same centerpiece. Jesus died for my sins, for Zack Ross's personal sins. He didn't use my name, but he made it clear again that Jesus was thinking about me while he was dying. Even when he came back to life, when he rose from the dead, he did it for people he loved. Ordinary people like me. People who did bad things, and thought about bad things, like I knew I did.

I was interested this Sunday in the "why" question. Why did God put his boy on the cross? You have to love people an awful lot to do that to your boy. Only it sounded like God didn't do it *to* his boy, he did it *with* his boy. Sounded like his boy was in on it. His boy agreed. He agreed that he loved people too, and he agreed to hang that love on an ugly cross. Which sort of made the boy just as loony as his pa. Loony with love. I couldn't relate. I was smart for my twelve years, but it confused me. I knew I couldn't love anyone like that. How did God and his son do it? What kind of God is this? It helped a little when Donnie's dad said outright that God was "foolish." He brought up the same Bible verses I'd heard him use before. He said even when God was foolish, his foolishness was smarter than when people are really smart. And even when God seemed weak, like when his son was stuck up on the cross, God was still stronger than all us humans.

I looked around the church. Some of the other people there looked a little confused too. It was funny, though. What Pastor White was saying sounded good to me. Maybe even true. No way could I have explained exactly what he was preaching. But it sounded like truth. Like the crack of a bat on a pitch.

Rebecca poked me and silently showed me the words right there in the King James Bible: *Because the foolishness of God is wiser than men; and the weakness of God is stronger than men.*

That was it then.

I was intrigued and a little puzzled with the preacher's words, but Rafer seemed positively mesmerized. His eyes stayed on Donnie's dad, even though the pastor moved quite a bit in the course of his message.

"They nailed Jesus to a piece of wood," Pastor White said. "They nailed him." He paused. "We don't want to remember the nails so much."

He held up an iron nail, bent in the shape of a cross, with a red string tied to it.

"Without the nails, there is no grave. Without the grave, there is no resurrection. And without the resurrection, our sins are still on *us*... instead of on *him*."

Rafer's eyes locked on the nail in the preacher's hand.

"You all get a nail today," Pastor White said. "I've asked the ushers to hand them out now. I also told them to say something to you as they put it in your hand. Listen to what the usher tells you."

The ushers came down the aisles, handing out the nails. It was hard to make out what they were saying until they got up close to us. Rafer got his nail just ahead of me.

"Remember this nail." The usher put it in his hand. "Remember the grave. Remember he arose."

Rafer stared at the nail in his open hand.

The man said the same thing to me and gave me my nail. As Rebecca was receiving her nail, Pastor White invited everyone to stand and sing hymn number 216.

Everybody stood up, except Rafer. He kept looking at the nail in his hand.

Up from the grave he arose, with a mighty triumph o'er his foes;
He arose a victor from the dark domain,
And he lives forever with his saints to reign.
He arose! He arose! Hallelujah! Christ arose!

Rafer never stood. He stayed fixated on the nail in his hand, touching it lightly with his other hand.

—

That evening, I lay awake in bed, Sawdust at my side. The day had been the most fun I could remember. Lunch was KFC, buckets of it, all you could eat. I didn't let the coleslaw and biscuits get lonely either.

I always fell asleep with the radio on low. Another Carpenters' song was playing, saying we need to look for a place to grow.

"Today was the best day of my life, Sawdust. So far, anyway. Sunday! Even church was a good time. Rebecca's as much fun as a guy. Maybe more fun."

Karen Carpenter kept singing—about horizons and sharing and just beginning.

"Playing football with Mr. Carson. You'd like him, Sawdust. He believes. He's like Donnie that way."

I stared at the ceiling, still petting Sawdust. Mr. Carson had ended up on the other team, which disappointed me at first; but then it proved a constant source of pride and achievement for me. I intercepted four of his passes. He really was a lame quarterback. But he was aces as a man. Strong and kind.

My dad was strong. And lots of people would have called him kind. But Dad didn't go to church. He didn't even pretend he'd like to. He didn't believe, period. Mr. Carson did. Both men were genuinely following what they believed and embraced, and distancing themselves from what they did not.

That puzzled me. Dad liked to say that everyone has to write their own story. As a kid, that always sounded good to me. Later I recognized we are not given the power to craft our own story, only the ability to find the tale the Storyteller has written.

I honestly didn't care if my life story was written by someone else. I'd rather someone better than me, and stronger than me, orchestrate my life.

"I don't get it, Sawdust. How can someone as big as God want to hang around somebody little like me? What's in it for God? I can see how he might want to run Pastor White's life. Or even Donnie's life. They're a lot nicer than me."

He disagreed, laying his head alongside mine and licking my face, my ear.

I kind of pulled away, but not really. "Hey now… that tickles. What's that? Oh no, I don't think so. They don't let dogs in the church. That's their loss, right?"

I rubbed behind his ears and the back of his neck, which always made him look like he was smiling. Maybe he was.

I closed my eyes. I didn't want it to end, but the day was done.

Turning over many times on my bed that May night in 1971, I wrestled, unaware, with spirits, deep into the Alabama evening and early morning.

CHAPTER 18

The week that school let out for the summer, I found myself with nothing to do and no one around to do it with. Donnie was visiting his aunt and uncle in Greenville, and Sawdust I guess was on a little vacation. He did that sometimes; just disappeared for a few days. The day was already turning hot and sticky, and I decided I wanted to go to the swimming hole—to swim a little, but mostly just to think.

Mom didn't seem to mind. "You're going to the creek?"

"Yes, ma'am."

"With who?"

"Well..." I hesitated. "Nobody."

"What about Donnie?"

"They went out of town. I'll be careful, Mom."

"I want you to stop by Mr. Miller's house on the way there and back."

"Paw-Paw's?" I said.

"Yes. Sit a while with Paw-Paw," Mom said. "He might want to go for a swim himself." She smiled.

I gave her a strange look. "Mr. Miller?"

"Oh, I'm just kidding around." Sometimes it makes a guy nervous when his mom "kids around."

"But you never know," she said. "Sometimes those older

folks surprise you with what they want to do." She looked at me. "He probably has days he wants to wear cutoffs and a sleeveless T-shirt, too."

I smiled my best sweet smile, hugged her quick and hard, and bolted out the back screen door.

"Stop and see Paw-Paw first," she called to me.

"I will."

"If he wants to go with you, you tell him I said he can go if he's careful."

"Okay, I'll tell… Oh, come on, Mom."

I started jogging toward the wood line that led to the streams that crisscrossed the base of Sand Mountain and came together in the creek we called Sandy. A couple hundred yards in, I saw the barn-red siding of Mr. Miller's house, and the man himself on the porch rocker. Everybody who knew him called him Paw-Paw. I had called him by his surname a couple years back, and he'd given me a forbidding, wide-eyed look.

"You a revenuer, son?"

"I don't think so." I didn't know what that was.

He smiled, but held his eyes in the same mock menace. "The only men who ever called me Mr. Miller were lawmen."

"I'm just a kid." I really wasn't sure if he knew I wasn't the law. Kids never know about old people.

"But you might be a lawman some day."

"I guess I might."

He smiled then, and ran his rough hand through my hair affectionately. "You'd be a good one, son. You know why?"

"Nope."

"'Cause you got a heart. And you're not afraid to use it." It was words like that that had endeared Paw-Paw to my mom and dad and the other parents in our neighborhood. People who hadn't gotten to know him thought there must be something wrong with him. People always think that about other people who live different or talk different. And Paw-Paw was different and then some. Nobody knew his age, and guesses ranged from seventy-five to ninety-five, or more. Some people wondered how he lived, but that was clear enough to anyone who visited him. There was enough garden and enough game to keep him alive and satisfied. He didn't want much.

I scrambled onto the porch, startling the old man just a mite.

"What in the... ," he turned and, getting good sight of me, beamed. "How are you doing, Little Man?" That was his name for me. It could have been much worse.

"I'm good." I plopped onto the crate that was my seat on visits. "I'm going swimming in the creek today."

He gave a look of soft surprise. "You all's outta school already?"

"It's been June for a week now. A week and two days. Today's June ninth. You don't know what day it is?"

"I know exactly what day it is." He leaned my way, looking me in the eye, but kindly. "It's the next day that God has made. Why we feel the need to put a name and a number on it is beyond me."

He sank back in his chair, and both of us were content to just look out over the rows of corn and other vegetables that were getting established in Paw-Paw's prodigious garden.

"Going swimming by yourself?"

"Unless you want to go with me." I thought it was a funny thing for me to say, but he seemed to take me seriously.

"I don't believe I want to go today," he said. "But thank you."

I thought maybe he was pulling my leg, but he sounded so genuine that I had to ask.

"Do you go swimming in the creek much, Paw-Paw?"

"Only when it gets real hot."

"Today feels real hot," I said simply. It felt like about a hundred and one to me.

"I don't mean... weather-hot." His eyes were still fixed on the corn rows. "I mean when it gets real hot on my inside. When I have to cool down on my inside."

I waited for an explanation, but it didn't appear he was going to give one unless I asked for it. So I did.

"Well, Little Man," he said in the sing-song tones that signaled he was going to share something unique to Paw-Paw, "every day we live, we get a few more coals poured into us. Some days, those coals are hotter than other days."

I wanted him to talk more, so I gently prodded. "Have you seen a lot of those days?"

"No, I haven't," he said. "Where I live, and how I live, the days are pretty still and mostly just cool or just warm. But where you live, Little Man," and now his eyes found mine, "where you live, you're going to have a lot of really hot days, and cold days too."

I decided to be a little bold. "You think people would live better out here—I mean, the way you live—than living back in my neighborhood?"

"No, I don't," he said in an even voice. "Fact is, I'm pretty sure you would see nothing but hot days living like me, and I would see nothing but fried days living where you live."

I was more than a little confused. But in a funny way, it didn't bother me. Paw-Paw's confusion seemed a little clearer than most people's regular conversation.

"So you beat the Hawks, huh? Pretty impressive."

That totally threw me. Paw-Paw never talked about the world beyond his corn and porch. He was still looking out over the fields.

"How do you know about that, about my team and all?"

"Rafer told me."

There are moments in all our lives when the world pauses and makes a sound like echoes from a falling rock hitting flat earth. Loud moments of silence. In those ricochets of stillness, we see past ourselves, past our rudderless lives. We grow older.

"Rafer talks to you?" I asked quietly.

"Sure."

"A lot? I mean, like, does he talk to you a lot?" My voice was rising. "Does he come by here and see you?"

"Sometimes."

"Sometimes?" I was incredulous, but discovering something.

The phone rang in Paw-Paw's kitchen behind us.

"That'll be your ma, Little Man. You answer it, would you?"

"What makes you think it's Mom?"

"Because your ma loves you."

I'm sure I looked confused. I went through the open doorway that led into the tiny kitchen. The phone, big and black and hanging on the wall, looked like something I'd seen in gangster movies.

"Hello?" I answered, feeling like I was in a dream.

"Oh, hi Zack," said Mom. "I just wanted to make sure you were doing all right there. How's Paw-Paw?"

"Rafer talks to him."

"Well, that's nice, but don't stay too long at the creek. You promised your dad you'd mow the lawn today, so you better get that done."

"Mow," I said. "Okay."

"That's right. I'll see you in about an hour or so, okay?"

"Okay, Mom."

I hung up the receiver and walked back out to the porch.

"Your mom all right?" Paw-Paw asked.

"She's fine. I gotta mow the lawn today."

I sat down and decided I really didn't feel like swimming.

"Does he talk a lot?"

"Who?"

"Rafer!"

"You don't have to yell at me, son, I'm not deaf yet."

"I'm sorry. I just ... I'm shocked to hear you say that Rafer talks to you."

"Why?"

"Because he won't talk to anyone else," I said. "Not much, anyway."

Paw-Paw's eyes flashed at me. "He told me that he talks to you, Zack."

"Well, yeah, he does. Short little sentences. Just a word here and there."

The man chuckled quietly. "Just a few words here and there," he repeated. "That's a book coming from Rafer," he said. "That's a long, tall tale, coming from Rafer's mouth."

"So, he talks to you about the team?"

"Nope."

I was past confused. "But I thought you said—"

"I said that Rafer told me y'all beat the Hawks. He told me that much about the team, and that was it. He doesn't really talk about the team much at all."

"But he's talked to you about other things."

"Not things, really. People. Rafer's not into things or games or happenings. He's into people."

"I find that hard to believe, Paw-Paw."

"Now, why do you say that?"

"Because he never talks to anyone. He doesn't even seem to look at anyone much, really." I wasn't mad about it. I was just describing Rafer the way I saw him.

"Now, I find *that* hard to believe."

"Well it's true," I said flatly. "The guy doesn't look at people."

"That don't mean he doesn't see them." He looked at me, smiling. "And it sure don't mean he's not interested in them."

I shook my head and he started laughing, so I did too.

"So..." I started talking through my adolescent giggles, "are you going to tell me what you're talking about... or do you even know what... you mean, or what?"

"I don't never know what I mean, Zack," he said between laughs. "My whole life is a quiet shot in the dark night."

"What?"

"I know enough to know I don't know nothing."

"Okay, whatever that means. But what about Rafer?"

"Rafer is like us, only more so." Paw-Paw had stopped snickering and was serious now. "He knows he's baffled, and I think..." He paused. "I think he wonders why everyone else is not baffled too."

"All I know is, he doesn't seem to even look at people, but you say he's interested in people. That doesn't make any sense."

"Maybe he sees people without looking at them. Maybe he sees more than we do—for all our lookin'." He leaned toward me, serious as the summer heat. "Here's what I want you to hear, Zack. Most all of us are blinded because we see too many things. We can't see what's real, and what matters, because we see too much of what is *not* real, what *doesn't* matter."

I stood up, ambled to the edge of his porch, and jumped off onto the Alabama grass, fried brown with the lack of rain.

"So I've run you off, have I, Zack?"

"I'm just going to go for a little swim. In the creek."

"Do you understand what I'm saying, Zack?"

"I guess I do, mostly," I said honestly. "It sounds like you're saying..." I thought about my words careful-like. "You're saying that people like Rafer might see things the rest of us don't. Maybe 'cause Rafer's not so busy going everywhere, seeing everything, and saying everything."

"That's a big part of it, Zack." He smiled and leaned back into his rocker. "Have a good swim. Tell the creek I said hello."

"Okay." I took a few steps toward the half-worn path we used to get to the swimming hole, and then turned back to call out, "Hey, Paw-Paw."

"Yeah," he answered.

"You never called me by my name before. You never called me 'Zack' till today. How come?"

"Oh, I don't know. 'Little Man' don't seem to fit like it used to. It's okay I call you Zack, ain't it?"

"Oh, yeah. It sounds good. See ya." I started jogging down the path, among and between the trees, thinking how cool the water was going to feel.

I didn't really swim so much that day. Mostly, I just bobbed in and out of the water and lay on the bank alone, thinking. Thinking about what I might not be seeing, and what Rafer was.

CHAPTER 19

The game against the Falcons was unforgettable for lots of reasons. One of the big ones was that Richard's dad got to see it. We were all pumped because Donnie's dad was going to follow through on his promise to have a picnic after the game on the church grounds.

After four days of meandering through the jungle bush in North Vietnamese territory, Captain Powell had stumbled onto a US Marine recon team that led him across the demilitarized zone to safety. It was big news. Nobody seemed to expect him to survive. In the newspaper, he thanked everybody for their prayers. I remembered Rebecca praying for him in the cafeteria. Really, I guess I had prayed too. I know Donnie had.

Just a few days before the game, Richard and his mom had met Captain Powell's flight home at Maxwell-Gunter, the air base outside of Montgomery. Of course, all us Robins thought we were pretty special to have Captain Richard Powell coming to our game. It was inspiring seeing him in the bleachers, still on crutches. Sawdust was especially taken with the man; he divided his time between watching the game from underneath the Robins' bench and watching it sitting beside Captain Powell on the bottom row of the bleachers. The captain obviously liked him too, petting him and talking to him like they were old pals.

Before the game started, I noticed Rafer handing Richard a black rock speckled with beige spots.

"What's this for?" Richard asked me, not Rafer.

"I think he's giving everybody one. I think it just means... I dunno."

"It means he's thinking of us," Jimmy drawled from behind me. I looked at him over my shoulder, surprised.

"I'm not totally stupid," Jimmy said, looking back at me. "Not like, ya know, totally, all the time."

The Falcons were competitive. They weren't as good as we were, but they were not the sort of team to be taken lightly. They were pitching Riley Brinkerhoff, whose fastball dominated a lot of Little Leaguers.

We got caught flat-footed. The Falcons jumped out to an early lead and stayed two or three runs ahead of us most of the way. As we came to bat in the sixth inning, we were down by two, 9–7. After Harold whiffed and BoDean grounded out to second, our bench was quiet, smelling our first loss.

Coaching third, Rafer's dad clapped his hands, encouraging Donnie, our last hope. "You can do it. Get us going."

But Donnie didn't step up to the plate. He jogged over to Coach in the first base coach's box and mumbled something I couldn't make out.

I heard Coach. "Are you sure about this?"

Now Donnie spoke clear, loud enough for me to hear. "He needs to play in the game, Coach. It ain't right if he don't play."

"All right," Coach said slowly. I could tell his thinking was not entirely in accord with Donnie's.

"Richard," Coach called to the little guy at the end of the bench, "grab a bat. You're pinch hitting for Donnie."

"Me, Coach?" Little Richard was as flabbergasted as the rest of us.

"Yes, you," Coach said a little too sharply. Getting his perspective back, he said in a warm tone, "Donnie thinks, and I think, your dad should see you play. Since he came all the way from Vietnam to see this game. Whaddya say?"

Now if I were Little Richard, and my team was losing with two outs in the last inning, and I knew I wouldn't even see the pitch, much less hit it, I would've been terrified. But Richard didn't see it as a terrifying situation. He had learned a little bit about what real terror involved, and this wasn't it. This was just a ball game.

The youngster grabbed a bat and the small batting helmet, pausing at the fence that separated the players from our parents in the bleachers. Captain Richard Powell, his crutches doing the heavy lifting, raised himself stiffly off the bleachers. His wife, Jackie, stood with him. They had been cheering their heads off the whole game.

"You gonna hit, son?"

Through the chain-link fence, Richard locked eyes with his dad. "I'm pinch hitting for Donnie, Dad. Some of the guys want me to get in the game."

"That's great, Richie." Captain Powell beamed.

"I hope I don't let the guys down." It was just a fact. He wasn't scared. He just didn't want to let us down.

"You can do it, son," said his mom.

"Batter up," the umpire called, but he was smiling.

Richard clamped the batting helmet onto his head. Peering out from under the brim, he said to his dad, "This is a lot of fun, isn't it, Dad?"

"That's right, Richie."

Seeing our smallest player at the plate, I wasn't very hopeful. Richard had been patiently riding the bench and cheering us on most of the season. The few times he'd gotten to bat, he'd struck out or popped out. He was still just too little to have much pop in his bat.

He took the first pitch for a strike and swung very late on the second pitch for strike two. The Falcon parents stood up clapping, smiling, and nodding to each other that the end had come.

Riley wound up dramatically and uncoiled toward the plate, an impressive combination of speed and fluidity. From my perspective in the on-deck circle, his fastball seemed to glide, traveling almost in slow motion. It didn't, of course, but it looked that way to me. It was one of those moments when a higher power pointed my eyes toward the action he wanted me to see. He stalled time, or so it seemed, so I could track it. Maybe those kinds of things only happen to me, or maybe you know what I'm talking about.

As I watched the ball glide toward the plate, it looked like a sure strike, right down the middle. Riley wasn't worrying about hitting the corners with this batter. Then I saw that Little Richard was made of the stuff of champions. He bent down, leaning over the better part of the plate. The ball smacked off his left forearm. Players, coaches, and fans collectively winced as Richard, hesitating only a second or two, started bravely trotting down to first base. It was a weird trot. His right hand was fisted and bent across his midsection in a natural runner's posture. But his left arm hung straight down, limp like the corner of a poster on a wall that's lost one of its top pushpins.

Coach and Mr. Forrester ran onto the field, stopping Richard halfway to first base. Coach put his big hand on Richard's little shoulder. "You all right, son? Let me see your arm."

Richard's mom and dad had come up to the chain-link fence.

"It's all right, Coach." The little guy smiled bravely. When we're older, we all learn that some things hurt worse than physical pain. Richard Powell knew that when he was ten.

The Falcons' coach ran up alongside Coach and looked at the arm, already darkening in a mean bruise.

"Is it broken, Wayne?"

"No, I don't think so. But he'll have a blue arm for more than a few days."

The Falcons' coach was Mr. Bob Irwin, a local county firefighter, and a bear for rules. His brother was missing in action somewhere in the Mekong Delta. He looked Richard in the eye. "Son, did you get hit on purpose?"

I could see Richard's face. His eyes, already brimful with tears from the stinging in his arm, gave way now. Through tears, he met Mr. Irwin's stare and said soft but clear, "Yes, sir."

"So you leaned over the plate, so the ball would hit you?"

"Yes, sir."

Coach Hornbuckle spoke. "Bob, I don't think that's right," he said, sighing heavily. "I don't know, but that's probably against the rules. He's probably out."

"No he's not," Irwin said quickly. He leaned in closer to the boy, his hand on his shoulder, and said quietly, "Your daddy must be very proud of you, son. I know I am. That took some guts."

The umpire was just now reaching them. "Coaches, is there anything I need to know?"

The Falcon coach smiled at Richard and nodded to our coach. He turned and walked briskly back toward his team's bench. "No, Blue," he said.

"Then let's play ball," the umpire said, walking back to the plate.

"I'm gonna put a runner in for you, Richard," said Coach.

"You can't do that to me, Coach."

Mr. Forrester spoke plainly. "He ain't doin' it 'cause you're hurt. It's on account 'a we need the run."

Just that quick, a light came on in Richard's head and his expression changed. Smiling up at Rafer's dad, he said, "Right, Coach Forrester." He jogged toward the dugout, his left arm hanging limp.

Coach clapped Mr. Forrester on the back. "Thanks, Cecil."

"I reckon I'm 'Coach Forrester' now."

"I reckon you are!"

Richard called out, "Hey Skeeter, get in there and run for me!"

His voice kind, Coach said, "That's my call who runs for you, son."

"Right, Coach," Richard said. "Sorry."

"Skeeter, run for Richard."

It was my bat. On his way back to coaching third, Mr. Forrester paused.

"Take aim," he said quietly. "Don't overswing. But still," his eyes danced, "knock the bejeepers outta what you're aimin' at."

"Batter up." The umpire glanced at me and put his face mask back on. I stepped into the batter's box.

You'd think Riley would be ticked the game wasn't over. But he looked like he was glad to face me again. He would end the game striking me out.

If you know what the pitcher's thinking, what he's *wanting*, it helps a lot. I decided to take the first pitch, no matter where it went. But I was pretty sure it would cross the plate.

"Steee-riiiiiiiiike." The umpire had gotten more animated in the later innings. He was having a good time. So were the Falcons' fans.

"That's the ticket, Riley," said the Falcons' coach. "You got his number, Riley." I decided to take the second pitch.

"That's a steee-riiiiiiike," the ump sang again.

As I stepped out of the box for a few practice swings, I caught sight of Riley's coach signaling him what to throw next. I guessed it was the sign for a curveball. I figured my guess was right when I saw Riley put his head down, pretending he didn't see the sign. He didn't want to throw a curve, even if that might get me out. He wanted to throw his heater, and if he had to pretend he didn't see the sign, then that's what he'd do. Especially against Zack Ross, who'd gone down swinging at the fastball two innings ago.

When you know what's coming, the world is like diamonds on your front lawn.

My goal was to get Rafer to the plate. I relaxed my stance a shade, making sure I didn't overswing. The pitch got to me in a hurry, but it was level, and I brought bat to ball in a simple, fluid swing. Solid contact, a line drive to straightaway center field. I started running to first, slower than I should have, admiring my work too much.

The center fielder for the Falcons was Larry Malone. He was a friend of mine, even if he was a Falcon. We'd swum the creek together more than one summer day, and we'd do it again many times in our teen years. Larry was tall for twelve, maybe a little too tall to still be in complete control of his hand-eye coordination and motor skills. He had started in as soon as the ball was hit, eager to snag the liner and end the game with a sweet-looking catch. But with the ball coming right at him, he misjudged the trajectory. Too late, he jumped straight up in a desperate try at the catch. He just clipped the bottom of the ball with his glove, keeping it from traveling all the way to the fence. He made a high-pitched sound, "Yaaaaaa," wheeled around, and gave chase. When I saw the ball tip the top of his glove, I was just getting to first. I kicked into overdrive, thinking triple. Almost immediately, I remembered I was either the last out or the tying run, and Rafer was coming up.

Don't take the bat out of Rafer's hands. It's not about you, Zack.

Some moments are large. Rounding first base, I changed. I became smaller and larger; life was not *about* me, but life *included* me. Both perspectives are priceless. They birth hope.

I eased up, coasting into second base while our fans shrieked with delight as Skeeter crossed home plate easily. Larry had hustled to the ball, and I watched him make a hurried, short throw that dribbled up to the third baseman's glove.

The shortstop, a kid I didn't know, gave me a wry smile. "You could've made third."

"Maybe," I said simply.

"I would've gone for it," he said casually. "Might've even gotten a worse throw from center. Gets by the guy playing third. Then I could shoot all the way home. Inside the parker, tying the game. I'm the hero."

I didn't say anything. I just smiled politely.

"That's what I'd have done. You missed it."

I got that funny, breezy feeling that the game was ours. I knew we would win. I *knew* it.

Dad knew it too, I could tell. I saw him and Pastor White laughing it up on the bleachers. Mom, though, looked anxious, rocking in fierce petition, her fists clenched.

Rafer walked in his familiar wooden gait up to the plate and stepped clinically into the batter's box. Right foot, left foot. His face looked, as always, perfectly calm and only slightly interested in the proceedings. It was really the same look he'd had the first time I saw him hit. Just another day slapping the ball with the bat for Rafer.

I prayed, *God, just let him swing. I really don't care if he flies out or lines out or whatever. Just let him swing.*

I thought maybe God had heard me and was answering no when the Falcons' coach called time and sauntered out to the mound. The catcher, Marty, met him there. From second, I could hear what they said.

"Riley, we're going to win this game. You need to walk him."

"Aw, come on, Coach."

"This is a big game, son. Are you going to help your team win it, or are you going to risk giving the game away because you want to do your own thing?"

Riley didn't say anything. He just looked away from his coach.

"Look at me, Riley." Riley lifted his head. "Walk him, and pitch like a champion to the next guy. We should win this game. Y'all boys are just better baseball players than them. Walk him. Okay?"

"Okay, Coach."

Mr. Irwin nodded and turned to the catcher. "Easy outside walk. You know the deal, Marty. Outside."

"I got it, Coach," said Marty, the Falcons' mammoth catcher, who looked like he was old enough to have a driver's license. He lumbered back to his spot behind the plate while Mr. Irwin walked back to the dugout, calling to the umpire. "Okay, Blue, we're ready."

Rafer hadn't moved out of the batter's box during the time-out, and Coach hadn't approached him to talk to him. Rafer just stood there waiting.

"Play ball!"

At the umpire's command, Riley glanced at me over his shoulder, and then started his windup. He tossed the ball casually, a good ways high and outside, and Marty rose and caught it.

"Ball one."

There were a few groans from our dugout and from some of the parents, but most of them expected this to happen.

Riley threw again in the same spot.

"Ball two."

Coach Hornbuckle called Duffey, the on-deck hitter, over to him and started telling him what to do when he got to bat. *Don't swing at the first pitch. Don't talk to the catcher. Remember to breathe.*

Riley wound up a little faster to deliver the third pitch and threw the ball a shade harder, still outside, but not quite as lame a toss. I saw Rafer cock his bat faintly; any movement was easy to see since he normally didn't move at all unless he was going to swing. The ball was outside but not as much, and Rafer stepped across home plate, swung hard, and just caught the ball on the end of the bat. It was foul, a weak ground ball to the first base side.

"Foul ball," said the umpire. "That's one strike."

Rafer had stunned all of us by swinging, especially by reaching out to swing at such a bad pitch. I had no idea what he was going to do next.

From our dugout Donnie shrieked in his preadolescent voice, "Time, ump!"

The umpire just looked in the general direction of our team.

Coach turned to Donnie. "You can't call time, Donnie. It has to be me."

"Call time, Coach!" Donnie's voice was shrill, excited. "Time, ump!" Coach called.

"Go ahead," the umpire said in a resigned tone. He turned to the crowd behind him and said, "So Orioles going to win it all this year like last year?"

The Falcon catcher pushed his mask up, resting it horizontal on his flattop haircut, and walked over to his teammates. "We got any cherry stuff left in that thermos?" Cherry Kool-Aid was big with all of us that summer.

Donnie scrambled out of the dugout opening and sidled up alongside Coach, Rafer's dad, and Rafer, still in the box. I ran in from second base.

Donnie put his hand on Rafer's shoulder. "Rafer…"

"No Donnie," said Rafer. "Donnie not bat. Rafer bat."

His dad put a hand on Rafer's other shoulder. "We know, boy. You're batting now. We know."

Donnie said, "That's right, you're batting, Rafer. Okay?"

"Rafer bat." The guy was born to hit a baseball. Just like Ted Williams.

"But listen, you can't hit balls that are way outside like that last one." Donnie turned to Coach. "He thinks he has to hit the ball, Coach. He doesn't understand an intentional walk."

Coach looked in Rafer's still face. "Just stand there, son, okay? The pitcher"—he pointed at Riley—"is going to throw balls, not strikes, so don't swing."

Rafer looked confused. "Rafer hit ball."

"No, not this time Rafer," said Coach. "Don't swing. The ball will be outside."

Mr. Forrester nodded to his boy. "It'll be off the plate. Not over the plate. You understand, Rafer?"

Slowly, Rafer's countenance changed, like some revelation was catching him full in the face. He spoke tentatively. "Rafer not swing. Ball off plate."

"That's it," Donnie smiled, nodding, and Coach chimed in, "You got it, Rafer."

The umpire leaned into our little powwow. "Are we ready to play, gentlemen?"

"We're ready, Blue." Coach tapped Donnie on his head. "Let's go. He's got it."

The coaches broke from the huddle, and I heard Donnie

mumbling as he went back to the dugout. "I dunno. You can't tell with Rafer."

Marty moseyed back toward his catcher's spot, his upper lip a bright red.

I wheeled to go back to second.

"Zack," Rafer said flatly.

I turned around. "Yeah?"

"Zack ready. Run ready. Ready run."

The umpire broke in. "Mr. Ross, are you still on base, or have you decided to leave this game early?"

It took me a few seconds to realize that "Mr. Ross" was me. "I'm in, Ump. I'm in. Gotta go, Rafer," I said, backpedaling fast from home toward second.

Then my friend Rafer did and said something that is still framed in my mind's eye today. He put the bat straight out toward me and said, "Zack come home."

I really had no idea, so I just repeated, "Don't swing, Rafer," and ran back to second.

"Play ball!" the umpire said, pointing at Riley.

Of course, Riley and everyone else had heard all these words. And Riley and everyone else knew Rafer was not like the rest of us. Only Riley thought being different meant being weaker. So Riley decided to strike Rafer out.

He wound up, a lazy exercise that looked like he was going to throw the intentional walk pitch outside, but let go a fastball down the heart of the plate. Rafer didn't swing.

"Steee-riiiiike two!"

Marty quickly threw the ball back to Riley, amid a rush of voices. But Coach didn't call for time, at least not quick enough for the umpire to respond. Riley wound up fast and let the next pitch go, and I had the sickest feeling Rafer was going to take strike three because we told him to. But I heard a strange sound. It was Rafer's voice, loud over the moment's noise, calling out, "Zack come home!"

Then I saw his bat cock, just a little.

The pitch came in fast, belt-high, and it was lunchtime for Rafer. His eyes widened, and he stepped into a swing that was graceful and strong at the same time.

The bat gave a crack so loud, I thought it might have snapped off in his hands. But it hadn't, and the ball lifted high and far into the Alabama sky like the little stones we used to hurl at other kinds of bats flying high in the summer air. And like those stones that disappeared in the rows of corn behind the house, Rafer's ball vanished over the center field scoreboard into the trees forty feet past the outfield fence. I jogged slow, watching the flight just like everyone else.

For Rafer, I think it really was just another game. When he rounded third base, he said aloud to Riley, who was still standing dazed on the mound, "Thank you." When Riley didn't say anything, Rafer called out again, "Thank you," before he stepped on home plate. To the end, he thought the point of the game was for the pitcher and batter to cooperate. I wonder if Rafer didn't have the best idea all along.

All of us grabbed him when he crossed home, a wild, festive affair that Rafer found a little unsettling. I think he was disappointed the game was over. He was always ready to play a little longer with his old friends, the Robins, and his new friends, the Falcons.

The whole team was so deliriously pounding Rafer and each other on the back and head, it took a few moments to see Rafer's dad standing awkwardly about ten feet away from our celebration pile at home plate. The other parents, including my own, were another ten feet behind Mr. Forrester, as if they knew he needed space for such a moment.

Rafer's dad looked like a different man; he was obviously thrilled with Rafer's home run and maybe even more moved by the celebration it had set off for all of us kids. But he wasn't jumping up and down or yelling anything. It was like he had surrendered, and he was glad he had. He stood there clapping kind of odd, his smile uneven, like his hands and face were getting used to these different things.

"That was... that was really good, son," he said.

Rafer, expressionless, looked directly at his dad. We had all stopped talking. Sometimes even kids recognize a holy moment.

"I hit," said Rafer.

"You sure do," his dad said, nodding. "I'm so proud of you, Rafer. And I'm sorry."

Rafer moved first, striding like a grown man to his father and extending his right hand. When Mr. Forrester threw his arms around his son, Rafer's eyes widened noticeably, like he wasn't sure what hugging was all about. But his face quickly turned peaceful, and he put his arms up around his dad's shoulders. We were watching new things.

Rafer turned to Donnie, who was still jumping around, hugging anyone in huggable range.

"Ball over plate," said Rafer to Donnie. "Ball over plate."

"That's right, Rafer, you maniac," Donnie said through a wide grin. "Rafer, you are a hitting machine, you maniac." He was laughing hard enough to cry, his voice cracking with invading emotions. "Ball over plate. Rafer swings. Ball over scoreboard."

Rafer had that grim look he got when he thought something was wrong. He wheeled around and started running out toward center.

"Hey Rafe, buddy," I shouted. "Where you going?"

He stopped at the pitcher's mound and turned around. "Rafer get ball. Ball lost."

"Come on back here." My voice was cracking too, from giggling and carrying on.

"We don't need the ball," I said. "It's okay, Rafer."

He looked at me, a strangely sympathetic look, and I sensed other things changing, bigger things. I felt fearful, disquieted, when I should have felt pure elation.

Rafer's eyes met mine, and without warning, the color completely drained from his face. He put his arms straight out to me and said, "Zack lost. Rafer get Zack. Zack come home."

Then my friend Rafer's eyes rolled up and back into their sockets, and he collapsed in a heap near the pitcher's mound, his arms and legs bent at odd angles away from his body.

I was sure he was dead.

CHAPTER 20

The ambulance was there fast; I thanked God that Rafer was getting what he needed quickly. It was scary. Rafer did not come to.

I can still hear the voice of one of the medics. "He's not coming around."

But there were other, more encouraging phrases. "His pulse is fine… everything's steady… he'll make it all right… they'll know what to do once he's there."

It was starting to rain when they lifted his stretcher and pushed him into the back of the ambulance. It looked like they were transporting a body, not a boy. Rafer's dad joined his son in the ambulance.

So much of what we do is in answer to our heart cries. There's nothing rational about chasing after an ambulance on a bicycle through the rain. But that's what we did. I mounted my bike and took off as soon as the ambulance doors shut. I heard Dad's voice behind me.

"You can't do anything for him, Zack."

I looked over my shoulder and saw Rebecca and Donnie hop on their bikes too. I was going to say "I know that" to Dad, but what I actually said was, "I got to go." I started pedaling fast, the ambulance just now pulling out of the long parking lot and onto the road ahead.

As hard as I was pumping the pedals, I was surprised to see Rebecca pull alongside me, Sawdust running beside her. Looking back, I saw Donnie not far behind.

Turning on the street the ambulance had taken, I was encouraged to see the road fairly empty of traffic, meaning the vehicle would have a clear path. But I was troubled to find the ambulance already out of sight. I was blessed; at twelve years old, I didn't know how to get to the hospital.

"Where's the hospital?" I called to Rebecca through the rain.

"I'm not sure."

Now, I harbor no illusion that Sawdust understood the King's English. All I know is that he barked and took off ahead of us. We followed after him. When he rounded a corner, we did too.

He got so far ahead that I thought we'd lose him. The rain was kicking off and on, sometimes steady, sometimes stopping, then coming back with a fury. Sawdust had bounded left far enough ahead of us that I thought sure we wouldn't be able to see his next turn. But when we took that left, there it was.

We were at the back of a long, flat brick building. A sign with a big arrow read "Emergency Entrance." Sawdust was barking, pawing the door. Rebecca and I dropped our bikes. I saw Donnie had just taken the final turn behind us and was pumping away, trying to catch up.

We ran to my dog and the door.

"Good boy," Rebecca stroked Sawdust's wet fur. He acknowledged us, whimpering, then pawed the door again, barking.

The door cracked open. A man peeked out.

"Is that y'all's dog?"

Sawdust growled. "Yes, sir," I said.

"Calm him down." Sawdust growled again.

"Can we come in this way?" I asked. "My friend—"

"Yes. But calm him down or take him away," he said, closing the door.

I took Sawdust's head in my hands and looked right at him. Kids and their dogs understand each other.

"You have to stay, Sawdust. Stay, boy."

He looked at me, concerned, his big eyes wet saucers.

"You have to wait for me. Stay." He didn't look convinced.

Rebecca put her wet head on his head. "It's gonna be all right, boy. But you have to wait for us." Sawdust licked her face. "You have to *stay*."

Sawdust lay down, his head on his front paws, whimpering in the soft rain. I guess he figured he couldn't fight both his master *and* his master's "special friend."

Donnie arrived, dismounting and dropping his bike, a single exhausted gesture.

"We're goin' in," I said. "Sawdust is staying, so don't swing the door wide open."

The big wet saucers were the last thing I saw before I pulled the door carefully closed behind us.

There was no one there but the receptionist and the man who'd told us to quiet Sawdust. He was in a room behind her, moving some chairs. I was glad the place was empty. Again, I silently thanked God that Rafer could get the attention he needed.

We looked quite the crew. Three kids, wet with rain and tears.

"My friend..." I said. "Our friend just came in."

"The ballplayer in the ambulance?" the receptionist asked gently.

"Yes, ma'am," said Rebecca.

"It's gonna be a while. They're with him right now." She smiled. "Do y'all want me to find some towels for you to dry off?"

I shook my head. "It doesn't matter."

"We're fine, ma'am," Rebecca said.

When there's nothing you can do but wait, the crisis cuts through you like late November winds. I sat on the floor, my back to the wall. Rebecca and Donnie sat beside me.

"You can sit in the chairs." The receptionist seemed worried about us. "And the couch. You won't hurt anything."

"We're all right, ma'am," said Rebecca. "Really."

In a few minutes, Coach and Pastor White came through the doors, the pastor talking. "I called the house and Patty, and the women have canceled the picnic."

I heard Dad outside, admonishing Sawdust to stay, to wait, and generally to be frustrated. When my dad came inside, Rafer's dad came out of the emergency room's closed doors. Everybody, including Rebecca and Donnie, gathered around Mr. Forrester. Everybody but me. I didn't seem to want to move. It was weird. I thought too much motion could hinder Rafer's recovery. Strange what we feel, what we believe, at such times.

After a few words and nods exchanged, Rafer's dad went back through the doors. The others came over to me.

Coach spoke first. "He's stable. Nobody but family can get in to see him, Zack." He waited. I didn't say anything.

Dad's voice was sensitive. "You can see him later, son. Tomorrow, maybe."

Over Coach's shoulder, I saw my dog's head in a window, looking in.

"I think we should all just go on home and rest," said Pastor White. "Rafer would want that, too."

I stood up then. Dad put his hand on my shoulder. "There's nothing more we can do," he said. "These things are out of our hands. They're out of everyone's hands."

"Everyone's?" I didn't really know what I was asking.

"That's just the way things are, Zack." His tone was not unkind.

We all walked outside. The rain had stopped entirely. Sawdust came bounding around the side of the building. I wasn't ready to comfort him, and he seemed to understand. I was starting to feel the whole heavy burn, the gravity of the emergency.

I got on my bike fast and started pedaling away, Sawdust beside me. Nobody tried to stop me. I heard Pastor White say,

"Just put your bike inside, Rebecca honey. I'll take you home. We'll pick it up tomorrow."

It's amazing to me now, to remember Sawdust knew where I was going. I was pedaling hard, but he stayed ahead of me, through the thick forest, the tight, bracken-carpeted paths behind the Mill Creek Fire Station.

We surfaced from the forest, onto the old ball field where Rafer had first said to me, "Rafer hit." I walked the bike slowly to the worn relic that still functioned as home plate for our practices. I slid from the bike and collapsed against the old chain-link backstop. Sawdust curled up next to me and put his muzzle in my lap. I let an arm rest on his side.

The sky was clear now. The sun was a perfect orange circle of descent, setting as if this day were no different from the days past or to come. I knew that wasn't true.

"Rebecca says you do everything." I spoke the words toward heaven, but they just hung there in the gathering dusk. Or maybe they didn't. "She says you got a *reason* for everything you do."

I listened. Not for an answer, but just for the sound of something other than my pain.

"I hope she's right about you. She's right about nearly everything else."

Sawdust was asleep, looking peaceful. I wonder if animals know—we surely do not—when to let go ... to wait for something greater than ourselves to deliver us from evil.

CHAPTER 21

We'll leave you two in here with him alone," Mom whispered to us. She tried not to break, smiling gently at Rafer.

Dad gave Rafer a little wave. "We'll see you later, Rafer. You're looking good," he lied.

Donnie and I came every day. We didn't want to be anywhere else.

We sat in chairs on either side of the bed. Rafer was either lying down, or like this day, propped up in a sitting position, leaning against the hospital's oversized pillow.

What are we to say at such times? Good things were collapsing. Our friend was dying. Mr. Forrester had asked a nurse to write down what the doctors said, so he could show it to us.

"It's a blood disease. The name really don't mean nothin'. Here's what the thing does." Mr. Forrester shook his head.

I unfolded the paper Rafer's dad put in my hand and read the words aloud to Donnie. "The toxins in the blood are not broken down the way they are in most persons. Instead, the brain stores them. After a while, these toxins affect the body adversely. The body's muscles, including the heart, rapidly deteriorate. The condition is terminal."

I folded the paper and gave it back to Mr. Forrester. Rafer's dad was sad, but he didn't seem angry. He seemed to want to tell Donnie and me everything.

"I know Rafer has… autistic. I mean, he *is* autistic. It's one of them funny words to say. That's why he don't talk much or smile. Felicia and I was told that some years ago. And we was told we weren't loving the boy enough. It was a blow, I can tell ya. They may as well have said we'd ruined the boy."

He brushed his eyes with the back of his hand. "But yesterday, this young doctor come by, real smart I can tell ya, and he says, 'Mr. Forrester, sir, the autism, it has nothing to do with how smart the boy is. And it has nothing to do with how he was raised, or what things were like at home.'"

He smiled, a soft peaceful expression. "That changed quite a few things in my mind, in my heart. I wish I could tell Felicia. We always loved the boy." He looked at Donnie and me. "Can y'all believe that?"

"Yes, sir," we said together.

"Now Rafer being real sick with the blood problem… this kind of thing happens sometimes, boys. And I decided I'm not gonna be mad about it. Not at God, or myself. Not anybody. I'm tired of being mad."

The girl in the room beside Rafer's was in her last days, too. Sherri was so small, it was hard to believe she was ten years old. I recognized her parents and her little sister, Jennifer, as a family I saw on my last visit to Silas Baptist.

Pastor White and others from the church came to see both Rafer and Sherri. Donnie's dad had an easy way about him. He could comfort and encourage people just by being in the room. His words weren't all "God-talk." I mean they weren't what you'd call pastor talk. He chatted about the weather, the hospital schedule, dogs, his family, and even baseball—and then, down and up a lighted path of phrases, he was talking about God. I started to recognize that all talk involved God, because all of life does. It's all from God, and about God, and our place in his world, in this story he has written.

I didn't know what Pastor White told little Sherri, or Sherri's parents, but I did notice that the family was always smiling. I started to see what warriors look like. An enemy was afoot in their daughter's body, and they were not happy about it. But they weren't afraid, either. I felt stronger, as a person, when they saw me in the hall and said hello. Why was that? But I didn't go into Sherri's room, even when Pastor White was visiting. I was afraid.

Death seemed to be on a kind of ugly parade those days. In the years ahead, I would see that is always the case. Here on Earth, death is ever with us. We try to ignore it, an impossible effort.

Rafer's dying was turning my inside upside down. I had known other people who had died. A kid in my third grade class was in a car accident that killed him. But he died instantly in the crash. When life recedes gradually, incrementally, and death leisurely sits and chats with us, the sorrow oppresses us. It is dead weight.

So it wasn't just Rafer's dying, even at such a tender age. The real tragedy, the hard, heavy thing I felt in my stomach's pit when I lay down at night and when I got out of bed in the morning, was "the hourglass." That's what I started seeing in my head.

The top of the hourglass was Rafer's physical body. It was emptying—slowly, steadily, his frame going back to fine dust, falling away. The bottom was his mind, and what we could now hear his mind saying. In the beginning, his mind seemed as silent as Rafer himself. You only caught a glimpse, and then only if you listened with real focus. Now, with the hourglass bottom filling, little by little Rafer was actually finding his mind *and* his voice. But he was losing his body.

I never knew what to say, but I noticed Donnie usually did. He even knew *how* to say things. He was connected to the truth. Donnie was also happier than anyone I knew. Rafer could see that too. We can all see happiness in another person, because it's a surprise. Like roses in winter.

On this particular afternoon, I waited for Donnie to say the right thing in the right way. But Rafer, who probably never had reason to know silence was uncomfortable, spoke first. Our season of surprises was still surprising.

"Zack I see... Zack talk," Rafer said slowly, in a voice flat and heavy. "Donnie talk. Donnie I see. God..." His shoulders dropped back onto his pillow, his eyes on the hospital room ceiling. "God I not see. God not talk... no."

He was asking us where God was. I didn't have anything to say. Rafer's question was my own.

But Donnie had things to share. In the dim yellow light of the room, the look on Donnie's face made him seem older than Rafer and me. Wiser. He was already free from the exaggerated self-importance of youth, from thinking life was all about him. Donnie was ahead of both of us in the real journey. He wanted to bring us with him.

"I don't see God either, Rafer," Donnie said honestly. "And I don't hear him talk. I don't see the wind outside. And the wind doesn't talk to me. But I know it's there because I see the leaves on the trees move. I see the grass bend when the wind blows over it."

Rafer lifted his head slightly in Donnie's direction and looked at his friend. Keeping his gaze on Donnie, he let his head sink back into the pillow. I thought how, just a few months ago, he never looked at anyone.

"God's like that." Donnie smiled. "We don't see *him*, but we see what he does. We see people's lives change. I mean, we see people bend when God blows over them. Don't we?"

"Rafer not see," said Rafer. "People bend. Rafer not see."

Donnie looked slightly taken aback, and I expected Rafer's words to frustrate him. But he actually seemed to be fired up by Rafer's words, by his honesty.

"Okay, maybe you don't see that, Rafer," Donnie said. "That's all right. But I believe God does touch people and change people. I believe God loves us and God wants to make us his children. He wants us to live in his big, wonderful house with him."

Rafer looked over at me. "Zack..." he said. "Zack in God's house? Zack and Donnie in God's house?"

I thought I should answer. Rafer deserved at least that. I knew God was real for Donnie. Donnie didn't just believe what his dad said, what his dad lived. Donnie had it, too. He had it for real. Like a line drive that smacks hard and deep into the web of your glove. You can't really drop a ball that's hit at you like that, after you catch it. But you can miss the ball altogether.

I spoke what I felt. If you can't be honest with a dying friend, you'll never be. "I... I don't see God's house, Rafer," I said. "And I don't hear God talk, either." I wasn't trying to prove anything or correct what Donnie had said. It was just the way it was with me.

Donnie didn't seem hurt by what I said. He still had that look of freedom, of peace, on his face.

We were silent for a while, a very odd threesome. The seeing, the blind, and the seeking. When you're born blind, you don't really know what it's like to see. I wasn't looking. But Rafer wanted what Donnie had.

"Rafer want... bend."

"What was that?" I leaned in over my friend's hospital bed.

"Rafer want to bend," he said again, only stronger, fixing his eyes on mine. "Rafer want to bend. Rafer want God's house."

I thought Donnie would jump in and tell Rafer how to do that, how to get there. But Donnie waited and watched. He watched me, to see how I'd answer Rafer.

"Rafer want God's wind... to bend Rafer," he said again, still looking at me, as if I were the one to help him. It struck me how he looked as normal, as rational, as I had ever seen him.

"I'm sorry... I gotta go." I hurried out into the hall and stopped suddenly to lean against the corridor wall. A torrent of quiet tears washed my face. I wrestled to keep from sobbing out loud. I wanted to hear what Donnie was saying.

"You love your dad, don't you, Rafer?" I heard Donnie ask. "I know you do. I see it. We all see it. But you know how your dad was always yelling at you? He was always mad at you, and it didn't matter how hard you tried to make him happy, he just stayed mad at you?"

"Dad..." Rafer struggled to talk. It wasn't his normal stilted voice. This was a different struggle. "Dad... hug Rafer. Hug Rafer."

"I know, and that was awesome, Rafer."

"Number one," said Rafer. "First... first Dad hug Rafer... first time."

"I know... it was so cool, wasn't it? That was cool as grits."

Rafer sounded faintly confused. "Grits?"

"I just mean that it was beautiful." Donnie laughed at himself. "A really cool thing to see you and your dad hugging like that."

"Number one... first time," Rafer said again.

"Rafer..." Donnie's voice was more serious and at the same time more excited. "Rafer... you can hug God like that."

Something gave way in my heart, and I couldn't listen anymore. I wiped my face hard with the sleeves of my shirt and hurried to the men's room at the end of the corridor. I thought I'd be a mess for a long while, but after about ten minutes I felt as if I had recovered completely. *There's nothing wrong with you. A friend of yours is dying, and your best friend is trying to make that hard thing go down easier. Of course you're going to cry some.* By the time I stepped back into the room, I felt all right about being blind.

Rafer's face and words when he saw me were not to be forgotten, by me or Donnie.

"Rafer bend," he said, his eyes shining. He was not smiling, but his face looked like someone ready for a good fight. Or a good flight. Or both.

"Rafer bend," he said again. "God bend Rafer."

CHAPTER 22

Our second game against the Hawks was a 20–3 train wreck. We were the wreck. The Hawks and their hotshot pitcher, Pepper Jasper, ran us over and left us for buzzards. I can think of some more metaphors, but it's painful even now to dwell on it too long.

It seemed like an eternity since we'd beaten them earlier in the season. Even then, we'd had to rally big time, and Rafer was at the center of the rally. Rafer wasn't with us anymore.

In that first game, because of Duffey's heroics (or poor sportsmanship, depending on your perspective and ethical base), the Hawks had played without their ace pitcher, Pepper, and their cleanup hitter, Booger. This time, we faced the juggernaut in all its fury. It was not pretty. As we sat on our bench licking our wounds, Booger walked by and rubbed it in a bit.

"Different game with me and Pepper in there, huh guys?" he sneered.

"Get lost, Booger," Batman said.

"Gonna make me? You and what army?"

I stood up and moved with malicious intent. Coach stepped in front of me and turned to speak to Booger.

"Son, don't you wanna join your team?"

I locked eyes with my antagonist. He stepped away then, walking toward his team's celebration. I sat back down.

Coach looked us over. "So they killed us. It's kind of exciting, really. We've both lost once, and that loss was to each other. Now it's a winner-take-all championship game in two weeks. We can beat Pepper, guys!"

"Get real, Coach." Jimmy spoke for the team. He wasn't buying it. "Rafer's in the hospital for cryin' out loud, and he and Zack are the only ones who can hit Pepper. If Rafer were here, we *might* have some kind of chance."

"I think Rafer is here with us, in a way," said Donnie. "Know what I mean?"

"He's not here!" Jimmy glowered at Donnie. "And I know *you* know what *I* mean!"

"Guys," Coach said in earnest, "it ain't over until the fat lady sings."

That mystified us entirely. We looked at each other.

Batman nudged Duffey. "Is your mama gonna..."

"You can just shut up right now!" said Duffey.

"C'mon guys," said Coach. "Yogi Berra? It ain't over till... ?" He shook his head and translated for us. "You gotta play it out. Anything can happen. Have some fun. How many people, in their whole life, get to play for a championship?" He paused. "Just think about it. Now go get some ice cream. I'm buying."

"But we lost, Coach," Tigger said.

"What?" Coach gave a friendly scowl. "You can't eat ice cream when you lose?"

"I can!" BoDean and Duffey said together, colliding in their frenzy to get off the bench on the path to the snack bar.

I stayed seated. Jimmy slid over next to me. "Where was Sawdust?" he asked.

"Sawdust?" I was a little confused.

"He came to every game except this one, and we won every game except this game."

Unbelievable. "He's a dog, Jimmy." I marveled at him. "A dog.

But I will invite him to join us for the championship game, if that'll make you feel better."

"That's great." He jumped up and ran after the others.

I was still shaking my head when Donnie whispered behind me, "Sawdust will be here for the game, right?"

I wheeled around and threw my glove at him. He dodged it, laughing at me. I picked it up and raced him to the snack bar.

When you're a kid, tragic and comic moments overlap. Your heart is light enough then to know the difference. Joy is our true, original destiny. Tragedy is the stranger.

CHAPTER 23

The next Saturday, we were watching NBC's Game of the Week, with Curt Gowdy and Tony Kubek at the mike. Even Rafer, who never wanted the TV on, seemed anxious to see the Pittsburgh Pirates and the San Francisco Giants go at it. Pittsburgh had always been my team, confounding a lot of my friends who were die-hard Braves followers. But I liked Pittsburgh's team persona. They could hit like crazy, and they had the fearsome pop of Willie Stargell's long ball. More importantly, they had the leadership, drive, and phenomenal abilities of Roberto Clemente. The Pirates reminded me of the Robins. They were always good, but never the best.

Rafer's dad was perched on the bed beside his son, his head tilted back into the pillow. He spent a lot of time with Rafer there, and Donnie and I had giggled at him snoozing on the bed with Rafer awake. The hospital pillows were pretty nice, I guess. And Mr. Forrester had been going through a lot of tiring stuff.

Donnie was sitting in an overstuffed chair we borrowed from the church's Fellowship Hall, his large Atlanta Braves baseball cap hanging too low over his eyes. The two of us had worked feverishly the day before to squeeze the chair's large frame and thick padding through the doorway into the hospital room.

I stood and turned to step out into the hall. "I'm gonna get a Coke. Maybe some peanuts."

"No, Zack," said Rafer. "Zack not go."

"I'll be right back, Rafe." I was already out the door and into the hall when Rafer's voice, louder now, caught me.

"Zack not go."

"He's coming right back." Mr. Forrester assured his son. "He's just getting—"

"Zack!" Rafer's voice cracked.

"I'm back. I'm back, man," I hustled back into the room. "See? It's me."

"No kidding," Donnie said.

"Shut up, Donnie." I frowned.

"Shut up, Donnie," said Rafer.

I laughed in the odd giggle-wheeze twelve-year-olds have and lose a short year later.

Rafer wasn't through. "Shut up, Donnie," he said again, in his flat tone.

Now it was Donnie giggling and wheezing at the same time.

"I never heard you say that before, son." Mr. Forrester looked at his boy, and I couldn't tell if he was going to reprimand him or laugh at him.

"Me either," I said. "I never heard you say 'shut up' before, Rafer."

"New words," said Rafer. "Shut up."

Donnie pounded the chair's armrest, laughing. "Hey, maybe we should teach him ... oh, never mind."

"Teach him what?" Mr. Forrester smiled.

"Never mind. Forget it. It wasn't nice."

"You surprise me sometimes, Donnie," I said.

"It wasn't a bad word, or anything," Donnie defended himself. "At least I don't think it is."

While we were carrying on laughing and expanding Rafer's vocabulary, Roberto Clemente hit a double into the alley between left and center field. Clemente was long established as an extremely gifted player. But he wasn't what most people would call a superstar. He was overlooked, playing in the long shadows of Willie

Mays, Hank Aaron, and even the Orioles' Frank Robinson, three of the greatest outfielders the game had ever seen.

"Who is this guy?" Donnie spoke through teeth tugging at licorice.

"You don't know Clemente?" Mr. Forrester was starting to look very sleepy, his head next to Rafer's on the big hospital pillow.

"Well, yeah, I heard of him and everything."

"You're lying." I shook my head.

"Okay, I'm lying." Donnie was at heart a truth teller. "I never heard of him."

"That's 'cause he plays in Pittsburgh," Mr. Forrester said, his eyes closed.

"Yeah, if he played for the Dodgers or any team in New York, you'd have heard of him. Pittsburgh is a small market," I said, parroting something I'd heard from a sportscaster.

While Donnie and I bantered, I noticed Rafer angling his head to look at whoever spoke. He did that regularly now, a big change from the Rafer of a couple of months ago.

"Well, I like the Pirates," said Donnie through a serious chunk of licorice.

"Oh, you do? Name one other player. I mean other than Clemente."

"Richie Hepburn," Donnie announced triumphantly.

I swallowed the two peanuts I'd been sucking on through a Coke, laughing hard, the way you did at that age. I kept myself from sliding out of the chair, but only with some difficulty.

"Hepburn? HEPBURN?" My voice choked with laughs.

"What the Sam Hill's so funny?"

Rafer bolted upright in the bed, opened his mouth, and said to the ceiling, "HEPBURN!" He turned his head to face me first, then back to stare at Donnie. For one beautiful and awe-filled moment, I thought he was going to laugh. But he didn't. He just leaned back on his long, tall pillow. His outburst hadn't seemed to bother his dad, who was now snoring softly.

"See, Pardner, now you got Rafer all worked up," Donnie said, trying not to laugh himself. When you're a kid, you laugh just because your friend is laughing. That good spirit escapes us when we become adults.

"You want to say something, Rafer buddy?" I know he heard me, but he just looked at the TV set. I chucked two more peanuts into the back corners of my gums. "It's not *Hepburn*, Donnie. It's *Hebner*. Third base. And how do you know Richie Hebner's name? I mean, you almost knew his name, anyway."

"I got his card. Well, I had it. I gave it to Rafer."

"Digs graves," Rafer said.

"What was that?" I asked him.

"Richie Hebner digs graves." Rafer held a Topps baseball card out to me.

I took it. Turning it over, I read aloud from the back of the card: "Richie has an unusual job in the off-season. He digs graves!"

The cartoonish image on the card's back was a ballplayer in a grave up to his neck.

"Who wants to dig graves?" Donnie frowned. "There's something twisted about that."

"He a rose," said Rafer.

"What's that?" Donnie looked at Rafer.

"He a rose," he said again.

"Who's a rose?" I asked.

From under his pillow, Rafer pulled out the cross nail tied with a red string that he'd gotten at church. He held it up in front of him.

He raised one finger. "Remember... the nail," he said. He raised a second finger and said, "Remember the grave." Raising a third finger, he said, "Remember he arose."

He looked peaceful, his eyes shining.

"Rafer bend," he said. "God bend Rafer."

The game came back on. Pittsburgh's catlike catcher, Manny Sanguillen was in his uneasy tiptoe batting stance.

"He holds his bat like Jimmy," I noticed. "Flat. Level, with his hands close to his head. Weird."

"Dad says he's a Christian," said Donnie.

I looked at him across Rafer's TV stare. "How's he know?"

"He read it in a baseball magazine. The Pirates' catcher has a copy of Billy Graham's book *Peace with God* in his locker."

"Peace," said Rafer quietly.

I leaned toward my sick friend. "What's that, Rafer?"

Rafer turned toward me. "With God," he said.

My eyes moistened. I really didn't know why. "Who's with God, Rafer?"

I wanted him to talk more but he turned his gaze back to the TV, and it was me who kept talking. "So he's got a Billy Graham book in his locker. Big deal. He's probably got some Caribbean lucky charms in there too."

"What do you know about stuff from… about Caribbean stuff?" asked Donnie.

Rafer chimed in again. He said, "Lucky charms" in a clear but flat tone, never moving his eyes from the TV.

Donnie spoke up. "Why are you such a hard sell, Zack?"

"Whaddya mean?" I knew what he meant, and I was relieved that he didn't get specific.

"Think about it, Pardner. If my dad reads about the Billy Graham book in a magazine, then it has to be something this guy, Manny Sang the Blues, or whatever his name is, wants to be in the magazine. He wants people to know he's reading Billy Graham's book. It *means* something to him. Right?"

I wasn't sure what to say. Donnie seemed smarter than me at such times. Or at least he had something I didn't.

I played the cynic's card, the card my dad always played with me. "Maybe the guy writing the story decided to put it in the magazine," I said. "Maybe it wasn't Manny's idea at all."

Sanguillen rapped a hard knock between third and short, rounded first, and skipped back to the base after the outfielder made a good throw in to the infield. The Panamanian catcher, a fan favorite, enthusiastically clapped his hands and called to his teammate, Clemente, to get him home. Before stepping into the batter's box, Clemente went through his odd ritual of pre-bat stretches, holding his bat at either end behind his neck, tilting and rolling his head. He was a panther, waking his muscles, getting them ready to pounce from hiding into the full view of the national television audience.

"It really doesn't matter, does it Zack?" asked Donnie. "The fact remains"—he stopped talking long enough to maneuver a significant chunk of licorice from the right side of his mouth to the left—"the fact remains that this Manny guy's reading a book about how people can have peace with God, how they can know God."

I didn't say anything. Clemente connected, a long drive.

"Look at that!" Donnie howled.

"There it goes," I said matter-of-factly.

We watched the ball drop into the stands. The camera followed Clemente's trot around the bases. Manny Sanguillen waited for him at the plate, hugged him, and welcomed him home. Safe.

I reached for the knob to turn the TV off, but something in the announcer's voice grabbed me.

"I am telling you this season is starting to look very special for the Pirates," Curt Gowdy opined. "The whole team is playing inspired baseball, like they have something to prove, something to say to the whole country this year. And Clemente seems like their mouthpiece."

Rafer's dad woke up and started for the door. "I'm going to get a snack. Anybody want anything?"

"No thanks," Donnie and I said almost in unison.

"Rafer?"

"TV" was Rafer's response.

"Okay. Just take me a minute or two." Mr. Forrester's voice trailed off as he walked out the door.

Suddenly I felt like I wanted to get away. I got up to leave the room, but Rafer's voice stopped me.

"Zack."

I turned around and saw the sick boy pushing his bed covers off, struggling to swing his legs around and down to the floor. Donnie was trying to stop him. "Whoa... Wait up, Rafer. Whaddya doing? You can't be going anywhere."

Rafer looked so different from that day when I had met him and he had lofted my pitches into the woods. Now he was straining, his thin arms stretched out, trying to push Donnie's hands away. And his face, always entirely blank before, now carried a clear expression. Growing concern. Desperate.

I took a step back toward him. "You need to stay in the bed, Rafer."

"Zack," he said. Then, much louder: "ZACK!" His put his arms straight out to me.

I went to him and put my hands on his shoulders, trying to sound calm. "Hey, hey... it's all right, buddy."

But it wasn't. At least Rafer didn't think so.

"Zack know God." It was the only time I heard him whisper, his voice gravelly but soft.

I was afraid I was going to cry, so I looked away from Rafer to Donnie. My friend had taken his Braves cap off and was squishing it in his left hand. His right hand was rubbing his face, his eyes wet with tears. He wasn't talking. I don't think he could.

I looked back at Rafer. Suddenly, without warning, I felt really mad. If anybody said "God" one more time... how can we know God? If he's there, why would he care? And if he *does* care, why is Rafer Forrester dying a pitiless death in an Alabama hospital? Why is the same thing happening to little Sherri in the next room?

Rafer opened his mouth and said, "Zack... Donnie... Rafer."

Before I saw it coming, he put his arms around my neck. It was like he was somebody else. Rafer didn't touch people physically like that. Then, slowly, he said, "Rafer … Donnie … Zack." And he let go of me, his body sinking back down onto the bed, his head finding the pillow, his eyes closing. It could have scared both of us, except that we could see him breathing very steadily, peacefully.

Donnie seemed a little calmer now, having cleared his face of the tears. He sat down abruptly on the edge of the bed and stared straight ahead, like he was thinking pretty hard about something. Then he looked right at me.

"What do you think he wants?" asked Donnie.

"I really don't know. What about you? Are you okay?"

"Yeah. I'm fine," he said. "It's not about me, Zack."

"What do you mean?"

"It's not about Rafer, either. I thought it was. But it's not."

I wasn't sure how to take him. Donnie was usually following my lead—on the team, in our friendship, and in our young lives. But here he was talking about something bigger and I was tagging along after him.

Mr. Forrester came back in, his face flush with discovery. "They got Reese's cups in the machine today. And M&M's with peanuts. See?"

"Hey, great!" Donnie and the older man had learned they had some things in common.

"Donnie," I said, "can we just walk around outside for a minute?" I knew it would take more than a minute.

"Sure."

There was a small, man-made lake behind the hospital. Donnie and I would eat lunch there a lot of days. We always sat on the short bank instead of the benches, our paper bags and sandwiches in our laps.

Today we just walked around the rim of the lake, counterclockwise.

"I know it works for you," I said. "But what I want to know

is ... how can somebody *know* God? I don't mean 'how does somebody join a church.'"

"I'm glad you don't mean that. I'm glad you don't think if you go to a building once a week you can get into heaven." He didn't say it to be funny. He just said it.

"But your dad's a preacher."

"Tell me about it. Just about every Sunday he says while he's preaching, 'Going to church does not get you into heaven.'"

"So why do people go?"

"Well, I can tell you why *I* go ..."

"Because your dad—"

"It's not because my dad is the preacher," he cut me off. "Just like you don't stay away from church because your dad stays away."

"Yes I do," I countered.

"You do?"

"No I don't," I said, a little confused. "I mean, I make my own decisions. My dad *wants* me to make my own decisions."

"So does my dad," Donnie said quietly.

I gave him a look that said I found that hard to believe.

"Okay," he conceded, "my dad being a pastor and all ... that's one reason I go now, while I'm a kid. But what about later? What about when I'm eighteen, or twenty-eight, or thirty-eight? Will I go to church then?"

"Maybe. You're used to it," I said. "Wait a minute, why am I telling you why you go to church? I asked you to tell me." We both laughed. We had walked halfway around the small lake. Donnie sat down on the bank, so I did too.

"It's not about church, Zack. It goes a lot deeper."

"I'm glad it goes deeper." It seemed to be the season, the year, for both of us to see that things went deeper. We needed them to.

"God is like water," he said.

I thought that was a little strange sounding. But then, we were talking about *God*. Everything was going to sound strange. "God is like water," I repeated after him, smiling.

"Yeah. God is water. What happens if you don't have water, Pardner?"

"You die."

"Bingo."

"Listen," I said, wondering if this conversation had anything to do with why my head always seemed crooked and Donnie's straight, "if God's water… and I need water to live… how come I'm not dead?" After I said it, it sounded really bizarre. But I still wanted to hear what Donnie would say.

"That's right, you're not dead, Zack." Then he looked at me with that sly, close-mouthed smile of his. "But you are dying."

I hesitated before saying the obvious. "I am not." He didn't respond right away, so I thought it was worth repeating. "I am not." Then I said aloud what both of us knew and neither had wanted to put into words until right now. "Rafer is dying, Donnie."

"So are you, Zack. So am I. Rafer goes soon." Donnie didn't care that he was starting to blink hard, and his voice was thinner, more high-pitched. I didn't care either.

"Rafer goes soon," he said again, "but we all go. Rafer didn't ask to go right now. He's just… he's just going. That's all."

It had always been hard for me to cry. Rafer was changing that. I looked at my friend rubbing his chubby cheeks and nose with both hands. And I looked out over the lake.

"Why would God do that?" I asked. "Why would he take Rafer so young?"

"So you *do* believe!" squealed Donnie, pointing at me like I'd just confessed to something.

"What are you talking about?"

"You want to blame God, to blame him for Rafer dying. That means you think God is responsible, God is real. Right? I mean, you wouldn't blame God for something unless you thought he was real. You think God is real, Zack!"

"Maybe I do," I said. I looked at my friend, and said it outright. "I know I think he's real, Donnie. I just wish I could… I could know him. You know what I mean? If he's real, I want to touch him. I want him to touch me." Turning my eyes away from Donnie, I relaxed my whole body, leaning my head back to rest on the ground. I saw clouds like cotton overhead.

Donnie leaned back next to me, his knees to the sky, his head resting on the earth like mine.

"Maybe he's already done it. Maybe he's already touched you, Zack."

"I think I would know. I think I would know if the Big Guy touched me."

"Really? So you know what God's touch feels like, what God's touch does to you, since you're sure you know when he's touching you."

"You're a real pain in the butt, you know that?"

Donnie let a comfortable silence settle in for a moment. "Rafer *is* dying, Zack. You know it, I know it, the nurses know it. Everybody knows he's dying. Am I right?" My friend turned his head to look at me. He seemed older. But it was the same squeaky voice.

What could I say? "Yeah. You're right."

"So where's he going?"

"Donnie, c'mon, you know that's what I'm asking *you*. I guess I don't think he's going anywhere. He's just going."

"How do you feel about that?"

"How do I *feel*? I think it's the pits."

"So do I. I mean, it hurts, doesn't it? Just about everything down here hurts."

"Down here?"

"Down here, on Earth. The whole planet hurts. People get sick, people die, people have horrible parents. Nothing's right, Zack. We try to pretend it is, but it's all wrong. You can see that, can't you?"

"I dunno. I think some people are trying to make things better. Your dad. He's doing what he can to help people."

"My dad would say to you..." He paused to think about what he was saying. "He would tell you that he does what he does because of what Jesus did for him, because Jesus loves him. Does that make sense to you?"

I didn't know what to say. I knew Donnie was big into Jesus. Truth is, I wanted to be too. But it wasn't real to me. Yet.

"Not really," I said. "Why couldn't your dad just help people, whether Jesus helps him or not?"

"Well, he could," said my friend. And here he looked right at me, almost right into me. "But people don't need to be *helped*. They need to be rescued."

"That sounds like something you heard your dad say." I smiled.

"It is." Donnie laughed. "He says it a lot."

"What's it mean?"

"It means that the reason people go through hard things, terrible things, is because of..." He stopped. "You're not going to like what I say."

"How do you know?"

"You're not going to like the word."

"C'mon, Donnie, just say what you're thinking. Let me decide if I like it or not." I was surprised I was so anxious to hear what he was going to say.

He took a long breath and decided to take me at my word. "The reason people go through hard things and then they die," said Donnie, "is because of... sin."

I thought he was going to keep going, but he seemed to want me to respond.

"That's it? Sin?"

"Yeah, that's it," he said. "I told you, you wouldn't like it, that you wouldn't agree."

I looked straight up at the sky. "What makes you so sure I don't agree?"

"Well, we talked about this last year and you said you thought the Adam and Eve stuff was made up." Donnie leaned back on the bank again, his hands cupped behind his head, eyeing the sky with me. "You said, 'cause I remember, Zack, you said you didn't believe all this sin stuff. You didn't believe that everything was all that bad in life. You remember you said that?"

"Yeah, yeah, I remember. It was a sleepover. We stayed up."

"Yeah," Donnie said. "And you said it a lot. You were sure about it."

I didn't say anything right away, just watching the clouds drift like they were on some big screen. I decided to say it. "I'm not so sure anymore. I mean, about the world. It seems pretty messed up." I was surprised my eyes were clouding over. "Rafer dying, that's messed up. Rafer dying," I said again, "right when he's kind of getting better. Talking, and everything. It's not right."

His next words caught me off guard. "So are you mad at God... for Rafer dying and all?"

"No."

"Really? Why not?"

"I don't know why not. Should I be mad at God?"

"Only if you think he's real."

I rose up on one elbow and faced my friend. "I thought you were going to talk me into it, Donnie. You know, talk me into believing in God, and all that stuff."

"I don't think I can do that."

I got a little concerned. "You mean, you think I'm hopeless?"

"Oh no. You can be talked into believing in God. But God has to do that. God has to talk you into believing in him."

"So why does your dad try to talk people into believing in God? Isn't that what he's doing every Sunday?"

"It probably looks like that." I was always surprised by Donnie's honesty. "I asked him about that, too. He said he's not trying to get people to listen to him. He's trying to get people to listen to God. He says only God can rescue people."

Neither one of us seemed to mind the break in the conversation again. After a long minute, Donnie ended the silence.

"So did I hear you right, Zack? Did you say you think the world's messed up?"

"It's messed up," I said quietly.

"How messed up?"

"Totally."

I looked over at my friend, and saw him smiling through some tears.

"What is *wrong* with you?" I said. I thought he was going to go to pieces, but he actually chuckled.

"Nothing," he said. "I just think it's cool, that's all."

"What is?"

"Last year, you were sure the world wasn't really that messed up. You didn't believe in this sin stuff, Adam and Eve and all."

"I still don't know about Adam and Eve. But sin... I think sin means there's something way out of joint in the world."

"What about in you? Is anything out of joint in you, Zack? Do you feel good all the time? Do you want to do good things all the time?"

"Who does?"

"That's it, Zack. Only Jesus. Only Jesus and his dad."

Just hearing the name Jesus made me feel scared and clean at the same time. I was ready to stop talking and come back to this God stuff later. When you're young, there's always "later." When we're older, "later" becomes "some other time." If we stall long enough, we might not have to bow down in this life. That's what we think anyway.

I got up off the ground, slapping stray grass off my jeans. "Let's go back to Rafer."

"Sure," Donnie said, standing.

Walking along the opposite side of the lake, back to the hospital, I opened up just a little more. "Do you think I'm running away from God, Donnie?"

He didn't look at me, but I could tell he was excited about something. "Can't be done, Zack," he said. "You can try to run from God, but you can't run *away* from him. He's God, right? If he's real, he's going to do what he wants."

"I'm not sure I like that."

"I understand," Donnie said simply. "We'd rather be God. But he is."

Sometimes Donnie was a real pain.

CHAPTER 24

It was Friday night. Rebecca and all of us Robins, except for Jimmy, were wearing our *R* caps and clustered at the hospital's front desk.

The nurse was pleasant. And suspicious. "I don't think so, Zack. You and Donnie is one thing..."

"But we're all Robins, just like Rafer is," Duffey pleaded. Realizing his cap was on backward, he turned it around so the *R* was visible.

Batman elbowed Duffey. "We said let Zack do the talking," he said, not low enough.

The nurse smiled, a good sign. "Where's your coach?"

"He said us kids would have a better shot... oww!" said Duffey, Batman poking him again, "... getting back there without him." Then to Batman, "Poke me again, and so help me..."

"We'll take five minutes," Duffey pressed the nurse. "Ten minutes max." He pulled out of the way of another elbow from Batman.

Richard gave her his sad little eyes. "Please, Miss Sarah Beth?"

"Now, how did you know my name, pumpkin?"

"Everybody knows Miss Sarah Beth. You're the best nurse in this whole place."

"Five minutes," she said.

"Let's go, guys." I started down the hall, the Robins flocking behind me.

"I'm coming after you in ten minutes, boys." Sarah Beth called after us.

I heard Richard, lingering at the desk. "Thank you so much, Nurse Sarah Beth."

"You go on now, precious," she said.

I heard Richard's little feet running fast. He hustled up beside me, Batman, and Duffey.

"We ain't got a lot of time," Duffey said.

"Should be enough," I said.

"How'd you know the nurse's name, Little Richard?" asked Batman. "I didn't see no name tag."

"The clipboard behind her," said the little guy. "The nurses' schedule was hanging on the wall."

Batman put a hand on Richard's shoulder. "Richard," he said, "you've got a lot of good, raw talent."

Tigger had bounced up next to us. "But how'd you know she was the best nurse?"

Batman whipped off Tigger's cap, ready to fling it down the hall.

"Hey, hey, hey," I stopped him. "No fooling around. We got three minutes to get him in."

Batman gave Tigger's cap back, and the two lookouts scampered in opposite directions, to either end of the hallway. The rest of us surrounded an exit door that led outside the hospital and opened it. Jimmy slid in, with a sheet-covered Sawdust in tow. Three rooms down the hall, a door started to open.

"Get back out," I whispered hoarsely to Jimmy, and he and Sawdust did a one-eighty back out the exit.

The room door opened all the way and a nurse stepped out and looked at us.

"Are y'all here to see the Forrester boy?"

"Yes'm," I said. I pointed to where Tigger stood at the end of the hall. "Could you please tell our friend where we are? I think he's lost, ma'am."

"Oh, the poor little darling." She walked away from us, in Tigger's direction. "I sure will."

I waved my arms in the air, so Tigger could see me. He started to "cry," just like we'd coached him. We could make out some of his words.

"I can't find… anybody. They's all gone."

I opened the exit door again, letting in Jimmy and the walking sheet. We all swarmed like bees into room 120, Rafer's room, buzzing as quietly as possible. Jimmy held Sawdust back, hiding with him against the wall. BoDean shut the door.

Rafer, paler than I'd remembered him just the day before, sat up weakly. And talked!

"All Robins. All for Rafer."

"That's right, Rafer," said Duffey. "All for you. And we mean *all* of us, buddy."

Jimmy let Sawdust go then. The dog bounded up onto the bed and licked Rafer's face. Rafer put his hands on the dog's head, "anointing" him in his usual fashion. The door opened partway, and we heard Tigger's loud sniffles.

"But they're not in there… I already looked, Miss Barbara, ma'am."

Jimmy and I collared Sawdust, picked him up, and pushed him under Rafer's bed.

I gave my dog that serious look that we think translates to them obeying us.

"Stay! Stay there, boy." He crouched under the bed, wagging his tail, reveling in this new game.

The nurse stepped inside. "My goodness, Rafer, you've got so many friends! I don't think we could fit another soul in this room."

"Under the bed," said Rafer.

"Yeah, I think you're right." The nurse laughed. "I guess we'd have to squeeze somebody under there, to fit any more bodies in here."

"Crowded down there," said Rafer.

Duffey snorted and Jimmy laughed hard and said, "That's a good one, Rafer. Crowded down there!"

Sawdust's tail wagged out from under the bed, and Rebecca pushed it back under with her foot. Tigger was in the room now, behind the nurse. He gestured to me, letting me know he'd done his best. When the nurse looked back at him, he started sniffling again.

"Now y'all can't stay more than a few minutes. Rafer needs lots of rest."

Batman came into the room just then, loud as a New Year's celebration. "Coast is all clear, y'all. Oooopps."

The nurse gave Batman a curious look as she walked out of the room.

"Way to go, genius," Duffey said to Batman.

"Way to go, genius," said Rafer flatly.

Sawdust scuttled out from under the bed and back on top of it. He lay his head on Rafer's chest. Mr. Forrester entered the room, real quiet-like. He smiled at me, but hung back, listening to us Robins chirp at our sick friend.

"Rafer buddy," said Duffey, "the big game's tomorrow. Championship. We're gonna miss you. You got any great advice for us?"

Rafer leaned forward in the bed and raised both arms up, extending them out toward us all.

"Be funny," he said. "Have… fun. Duffey?" He stared at Duffey. "Bat… choke up. Choke up bat."

Duffey grimaced. "Duffey can't… I mean, I can't hit like that, Rafer."

Rafer moved his gaze to the Robin on his far left, Skeeter. He pointed at him, and then moved his arms left to right, from Robin to Robin.

"Robins for Robins," he said. "Robins choke up."

"But Zack hits Pepper without choking up," said Batman.

Rafer shook his head, a new gesture for him. "No Zack. No Duffey. No Rafer. Yes Robins. Robins for Robins."

"We can do that." I nodded. "Robins for Robins."

"Bring it in, guys," Donnie pressed in toward Rafer and the rest of us pulled in as tight as we could to Rafer's bed. We took off our caps and bowed our heads.

"God, your boy Rafer's pretty sick," prayed Donnie.

I looked at Rafer. He and I alone had our eyes open.

"Take care of him, would you? You know what he needs. You can heal him, God. And, about the game, God . . . I don't really hate the Hawks. Except for Pepper Jasper."

"And their catcher, Booger . . ." Duffey broke in.

"And their catcher . . ." Donnie pulled up, looked at Duffey, then closed his eyes again.

"God, we don't want to hate any Hawks," he prayed. "Just help us to play like a team. Thanks, God. Amen."

"Jesus name," said Rafer, eyes still open.

"In Jesus' name," Donnie agreed, "amen."

Duffey drawled "amen" again, and Sawdust barked. Jimmy threw the sheet back on the dog, and the Robins started slipping out the door.

Rafer called to me. "Zack."

He pulled something from under his pillow and held it out to me. It was the cross nail, the one he'd gotten at church, with the red ribbon tied to it. He put it in my hand.

"I can't take this, Rafer. It's yours."

He was, as ever, without expression. But his eyes were clouded. One of them gave way and a single tear streaked his face.

Rebecca was still beside me. "He wants you to have it, Zack."

"Zack please," he said.

I took it then, squeezing the nail tight in my hand.

Duffey stuck his head back in the room. "Nurses coming this way, Zack-man. A whole posse of 'em."

Rebecca hugged Rafer's neck and kissed him on the top of his head. Rafer said, "Magically delicious."

"See ya tomorrow, Rafer," I said. "After the big game, buddy. When it's all over."

"When it's all over," he said.

Rebecca and I were halfway out the door when Mr. Forrester touched my arm gently.

"I'm glad y'all came by, Zack. All y'all." He smiled.

I nodded. "So am I."

"Good night, sir," Rebecca chimed.

"Good night, kids," he said.

Just outside Rafer's door, Rebecca and I bumped into Donnie. We watched my teammates down the hall pass a posse of laughing nurses.

"Nurses everywhere." Donnie's unease started to sound like panic. "It's the gestapo."

"Where's Sawdust?" I asked.

"I had to put him somewhere fast."

"Where is he, Donnie?" asked Rebecca.

He pointed to the door next to Rafer's.

The three of us fluttered into room 118. Sawdust had his paws up on Sherri Carpenter's bed, delighting the little girl.

"Aren't you a nice doggie?" She was petting his head, rubbing his back.

I darted over to Jimmy at the window. He was pushing it open.

"You go first," I said. "I'll hand him to you."

Jimmy crawled through and dropped from sight. I heard his body thump on the ground. He moaned like a drunken cow. Rebecca ran to the window and I ran to grab Sawdust. I gathered him quickly in my arms, sloppily, dog legs sticking out in all directions.

Rebecca called out the window. "You all right, Jimmy?"

I heard the drunken cow again.

"Jimmy got the wind knocked out of him." Rebecca looked concerned.

"I'm gonna knock something else out of him." I started easing Sawdust out through the window. "Get your butt off the ground!"

I hollered down to Jimmy. Sawdust licked both our faces as he passed from my hands to the groaning Jimmy's.

I closed the window just as the room door opened. It was the nurse Tigger had cried for. "Oh, I thought y'all were with Rafer," she said.

Sherri, her eyes alive with mischief, said, "Miss Barbara, I'd like you to meet my cousins. This is Homer…"

"Zack," I said. "I'm… I'm Homer Zack."

"And my other cousin…"

"Rebecca," said Rebecca. She was always quicker on her feet than I was. "Well, Homer, we had better get a move on," she said, smooth as polished marble.

"Don't leave on my account," said Tigger's nurse.

"Oh no," Rebecca's tone was breezy, "we've caused enough trouble."

"Come on back, Homer Zack," Sherri hooted. "Rebecca too. And bring you know who."

We shot out the door and scurried down the hall. Just outside the hospital's front door, Jimmy met us, still kind of bent over.

Rebecca put her hand on his back. "You all right, Jimmy?"

"I been better," he said through gritted teeth.

"He's fine," I said. "Where's Sawdust?"

"Took off," Jimmy muttered. "Rabbit or something, I guess."

"Best news all night," I said. I spotted Pastor White, Coach, Mr. Forrester, and Dad next to four parked cars in the hospital lot. "Let's go, Jimmy."

Walking away, I heard Jimmy say, "Your boyfriend's all heart, Rebecca."

I stopped and looked back. She was looking at me, smiling warm as the summer night. "He could use a little work," she said.

"What?" I tried to look disappointed. "A little… oh please."

The other Robins began to gather at the cars with us.

"How'd it go boys?" Captain Powell asked, obviously enjoying the hijinks.

"Mission accomplished?" Dad raised his eyebrows.

"It was great." Duffey was enthused. "'Course Batman almost blew it for us."

I didn't see it, but Batman must have elbowed Duffey. "I told you..." Duffey squawked, and like bobcats they were all over each other, kicking and clawing on the ground. Coach and Dad and I pulled them off each other before there was any real damage. We held them apart, still breathing heavily and giving each other the evil eye.

Donnie got in between them. "Guys, remember what Rafer said? Robins for Robins."

Duffey broke. "I'm sorry, man. I'm sorry."

"Me too," said Batman. "Forget it. Shake?"

They shook hands to audible sighs of relief from the rest of us. Kids can do that. Be at each other's throat and then decide they'd rather pal around together. Losing that ability may be the heaviest casualty of aging.

A passel of kids climbed into the back of Captain Powell's pickup. Dad drove a group of us home in his Buick, with Pastor White sitting in the front passenger seat. Donnie, Jimmy, Rebecca, and I were crunched together in the back, not saying anything. We were fairly played out, I guess, from our successful, harrowing mission.

"Y'all don't have to answer this if you don't want to," Pastor White said over his shoulder, "but did y'all sneak Sawdust in to see Rafer?"

We didn't answer at first, looking at each other and thinking about the consequences that might flow from lying to a man of God.

Rebecca rescued us. "Pastor... if we try to answer that, we'll probably break a commandment."

His smile connected with ours before he turned to face the front again.

"Well, I think that's all right," he said with grace. "I'm pretty sure God is smiling on all of you. Smiling on Sawdust, too."

"He's smiling on Rafer," I said. "Don't you think so, Pastor?"

"Especially Rafer. Rafer's his boy."

I opened my hand and looked at the cross nail.

CHAPTER 25

As far back as I could remember, going to bed for me was not a gentle drift toward sleep. It was more like punching my ticket to end the day. My head would hit the pillow, and I was out. Dreams were rare—at least dreams I remembered. Sleeping like that ushers in alert mornings, with a rested mind.

The night before the championship was different. I didn't really care about sleep. When you're twelve, you don't worry about being tired the next day. I just lay there and let my mind drift. Images danced in front of me; it was like a carnival. I kept thinking about Rafer.

I left the radio on, playing low enough to sleep but loud enough to speak to me. The last song I remembered, before sleep pulled me in, was about something coming at us from just over the horizon, something radically different, brand new. Things as we knew them were ending, and things we had longed for—some so magnificent we hadn't the nerve to imagine they could be—were even now on their way.

Sleep brought a brilliant dream. Thirty-six years have followed in the wake of that night; I have dreamed multitudes of other dreams, but that night's reverie remains my most beautiful haunt. It plays on, luminous, in my mind's recesses.

A man, whom I know is Rafer but about thirty years old, is teaching a class. I guess it's a class. He's on a beautiful stage in an auditorium, with rows and rows of people seated, listening to him. Everybody, including Rafer, is wearing jeans and some kind of off-white shirt or blouse. I don't know why. It's a dream.

Rafer's half sitting, half standing on a tall chair with spindly legs, the way young seminar leaders teach—so they can spring to life, walking with fierce animation from one end of the stage to the other. He is talking and making dramatic gestures, at points rising from his seat, taking a few steps, and then returning to the half-seated position.

I can't make out what he's saying, but the audience is totally into it. Everyone's out of control with laughter. I look closer and I see some people crying. Then I realize they are all laughing and crying, all of them weeping and hooting at the same time. They're obviously enjoying it, and it's obviously changing them, too. Rafer's message is undoing them and putting them back together.

The people in the audience appear to be at different stages of growth, and yet all the same age. I know. It doesn't make sense.

Rafer's words seem a spoken opera. It's not a common language. He speaks with eloquence in dramatic tones, alternating in three parts between tragedy, humor, and silence. When he stops talking, I hear the sound of many waters. When he starts again, the hum of the waters subsides.

The air smells like honeydew melons. Sometimes. Then it smells cleaner than wet pines—like you just stepped out from under tree leaves still holding water from a rain, and onto a meadow still wet from God doing his laundry.

Now a little boy with olive skin and pitch-black hair, wearing cutoff jeans and a white T-shirt, comes onto the stage from Rafer's left. He's carrying a baseball bat. In our world, awake, we'd say he was about ten years old. But in the dream, his age seems beside the point. He looks timeless. Weird dream stuff.

The boy walks up to Rafer, gives him the bat, and says with a smile that's serious and frivolous at the same time, "Merry Christmas, Rafer." The bat's a gift. Taking the bat, Rafer stands up, laughs hard and choppily, and puts his arm around the little boy's shoulder.

For the first time I understand Rafer's words.

"I don't know how I can ever thank you," he says to the little beaming boy. "How did you know I'd want this?" Rafer looks amazed at the gift.

The little boy acts a little shy. "Well," he says, his voice liquid, "I can't take all the credit. I had some help picking it out."

"Help?" says Rafer. "From who?"

"My dad said you'd like it."

"But how did he know?" Rafer asks.

The little boy turns to face all the people, who are riveted, absorbed in this simple exchange. "He wants to know how Dad knows this!" He beams at his audience and scratches his head—a mindless motion of someone who appears preoccupied but is in fact free of any and all real cares.

Then he starts to laugh. It's the laugh you hear from little boys. Richard laughs that way when Donnie or I tease him. He knows we're really his buddies. It's as if he enjoys the revelation of his own shortcomings. It's like he'd rather be a source of fun and recreation for all the rest of us than be cool.

The boy's laughter gets louder quickly, stronger by leaps, a magnificent virus sweeping over Rafer, the crowd, and me. It takes over the world, because in the dream, that's everybody. That's the whole world. All laughing. And the laughter feeds us, makes us stronger. We are re-created.

Then I woke up.

It's funny; the dream seemed to last a long while. But when I awoke, the same song was playing on my radio. Peaceable things were coming. Love untroubled.

I wanted to go back into the dream. I still do.

I feel as if someday I will.

CHAPTER 26

In my first minutes awake, scrambling out of bed, I felt sharper than normal, more alert than if I'd had my regular nine hours.

I poured milk over Cheerios and Wheaties mixed together. My pregame meal.

If we beat the Hawks in this final game, we would win the 1971 Silas Little League championship.

For Donnie and me, this game was the end of a dream. The home movie of this game had run in our minds at least since mid March. The dream would end today, in one way or another. And we would walk about in its mist for years to come.

People were kind enough not to come right out and say so, but it was pretty obvious nobody thought we could win. I couldn't blame them. We had barely squeaked by the Hawks when they were missing two of their best players. And the Hawks were as close to a winning machine as preteen ballplayers get. They descended on weak teams like... well, like Hawks descend on sparrows. Or Robins.

In Eddie Glass, they had a twelve-year-old version of Willie Mays. Eddie ran around the bases and across center field like a deer. He pinched other kids' extra-base hits with his glove. So when he came to bat, it was like he pulled *that* hit, the very one he had stolen in the field, out of his back pocket, cocked his bat, and recast the ball as his own long liner out into the other team's left-center gap. He ended up on third with what you might call a six-bagger (one triple stolen and one triple hit). Twelve-year-olds don't do that. Except for Eddie Glass of the 1971 Hawks. The Hawks' coach liked to switch Eddie to shortstop in the later innings. It was kind of a signal that the coach believed the game was on ice. Eddie was a killer shortstop, too.

The other Hawks were only slightly less formidable. They were a scaled down version of the Baltimore team that stormed through the 1971 Major League season with no observable weaknesses. The Hawks were way more consistent than us Robins. Swinging at the right pitches, taking balls and connecting with strikes. Their fielding, too, was way more consistent than any Little League team I'd seen.

We Robins swung at balls we should have taken and took strikes we should have jumped on. There's a good life lesson in there somewhere about opportunity, and maybe about desire. You can get away with swinging too aggressively. You can't really do anything about the strikes you let go by.

We won a lot of ball games by being aggressive. We weren't the "Hawk machine," but we were a good team. If we won this game, it would not be because our pistons were well oiled and we were firing on all cylinders. They weren't, and we weren't. If we won, it would be because a spirit invaded the playing field. Or maybe invaded our arms, legs, and hearts. Coach told us so in his pregame talk.

He had us sit in a semicircle on the ground in front of him and Mr. Forrester. I think he tried to keep the talk low key. He understood that kids just want to play. On the other hand, kids aren't stupid. This game was different.

"You guys have a chance." Coach turned his head from side to side, eyeing all of us seated on the grass. "You guys can win the whole thing," he said in a serious tone. "The championship. Your parents want to see that happen. I want to see that happen. And I know you want to see that happen."

He looked at Mr. Forrester. "We appreciate you being here, Cecil."

My teammates agreed: "Yes, sir." "Thank you, sir." "Thanks, Mr. Forrester."

The man laughed. "Rafer kicked me out of the hospital. He said 'Game go, go game,' so I went. Here I am."

We chuckled with him. Just as quick, I felt like I could cry. So much was crammed into that moment. Just as in that whole season.

I glanced around. Everybody was looking at Coach now.

"You know how many times in life you get to play for a championship? Not many times, guys." For a scary instant, I thought he was going to give us some history of real teams playing for real championships. *Don't do it, Coach. We're kids. We're having fun. We'll play hard, do our best. But it's just baseball. It's not something else.*

He smiled. "Hey, this is just baseball, right?"

That scared me a little. What else did he read in my mind?

"This is not..." He paused and my heart gave a little jump. "This is not something else."

Jeepers!

"But we want to win. And I'll tell you something more, guys. I think you're going to win. You want to know why?"

Nobody said anything right away, and then Richard piped up. "Yes, Coach. I'd like to know why."

Skeeter frowned at the little guy, but Coach said, "Thank you, son." He looked right at me then. "I think you guys are going to win because... because you play with your hearts. The Hawks are good... real good. They *could* win. They could win easily, if we don't play with all our hearts."

I thought what Coach was saying *sounded* good, but I really didn't know *what* he was saying. And if *I* didn't know, the odds of more than two or three of the others knowing were very slim. Of course, Little Richard seemed to know more about everything than the rest of us put together. Richard seemed to have even

Coach's adult brain beat. Then there was Rafer. I had long suspected Rafer's mind, though veiled, was north of ours too. Closer to the source.

"What do I mean by playing with all our hearts? I mean playing aggressively. Going for it. Taking some risks out there. You've done it all season and all season the other teams have been caught off guard."

He took a healthy pause. I thought he was through, but he wasn't.

"In games like these, the winner is the team that dares the other team to stop them. Skill only goes so far. Then it comes down to heart," he said, tapping his chest, and looking away from us for a second.

"Guys, win or lose, I will never forget you. You guys have a heart the size of Alabama..." He looked away again. "And it's been my privilege... my privilege to know you and coach you."

I know. It's what the world calls corny. But it's what people with heart call real.

Coach pulled himself together, smiling, and pointed toward the playing field. "Let's go play ball!"

"Rockin' Robins!" I tried to holler just like everybody else, but it was a little harder than usual.

We all knew that Pepper Jasper had a wicked fastball. He also had a working curve. By "working," I mean it really curved and he could reasonably spot it in certain locations. Only he didn't like throwing it. I'd noticed the year before that Pepper had the same disease the Falcons' Riley Brinkerhoff had. He liked to shake off his coach's call for the curve. It intrigued me that his coach never chided him or looked upset by his pitcher's overruling him. I guess Pepper thought he knew better than his coach—or, more likely, he was just in love with his fastball. Every Little League pitcher is. Maybe every pitcher, period.

Truth be told, our pitcher, BoDean, was average. In a couple of years, that would be common knowledge, and BoDean would quit pitching in junior high. But in 1971, he had a reputation as a winner in Little League ball. He never seemed to dominate a game, but he always seemed to win. A lot of people call that luck. I've learned to recognize it as seizing opportunity.

Everybody, adults and kids included, had the impression that BoDean wasn't bright. He liked a good nap. Sure, he sometimes moved slower than molasses, and he always talked slow. But that was his way of conserving energy, storing it up so it would be there when he needed it. If he had to move quickly, he could. He'd snagged more than one line drive fielding his pitcher's position, and he'd also let more than one soft grounder go by the mound when we were up big and the game was practically won. "Why burn yourself out over a ground ball that don't change nothin' no how?" he'd say.

I don't know how he made such computations in his mind and muscles, but he seemed to do it consistently. He builds houses these days, and I'm told he adjusts his construction speed in accordance with the buyer's schedule and motivation. Some things never change.

We all knew Pepper was the cream of the pitcher's crop that year, but we still felt confident about winning with BoDean on the mound. Confidence can go a long way sometimes, even further when you're young.

Warming up, I heard a couple of Hawk parents in the extra makeshift bleachers talking about the lineups.

"They just don't have enough stars to match up with us. They're top heavy. The top of their lineup is fun to watch. That Rafer kid eats fastballs like candy corn. But he ain't here."

"Zack Ross is a player."

"Oh yeah, he's big time for Little League. Be a good kid to watch for at the high school in a few years."

"But you don't think they're gonna give us a game today?"

"Nah. After number four, they can't stay with us." He laughed the laugh of the convinced. "They got two, three real players. We got an all-star team."

Suddenly I felt very confident. I caught Donnie's warm-up throw and held it, walking toward him.

"What're you doing?" asked Donnie.

"We're gonna win," I said.

"I know that." But of course, he didn't. "How do you know?"

"Get the guys over here," I said. I called to them myself. "Hey guys, c'mon over here, will ya?"

They fluttered over to me, most of them already looking nervous.

"Guys, I got a great feeling about this game. We can beat these guys. They're not expecting to have any trouble from us, and that's going to work in our favor big time."

They started to look hopeful.

"Listen," I said, "'member how Rafer gave all of us a rock?" I pulled my own out of my pocket. Every Robin, except for Duffey, pulled a rock out of his pocket and held them up for me to see.

"This is just a rock." I tossed mine a couple times in the air. "There's no power inside it. Except that it reminds me that I got a friend named Rafer, who gave me the rock." I paused. "And then that reminds me, too, that Rafer is really with me today, in the way that counts. He's pulling for me."

"He's pulling for all of us," Jimmy said. "He gave one to all of us this season. I got mine the third game."

"I got mine the fourth game," BoDean said.

"He always liked me better than BoDean," Jimmy hooted.

"Why don't you go pick your nose?" BoDean suggested.

"Is there something hanging out of there?" Jimmy rubbed his nose.

"Robins for Robins," I said. "God help us. I believe we're gonna win."

"Batman believes too," said Batman.

"Let's stay loose, have fun, and play some baseball today," I said.

The Hawks' first at-bat was the thunder heard in a distant storm. You know the storm took off somebody's roof, but then you see it pass your house without incident. After their first two batters lined out, Eddie Glass stroked the ball over my head in center, but I hustled it down, holding him at second. BoDean walked Booger. I wasn't sure, but I seriously hoped he did it on purpose. Their number five hitter, a long-haired kid we called Greaser, swung through strike three around his ankles.

"You feel like your control is there today?" I asked BoDean while we jogged in.

"Never better, Zack-man."

"Got lucky with that third strike."

He gave me a disappointed look. "That pitch went right where I put it. Greaser's a sucker for blue-darters."

I knew BoDean always told the truth.

We reached the dugout at the same time, and Coach looked more than a little concerned. "Your control gonna be a problem today, BoDean?"

If it'd been me, I probably would've got a little angry. But that would cost BoDean too much energy. He just smiled up at Coach and said, "If my control's a problem, Greaser walks. When I strike him out, my control ain't a problem, Coach."

"You're up, BoDean," Duffey drawled.

"Stand back, non-believers," said BoDean breezily. He picked up his bat and glided to the plate, smooth as syrup.

After BoDean took the first pitch for a strike, I was sure I saw him step a hair closer to the plate. The next pitch plunked off his left thigh.

"You all right, son?" Coach called.

"No sweat." BoDean sauntered to first, rubbing his wound but not overdoing it. "Never better, Coach." That ball had to hurt like a house of fire, but BoDean wasn't letting on.

The second Robin in the order was Donnie. I watched my

friend top the ball, dribbling a slow roller toward third. The third baseman fielded the ball clean, but the grounder was so slow, he had no play.

"Now we're moving!" Coach clapped his hands.

Batman stepped in, looking a little nervous and a lot excited.

"Just meet the ball," I encouraged him from the on-deck circle.

He got a piece of the first pitch and blooped it just past the reach of the shortstop. Gator, the left fielder, had raced in with the hit. He picked up the ball and fired home, holding BoDean at third.

Walking to the plate, I looked at my friends on first, second, and third, clapping their hands. They were almost bouncing up and down on the bases, keyed up something fierce. I didn't look, but I heard and felt our fans calling my name. It was a great moment.

I glanced at Coach to see if he wanted me to bunt or if he wanted to call time and tell me anything. But he did the same thing he always did with me. He touched his belt buckle, repeatedly. That was our team signal for the batter to do whatever the batter wants. Of course, most twelve-year-olds want to swing away. I was no different.

I figured Pepper would come straight at me. He was cocky; he knew he was good. Sometimes you can turn that coolness around on a guy. But you better do it right away.

The first pitch split the plate, low and fast enough that I couldn't really get full extension. But I knew right away I'd got enough of the ball to make a difference.

Racing to first, I heard Coach's voice. "Get outta here!"

I looked up in time to see—and hear—the ball clang off the right center field fence, just inches from the top.

The Hawks' right fielder was pretty big, but his throwing arm wasn't the strongest. On my way to second, I saw him get to the ball ahead of Eddie. That told me to go for it. I caught the inside of the base, pressed off, and headed for third. The third baseman was so prettily poised to catch a throw and tag me out that I knew he was faking. I slid anyway—a pop-up slide—and watched as the third baseman scurried to his right to scoop up the errant throw before it could get past him.

I relished triples, even more than home runs. It takes a little extra something, a little bit of the gambling spirit, to reach third when your hit doesn't leave the field.

I looked at the scoreboard and watched the guy put up a numeral three in the bottom half of the first inning. In the top panel was a zero for the Hawks. Hearing the cheers, I looked at my parents and gave a little wave. Even at that age, it seemed to me that the parents got more of a rush out of such things than the kid. Now, I know that's the case.

Duffey was up.

Coach tried to help him out. "You can take a ball or two, Duffey. Let's make him work a little bit."

Duffey had the same idea I did, though, about jumping on the first pitch. Only his "jump" resulted in a pop-up to the second baseman, while I held my ground at third. I felt for Duffey, but I still had a cool sense that I'd be scoring before the inning died.

I didn't have to wait long before Jimmy slapped a grounder between first and second and I raced home. The scoreboard guy switched the three to a four and Robins on the bench all cheered.

We still had only one out, with Skeeter at the plate. He swung through a fastball for strike one, and then laid off a ball in the dirt. With the count even, he tapped the plate and prepared for Pepper's third offering. What happened next is one of those "breaks of the game" situations that nobody can control. Unfortunately, this one did not end in our favor.

Pepper wound up a delivered a pitch that looked like it was headed straight for the ear hole on Skeeter's batting helmet. Skeeter hit the dirt, but he forgot to bring his bat down with him. The ball glanced off the barrel of the bat and rolled out in front of the plate.

"Fair ball!" the umpire shouted.

Booger pounced on the ball from his catcher's position and

fired it to second base to nail Jimmy. With Skeeter having to scramble to his feet before he could run to first, the Hawks had no problem completing the double play. Tough luck for the Robins—but hey, we had four runs and that was a good start.

Booger had made a really excellent play. Duffey, in a genuinely sportsmanlike instant, told him so.

"That was a great play, Boog! I don't think I could do that."

"I *know* you couldn't do that, Francis," Booger answered. I guess he didn't get the sportsmanlike gene. "You're just a Robin. Hawks eat Robins."

"Oh yeah?" Duffey sounded off, ready to rumble. "What was I thinking? I guess when we got four runs and y'all got zero, I got confused."

"Get lost, chump," Booger spat.

"Gonna make me?"

As I came out of the dugout, I saw Rebecca approach Duffey with his chest protector in her hand.

"Here you go, Duffey," she said. "I know it takes a while to get all this stuff on."

It was an odd sight, a little comical, but not entirely harmless. Two catchers staring each other off, one still in his full catcher's gear and the other with his chest protector being fitted on him by a smiling twelve-year-old girl and would-be peacemaker.

Coach yelled, "Get in here, Duffey, and get the rest of your gear on." Duffey started moving toward our bench.

Mr. Forrester was chuckling on the bench. I heard him tell Coach, "We're gonna win, Wayne. We're gonna win."

I raced over to Booger, who watched my approach like it was the unhappy arrival of early winter. I said, "I wouldn't mess with Duffey. He's Cherokee."

"Really?" He was genuinely surprised. "I didn't think Indians were supposed to get fat like that."

Duffey must have heard him because he hollered from our bench, "Only us mean ones!"

"We're going to win," I said to Donnie, passing him on my way to center field.

Batman heard me and beamed. "I'm starting to think you're right, Zack-man."

"'Course we're gonna win," BoDean said in his "standing sleep stance" on the mound. "I don't know how to pitch to lose."

"Don't get too cocky, BoDean." I didn't know what else to say. "Just do your best."

"Nothin' else to do," he said. He wasn't arrogant. He was just BoDean. "Ain't nothing but a thing." That was one of his favorite expressions. I still don't know what it means. But I did know I didn't want anyone but BoDean and his stress-free attitude on the mound in this game.

As it turned out, we needed every bit of his attitude and more. The Hawks threatened to score multiple times, but only managed one run in each of the second and third innings, leaving the bases loaded both times. BoDean wasn't cutting the Hawks down, but he was frustrating them to no end. That was working, for now.

Meantime, Pepper Jasper had clamped down on our bats like a shop vise. After going down one-two-three in the second, we got another run across in the bottom of the third—and we might have gotten at least one more if I hadn't fantasized about being Lou Brock. After Pepper uncharacteristically walked Donnie ahead of me and Batman popped out, I swung late on a fastball, drilling it past the first baseman and into right field. Donnie hustled all the way home.

I thought the outfielder was slow getting to the ball. Picturing two triples in my box score in the *Silas Town Crier* the next day, I tried to stretch the double and was thrown out easily at third.

I had driven in our fifth run, but I felt terrible. My bravado had cost us not just an out, but also a run. Duffey got a little too far under Pepper's heater and lifted a long fly to left. I could've eaten a doughnut and coasted in from second on that sacrifice fly. Instead, it was the third out.

The Hawks got another run in the fourth, and would have gotten a lot more if Tigger hadn't robbed Eddie Glass of a grand slam. With two outs and the bases loaded, Eddie hit a deep shot to right that backed Tigger to the fence. It looked like the ball was headed for the trees, but Tigger leaped like his namesake and snagged it in the web of his glove. Eddie and the three other base runners shouted something obscene, our team shouted something sacred, and just like that, the top of the inning was over.

This next part might be hard for you to believe. But I'm not making it up. I was cheering with everyone else, running in from center, when I heard Tigger's cry.

"Zaaaack!"

In his descent from the top of his leap, Tigger's belt loop had caught on the top of the fence. The little fellow was hanging out there like a rag doll. Batman and I ran over to him.

"Holy chain links!" Batman was impressed. "Lookit that!"

"I'm stuck."

I looked at Batman. "How come everything's *holy* with you? Everything's not holy, ya know."

"I can't get down." Tigger wiggled.

"That's Batman and Robin talk." Batman shrugged. "Holy Metropolis and stuff."

"Holy get me off'a here!" Tigger squealed.

I lifted Tigger like a sack of grain and held him there while Batman worked the belt loop free. Both sets of fans applauded as we three jogged in.

Coach slapped Tigger on the back. "That's a new one! I've never seen that before."

"Everything happens to me," Tigger moaned, slinking away.

Coach took Tigger by the arm and turned him around gently. "I meant the *catch*, son!" He nodded seriously at Tigger. "I've never seen one like that before."

The boy threw his shoulders back, a giant now. "Ohhhh. That was nothing, Coach."

"Still think we're gonna win?" Donnie asked in a low voice meant for my ears only.

"I do." I tried to sound confident.

But we hadn't been in the dugout three or four minutes before Jimmy, Skeeter, and Tigger all struck out. Pepper walked off the mound pumping his fist in the air and chanting some kind of war cry with his teammates. I couldn't make out what they were saying. It sounded like the Italians yelling on those old Chef Boyardee commercials, when they tell their children to run home for supper.

"What are they saying?" I asked Batman when I passed him at shortstop on my way to the outfield.

"I don't know. But I'm getting hungry."

"You gotta be kidding me. There's only two more innings, Batman. Think about the game, all right? Stay in the game."

"I wonder what's for supper tonight."

I started to say something else, but decided not to. Trotting out to center, I could still hear him muttering, explaining to anyone in earshot how even Batman has to eat.

The Hawks scored two runs in the fifth inning, tying the game at five runs apiece. Harold was first up for us in the bottom of the frame. Pepper struck him out on three pitches. But BoDean hit a ground ball hard up the middle and Eddie struggled to field the ball cleanly. It was an infield single, but the way BoDean strutted on the first base bag, you'd think he lined a shot off the fence.

Then Donnie got just the tail end of his bat on a pitch, and the ball squirreled out toward the second baseman, slow enough that he had to throw to first to make sure they got one out while BoDean hustled into second. Two outs.

I watched Batman settle in at the plate, a very serious look on his twelve-year-old face. I found myself praying again, a short arrow-prayer. *C'mon God, let him rip one. Just a clean single up the middle.* I was bold with my next little arrow. *Don't you wanna see that, God?*

He must have. Batman kept his head down on a knee-high

Pepper offer, and lined it to dead center. He hit it so sharp it got to the center fielder on one clean bounce and he hurled it home, holding BoDean at third.

With Robins at the corners, I stepped in. *Just get good bat on the ball*, I told myself three or four times.

"Time!" The Hawks' coach walked to the mound with a serious stride. I couldn't hear their hushed tones, but Mr. Malcomb's stern countenance looked like it overruled Pepper's pleas. The coach walked back to the Hawks' bench.

I saw four pitches, all of them wide of home plate by a good foot.

"Take your base," the ump drawled. I jogged to first disappointed, but excited that Robins were on every base.

Duffey was up. On his way to the plate, Tigger stopped him and put a "Rafer rock" in his hand.

"But that's yours," Duffey objected. "Rafer already gave me one."

"But you don't have it anymore," said Tigger. "Take it."

The big guy started to say something else, and Tigger pressed in closer, looking up at his teammate towering over him. "Take it!" He shoved the rock into Duffey's pocket, whirled and hopped back to the bench.

"Okay," said Duffey sheepishly. "Maybe I will."

In the box, Duffey swung at the first pitch, lofting a long foul ball down the left field line.

"He's swinging for the fence," I heard Donnie moaning from our bench. "He's gonna strike out."

I yelled at him. "We need base runners, Duffey! Think about your team."

"Duffey!" It was Rebecca. Duffey looked at her. "Remember 'Robins for Robins'!" she hollered.

Suddenly, Jimmy was rattling the chain link in front of our bench. "I knew he'd show up! Over yonder!" Jimmy pointed at Sawdust waltzing merrily out of the edge of the wood line.

"Sawdust!" he called. "Get over here, boy!"

Sawdust barked. Pepper fired. Duffey squared around and bunted the ball down the third base line. The Hawks' third baseman was stunned, temporarily paralyzed. BoDean raced past him down the line toward home, and by the time the third baseman had scrambled to the ball, BoDean had scored. Duffey, all one hundred and forty pounds of him, huffed and puffed toward first like the A train.

"Go, big man!" Rebecca screamed. "Go!"

The third baseman threw wild past the first baseman. Batman dashed home too, and I went into third standing up. The A Train chugged into second, smiling and tipping his cap like you saw in the old pictures of the Babe. The cheers of Robins and their fans mingled with Sawdust's raucous barking as he ran around to our bench and into Jimmy's hugs.

A minute later a distracted Jimmy struck out, but I didn't think it would matter. We were up 7–5.

Duffey and I ran into the dugout together. "We're up 7–5, Duffey. Three more outs, and the game's over."

"Piece of cake." He walked into the dugout for his gear and I scurried to the outfield.

It was stale cake, and we were made to swallow it. The first Hawk batter slapped a double to right center, a ball I was fortunate to stop before it got by me. I was still congratulating myself on my crucial defensive play when Booger got all of BoDean's six-inning-old fastball and cleared the right field fence by about ten feet. The game was tied, and just that quick, we had gone from the cusp of winning to the precipice of losing.

I thought we'd at least get out of the top of the sixth tied with the champs, but after Greaser singled, Red from tryouts homered. Hawks 9, Robins 7.

My faith flickered off and on, a once-hot coal not yet cold.

The next two batters singled. We still had no outs.

Coach called time and walked out to talk to BoDean. Donnie and I rendezvoused with them at the pitcher's mound.

"Son, maybe it's time for Batman."

"Whatever you say, Coach." BoDean gave Coach the ball. "I don't have to pitch. I just want to win."

"There's no shame, BoDean. You did great. Everybody knows the Hawks usually score twenty, twenty-five runs a game."

Donnie gave BoDean a glove-tap on the shoulder. "You kept us in it, man. The game's not over."

BoDean looked at me then. I'd never seen him misty-eyed like that. "I thought we could take 'em this year, Zack-man. I thought I had 'em."

"You did," I said. "For five long innings. Nobody can ever take that away from you."

BoDean nodded at me. He had an odd expression. I think he wanted to smile, but he couldn't.

Coach waved to Batman, who left his shortstop post and walked up to the mound.

"I still need you in the game," Coach said to BoDean. "I need a good glove at shortstop."

BoDean looked at our bench, eyeing the Robins yet to get in the game—Little Richard and Clay.

"Let's put Richard in, Coach," said BoDean. "I can sit out now."

Batman couldn't see it. "Are you brain-dead? He's too little. Holy Metropolis, this is the championship!"

"He can't play short, BoDean." Coach was emphatic. "I don't want to embarrass him."

"Put BoDean at short," Donnie said. "Let Richard play second. I'll sit out."

"You're sure about that?" Coach asked.

I was surprised. I shouldn't have been. Donnie was aces.

"I'm sure," he said simply. "I think his dad should get to see him in the big game, don't you?"

Coach waved to our bench. "Richard, let's go."

Richard hesitated. "You mean me, Coach?"

"No, I mean the other Richard, Big Richard." Coach smiled. "Let's go, son. You're playing second base."

Richard ran onto the field.

In the bleachers, Captain Powell stood up. "Hey! That's my son! That's my boy out there!"

"Richard," Coach called. Richard stopped. "Get your glove, son," Coach said simply.

"Oh yeah." The little guy ran back to the bench and got it.

Batman was shell-shocked. "Batman's got a bad feeling about this," he said.

But Richard was playing second, BoDean was at short, and Donnie had gone to the bench.

The ump pointed at Batman. "The new pitcher can take warm-ups."

"Batman don't warm up," said Batman.

"Whatever Batman says..." The ump smiled. "Play ball!"

Coach's voice echoed over the field. "Be ready! First and second, no outs!"

From center field, I saw Rebecca jumping up and down and heard her calling to Richard.

Richard waved to her. "Hi, Rebecca! I'm playing second base!"

"Move toward the base, Little Richard!" she yelled.

He moved toward it, all right. He was on top of it now.

"Not that close!" she hollered.

I was going to have Coach call time and position him myself, but Batman's pitch was on the way and the Hawk batter connected. The ball zeroed in on Richard like a smart missile. He turned his head, afraid, and stuck out his glove. The liner disappeared in the webbing, knocking him over on top of second base. That doubled up the Hawk on second who took off with the hit.

"Throw to first! Throw to first!" Rebecca and somebody else were shrieking. It was me.

Half sitting, half lying on second base, Richard managed to

toss the ball in a slow arc toward Harold at first. It just barely got there, but it did, right before the runner.

I heard Captain Powell's booming voice. "Triple play! Triple play! That's my son!"

I had run in, and was picking Richard up off the second base bag.

"What happened?" he asked.

Duffey was congratulating him, a little too aggressively, and I thought Richard might even get hurt by Duffey's back slaps.

By the time we reached the bench, reality reared its head. We could hear the Hawks singing the Chef Boyardee chant while they raced out to the field.

Coach was clapping his hands, trying to rally our spirits. I got the idea he didn't really believe in miracles any more than we did right now, but he wanted to fulfill his "coaching obligations."

"We can do it, guys. Two to tie, three to win. C'mon now, we can do it. Tigger, I'm putting Clay in for you. Everybody gets in the game today."

Clay looked like he'd just been sentenced to hang. "Am I up, Coach?" he managed to ask.

"You're on deck. Skeeter's up."

Skeeter hit a weak one right back to Pepper, who fielded it like it was a precious gem and threw it to first base for out number one. I noticed that Skeeter hustled all the way, right out of the box. Skeeter was the kind of guy I wanted to go to war with. He never said die.

From his coach's box, Mr. Forrester clapped his hands and yelled, "Good try, son! That's the way to hustle down the line!"

Tigger gave Clay his best fellow ten-year-old advice for such a time. "Don't swing. Maybe he'll walk you. Don't swing unless the ball's right where you like to swing at it."

Clay stood still as pond water through the first five pitches. He was short; he rivaled Richard and Tigger for "Most Likely to Go Undetected." On a 3–2 count, he decided to swing at a pitch over his head, fouling it backward over the backstop.

"What are you doing?" Tigger was incensed. "That was ball four!"

"That was right where I like to swing at it," Clay announced.

Pepper must not have heard. His next pitch was across Clay's ankles for the fourth ball. Clay raced down to first before the hangman might discover he'd been cheated.

Harold was a good first baseman, but Pepper had his number at the plate. He struck out swinging. I felt for him. He would probably remember that at bat all his life.

I saw our season slipping away. I felt like I had lain down two innings ago in a field of cool green grass, and awakened now on stones.

Donnie stood beside me. "We came so close, Zack. So close."

BoDean was up. He must've been nervous, because he yawned. I'm just telling it like it was. BoDean is the only guy I ever knew who yawned when he was nervous. Psychologists would say it was a defense mechanism, but who really understands these things?

"Son," said the ump, "you're awake enough to get out of the way of a fastball, aren't ya?"

BoDean backed out of the box. "He ain't fixin' to throw at me, is he?"

Booger snickered through his catcher's mask. "Baby wants to go beddy-bye."

BoDean stepped back in and took a practice cut, "accidentally" hitting Booger in the mask on the backswing.

"Hey!"

"You might want to back up," said BoDean. "Ump says he don't want nobody gettin' hurt."

Choking up on the bat, BoDean went with Pepper's first pitch and drove it to right field. Clay scampered to second, but BoDean barely beat the throw from right field to first base. Coach had a cow and gave him a "what's up?" gesture.

"I had it all the way, Coach." BoDean smiled.

"Need a batter, Coach," said the ump, looking our way.

Nobody stepped up to the plate.

Coach scanned his clipboard quickly. "Richard! Richard, you're up!"

Richard grabbed a too-big bat and a too-loose helmet that would have to do.

Coach called time and stopped Richard on his way to the batter's box. He put his arm around Richard's little shoulders.

"This guy's had some control problems today. You don't have to swing, Richard. You understand?"

"Okay, Coach." Richard's serious tone and face matched Coach's. "Okay."

"Good man. Just do your best, son." Coach turned around and started walking back to the coach's box.

"Hey, Coach," Richard called out to him.

"Yeah, son?"

"This is *fun!*" said Richard, his face beaming. He raised his head and shoulders to their full height, all of about four feet, and strode into the batter's box to do battle with the dragon. All of us were standing in the dugout, leaning against the chain-link fence, peering through it, our hands gripping the wire in front of us. Batman asked me, "Did he say this is fun?"

I nodded.

"Hey!" Batman called out. "This ain't fun. This is baseball. Get your head in the game."

I thought that was kind of a funny thing to say. I mean *funny* both ways. *Ha-ha* funny and *strange* funny. But I knew it wouldn't help Little Richard to hear it.

"Take it easy, Batman." I laughed. "If he thinks it's fun, let him think it's fun. Anyway, he's right." I turned to Donnie. "This *is* fun, don't you think?"

"I'm having fun." Donnie's smile was big as life. And just as real.

"You guys are weird," said Batman.

"That's another ball," the ump said.

The team hollered. The count was already two balls, no strikes.

Little Richard had no knees or chest. Even when he didn't crouch, he had the same strike zone as G.I. Joe.

Abruptly, the umpire called time and motioned to both teams' coaches to come over to him. He took a few steps in our dugout's direction. From our bench, I could hear every word.

The umpire shook his head. "Lonnie, your catcher is harassing the batter."

"What do you mean?" My recollection of the Hawks' coach is a man who didn't seem to know how to smile. When he tried, it was always a sneer.

"He's mumbling about the kid's dad. You know, serving in Vietnam."

"Has he called the kid by name?"

"No."

"Well then, everything's okay, right? Felton, you know the rules. A catcher can chatter just like everyone else, so long as he doesn't call the other player by name."

The umpire frowned. He turned to Coach.

"What do you think about that, Wayne?"

Rafer's dad broke in, answering for Coach. "I think it stinks." He looked Mr. Malcomb in the eye.

"So do I—" the umpire started.

"But," Coach interrupted, "it's perfectly legal." He looked at Mr. Malcomb. "And this game is going to be played by the book. So when it's over, and somebody wins, and somebody loses, it happened by the book."

The Hawks' coach, his eyes frozen on Coach, said, "You're a wise man, Mr. Hornbuckle."

"Not really. I just want the game won and lost, fair and square."

I could tell the umpire was not happy, but he was also not going to add any of his own rules to doctor the game. He put his mask back on hastily, saying, "Let's play ball, then."

The coaches trotted back to their places, and I looked at Richard in the batter's box. His bat was propped, leaning against his legs, and he was rubbing his face and eyes. Booger was still talking, snickering.

I was mad, and I started out toward the plate, but Coach grabbed my shirt.

"Where are you going?"

"I'm gonna kick—"

"No you're not, Zack." He pulled me back toward the dugout and put his arms on my shoulders, looking right at me. "It's not the catcher, Zack. It's the coach. He's just doing what the coach told him to do."

"It's not right."

"No. It's not. But it's bigger than us, right now. Do you understand?"

"No!" But I was starting to, and I didn't like it. I wanted to make things right, and I couldn't. This is our wretched curse.

"We have to stay inside the rules. We're not God, Zack."

"Okay. Okay, Coach." I wheeled sharply and darted into the dugout with my teammates. I wanted to believe I didn't understand what Coach was saying. But I did. The world's problem isn't just catchers and coaches. It goes deeper.

I got a strange sense of seeing something that had not yet happened. It's hard to believe, but I saw the next pitch before it was thrown. And I saw Richard seizing the day, before the day dawned.

Coach must have sensed the same omen. He hollered at BoDean on first. "BoDean, you better be on your horse, boy."

BoDean gave a quizzical look and started to say something. "Ain't the count three balls—?"

The crack of the bat stopped him in mid-sentence. It really seemed to stop everything. I don't think Richard had swung at a pitch more than three or four times the whole year. And he sure hadn't hit the ball solid. Before now.

This pitch was down the pipe. Richard's swing in batting practice was never that bad, just slow. Now, he was a little late, but in line with the pitch. The ball shot down the first base line, just fair.

With the count 3–0, the first baseman had been almost comatose. He flailed meekly at the drive as it passed between him and the bag, about head level.

"Come on home, Clay! Run, BoDean! Go, go, GO, BODEAN!" Coach was jumping up and down like a crazy man in the first base coach's box. Little Richard was sprinting down the line as fast as his no-knees legs could travel.

BoDean was doing his best Tigger impression. At the crack of the bat, it honestly looked as if BoDean had gone vertical. He was in the air for what seemed like two or three seconds, like something had exploded underneath him. When he came back to terra firma, he was pointed in the direction of second base, which was where he wanted to run, but it took his feet an instant to get traction, like a cartoon character. Meanwhile, Little Richard was pumping hard behind him with his little arms and legs.

The ball landed fair, about a foot inside the right field line, and bounced cockeyed away from the Hawks' right fielder, who was trying to run it down. He was wheezing like he had a flat tire or something. Right fielders don't normally run very much in Little League.

Clay crossed home plate. BoDean was rounding second with Richard in hot pursuit. The guys around me were jumping up and down, yelling, some of them trying to help Coach get Richard's attention.

"Stop there, Richard!" Coach roared, and the players screeched: "At second, Richard! Stop!"

But Coach bellowed too late. Richard was running hard, pressing BoDean, both of them barreling toward third.

To this day, I can see Rafer's dad frantically waving to Richard: "Go back! Go back, son!"

Of course, BoDean thought he was yelling at him, so he stopped and started to backpedal in a confused stagger.

"Not you, son! C'mon, c'mon, What's-your-name!" he shrieked in a high-pitched voice. He couldn't remember BoDean's name.

"C'mon BoSeefuss, run BoJangles!"

The Hawks' right fielder had finally corralled the ball, picked it up, whirled, and thrown the ball in the general direction of the infield.

The second baseman, Red, lined up in short right to act as cutoff. But the throw was seriously off, forcing him to race it down as it dribbled just behind second base, in short center field.

The BoDean–Richard train chugged around third, to the odd chorus of the fans, Coach, and my teammates, all yelling like the county dam was bursting.

"Run Beauregard!" howled Mr. Forrester from the third base coach's box. "Don't let him pass you!"

"Stop, Richard!" bawled Coach from the first base coach's box. Then, seeing that Richard heard no sirens today but those singing inside him, Coach yelled, "Go, Richard! Go!"

It was going to be close. Booger was an all-star catcher and a smart player to boot. He adroitly let BoDean slip over the plate safe, avoiding any collision that might have taken him off mission. His sights were set directly on Richard, and he capably aligned his body to take the throw and tag the runner out.

This short a throw from Red should have been squarely on target, but nothing about this scenario had been normal. He let go a missile and we watched the ball and Richard zero in on home plate and the waiting Booger Clark.

I was terrified for Richard, because I thought he was going to try to plow into the catcher to dislodge the incoming ball. *Don't do it, little fellow. It's not worth it, Richard.*

Coach was yelling something different now. "Go back, son! GO BACK!"

My mind had already finished the scene, replaying last year's All-Star game outcome, when Pete Rose barreled into Ray Fosse. Only, this time, the runner would suffer the career-ending injuries.

The throw was high, giving Richard an extra split second. He needed it. Booger extended to catch the ball cleanly. Richard, to my everlasting surprise and relief, went horizontal. He threw his feet forward and let his back glide in concert with the Choctaw County earth around home plate. It was a perfect slide, except that Booger's muscular legs and body were blocking the plate. When Richard's sliding legs hit the catcher's solidly planted feet and shin guards, his legs folded back into where his chest would be in a few years when he had one.

Booger confidently brought his mitt down to make the tag, but it seemed Richard's left hand had become a fist. He swung it with all his might into the catcher's mitt. The ball jumped out like a kernel of popcorn. With his right hand, Richard reached behind the catcher's massive frame and slapped home plate.

The umpire had already positioned his body and hands to make the out sign. Now he spread his hands wide, palms down.

"Safe!"

Nobody made a sound for likely three full seconds. The umpire, looking faintly surprised at the stark silence, signaled again and said, "That man is safe. That's the ball game."

Pandemonium ensued. Richard was lying flat on his back, staring up at the Alabama sky like he'd just fallen from it. We rushed him in a group, yelling at the top of our lungs. Coach picked up Richard and set him on his feet. We pounded on his oversized batting helmet. He fell over, collapsing under the weight of our head and shoulder slaps, but he was giggling. And crying. So was I. So was Coach.

I heard Red and Booger talking as they drifted with their teammates back toward their own dugout.

"It's my fault. It was a bad throw."

"No, no. He popped it out of my mitt. Before the tag! How could his little hand *do* that?"

We were still knocking Richard over and picking him up, and Richard was trying to say something to Coach.

"I'm sorry. I just couldn't stop. It was like I had no control."

"Like you had no control, huh? But did you have fun, Richard?"

We were all listening now, and Richard looked serious.

"Well," he said, smiling softly. "Hitting the ball was a lot of fun. And running was a lot of fun too, most of the way. But when I saw Booger waiting for me, it wasn't fun anymore."

"Yeah, I understand. Got kinda worried there, didn't you?" said Coach.

"Yeah. I thought I might hurt him."

Everybody roared, and Coach had to raise his hands to get them to calm down. "Wait a minute, guys. Let him talk."

"I mean, I know he's bigger than me. Everybody is," said Richard. "But, well, I was worried because I felt like I wanted to hurt him." He looked around at his teammates. "I wanted him to get hurt, and I wanted to do it. I hate that feeling."

"But you kept running at him," Coach said.

"Well... I reckon there wasn't much else for me to do."

That sounded funny too, and all us Robins cackled like happy hens.

The parents had followed our little victory parade, but kept to the side to let us celebrate as a team. Now Richard saw his mom and dad.

"Hey Dad, did you see that?" He forgot to be cool, and just ran like a three-year-old to his dad's arms. Captain Powell lifted him off the ground and hugged him close.

"I saw it, son! It was amazing!"

Coach was still looking at Richard. "No hits on the year until today. You swing at a three-and-oh pitch, you hit it on a line to right, and you race all the way home, worrying about why you're so mad at the big bully catcher." Coach couldn't stop shaking his head.

There was an eerie silence, lasting about five seconds. I think we were all just learning how to breathe again.

Donnie said it out loud, but quietly. "We're the champs, y'all."

We all looked at each other like we'd just come off a battlefield, lucky to survive. "I wish Rafer was here," said Duffey. Everybody murmured assent.

Batman said, "We wouldn't have been here without him."

"It wouldn't have happened," Jimmy said.

Donnie motioned, "Bring it in, guys." Richard scuttled out of his dad's arms and all of us clustered around Donnie, hats off, arms on each others' shoulders. Parents were watching and we sure didn't care.

"You been good to us, God," said Donnie. "Real good. We thank you. And tonight, when we go see Rafer, we want to be thankin' him too. And we're gonna keep asking you to heal him, God. He's a good kid, God..."

His voice cracked a little, and I thought the prayer was done for. But he got it back, real strong. "Now, God, help us to celebrate this game, and this whole season, and... just everything, God! In Jesus' name... AMEN!"

His "amen" tore the roof off the sky and sort of set us all free to raise a ruckus. We hollered like dogs on the hunt, our gloves flying high, and we chased each other like it was capture the flag, yelling all the way. Batman ran into Jimmy, and Duffey ran over Donnie, and I ran into Rebecca (I swear it was an accident). She didn't seem to mind at all.

Duffey's dad picked up his boy and military pressed him over his head. Airborne, Duffey let out a war cry and his dad answered. The rest of us found our parents. They said they couldn't lift us over their heads, and maybe Duffey's dad would be nice enough to lift us for them. He was, and Robins were raised in pairs on the big guy's shoulders.

I'll never forget those moments. And I don't think it was just winning the championship that set those postgame feelings in my heart forever. It was deeper. It *is* deeper. It was the team. And something beyond them. Rafer. Even something beyond him.

Truth... setting me free.

CHAPTER 27

We wouldn't be in no championship game if it hadn't been for you," said Duffey. It seemed like a good idea to let Duffey tell Rafer. The rest of us stood in a semicircle around Rafer's bed. He was sitting up, emaciated and pale, but alert.

"I'm not talking about your hitting and stuff..." Duffey broke a little, rubbing his eyes with the back of his big hands. "I mean, you pulled us together. So, we all talked about it and everything... and we all thought you should have this."

Donnie and I picked up the sizable trophy from the floor at the foot of the bed and held it high so Rafer could see it easily.

"For Rafer." Rafer really was asking, but his inflection was flat as ever.

"That's for you." Batman grinned. "For you, big guy."

Mr. Forrester said, "Rafer and I'll be privileged to hold it awhile, boys, but it belongs to all of you. And when Rafer goes home, we'll move it from one house to the next. Everybody'll get to have it."

Rebecca leaned toward Rafer. "We brought you something else, too."

She nodded to Richard, who went to a little table in the corner of the room. He picked up a poster board and carried it level and flat to the bed. Rafer wasn't strong enough to take hold of it. Richard laid it face up on the boy's lap.

It had all his rocks on it, the ones he had given his teammates. The top of the board read, in large letters, "All Robins for all Robins." The rocks were glued in a baseball field design, each rock next to our names, at the position we had played in the field.

He said the same thing. "For Rafer."

"For you, Rafer." Rebecca looked straight into his dim eyes, her own eyes shining.

"Rocks," he said. "Rafer rocks."

"Them's the very ones that you gave us!" Tigger said, with a slight hop.

Duffey was sniffling a little louder. Coach put his hand on his shoulder. "It's all right, son."

"No," the big guy wouldn't be consoled. "That's not the rock he gave me." He looked at Rafer and confessed. "I'm sorry, Rafer. I threw it at Booger. Then I couldn't find it."

That was funny. We all smiled, but had the presence of mind not to laugh out loud. Tigger put his little hand on Duffey's other shoulder. Mr. Forrester patted Duffey on the back.

"Don't worry about it, kid," said Rafer's dad.

Doctor Dale, a kindly, older physician, came into the room. Through the open door, I saw Pastor White and Nurse Sarah Beth in the hall. The nurse looked pretty broken up.

"Rafer, son, I see you're very popular today," the doctor said. "But I think all you Robins had better say good-bye for today. Rafer needs lots of rest."

My teammates filed by the head of the bed, one at a time.

Jimmy patted Rafer on the shoulder. "You're the best, Rafer."

BoDean said, "You get well now."

Harold was next. "See ya soon, Rafer."

Skeeter pointed to the poster board, still resting on Rafer's lap. "I got the coolest rock. Thanks!"

Batman mumbled, "You're the best hitter I ever seen. Probably ever will see."

Tigger chirped, "Thanks for giving me a big rock!"

Duffey said, "I won't never forget you." He put a hand on Rafer's arm. "Never."

Coach patted Rafer on the arm and said, "You get outta here soon, son. We got the all-star game to play."

Richard reached up and hugged Rafer as best he could. "You're my hero, Rafer."

Rebecca got close enough to whisper in his ear, "Jesus is inside you." She kissed him quickly on the top of his head.

Then Donnie spoke up. "We're gonna have a big picnic at the church when you get out of here, Rafer. The biggest ever."

Rafer's dad said something to the doctor, who nodded. They both followed Donnie out the door.

Now it was just me and him. I was still at the foot of the bed. We just looked at each other. A good while.

"You're the best, Rafer."

"No... Zack best baseball."

"I'm not talking about baseball."

I didn't think he could move his arms. He'd kept them still at his side while we were talking to him. But now he raised them both. He put his left hand on his chest and his right on his forehead.

"Jesus... inside Rafer... Jesus inside."

I heard the door open, my eyes still on my dying friend. Doctor Dale came alongside me. "You can see him tomorrow, Zack. He really needs to rest."

He moved to Rafer's side and my friend moved his eyes away from me to look at the doctor.

"How are we feeling today, Rafer?"

"We don't know," he answered.

I pulled the cross nail out of my pocket. "This belongs to you, Rafer," I said.

Then it happened. For the first time ever, Rafer smiled. His eyes shined so big, I thought he was a different person.

"Bring Zack home," said Rafer. "The nail," he said, raising one finger. "The grave," he raised a second finger. And then a third finger, "He arose ... bring Zack home."

He laid his head back on the pillow then, his eyes closed.

"That's good, Rafer," Doctor Dale said. "Get some rest." He nodded to me. "You can see him tomorrow, son."

Mom and Dad were waiting for me in the hall. Mom put her arm around my shoulder. "Did you get to tell him good-bye?"

I guess I didn't answer right away.

"Zack?"

"Rafer didn't want to say good-bye," I said.

"Zack, he may not be here tomorrow," she said gently.

"He's gonna be all right," I said, feeling a sudden strength. "He's all right. Is it okay if I go to the swimmin' hole this afternoon?"

Dad looked unsure.

"You can go," said Mom.

Dad looked at her. "Paulette, it's not really a time to go swimming."

"Absolutely, you can go." Mom's voice was strong. "Try to be back before dark."

"Try?" Dad balked. "Son, there's no reason for you to be out there after dark."

I nodded. "I don't plan on it."

"But if you are," Mom said, looking at Dad, "that's okay too."

It was dusk; the day was letting go. We sat, Sawdust and I, at the base of the take-off tree. The air was cool, still. Shadows lengthened, ushering the evening in.

I felt Sawdust recognizing the event before I did. He would not lie down, or sleep, though he had done so many times in this place.

"What are you thinking, boy?" I rubbed his ears. He just looked at me, his eyes serious, faithful.

Belief came to me. It had flown after me that whole miraculous season. It soared over me while I played, and carried me on wings over many fires. Now it was coming home to settle in my heart.

"Here I am, God," I said for the second time that year, only this time I was not drifting off to sleep.

"And... I know I need you." Something turned inside me.

"I know he's dying," I breathed aloud, "but it feels like he's not."

Sawdust's tail thumped the ground peaceably. "He's leaving," I said quietly, "but it's like he's just now coming alive."

I closed my eyes and listened to the breeze. "That's what I want, God."

I laughed then, a strange sound for such a moment. I said it again. "That's what I want, God. I want to be like Rafer." I paused for a second before continuing. "I want to be like... your son."

I broke then, weeping in stops and starts. I took the cross nail from my pocket and said, "He arose." The words floated out of my heart, and milled about in the Alabama air, refusing to leave.

Sawdust cocked his head. "It's okay, boy." He didn't look like he needed to hear it as much as I needed to say it. "Everything's gonna be all right."

For the first time in my life, I felt alive.

I lay on my bed that night, unable to sleep and not caring to. For the first night in a long time, I left my radio off.

The phone rang. I heard Mom's voice as she answered.

"Yes. I'm so sorry. I understand. Let us know, Pastor, what we can do."

I walked into the kitchen, quiet, and listened.

"Yes, I believe that," she said. "I do believe that, Pastor. I'll tell him. Thank you so much for calling. Good-bye." She hung up, turned around, and saw me.

"Oh, honey, I'm so sorry." We hugged. "He had just started talking so good and everything. Donnie's dad said he even sang a little yesterday morning. He said he liked that 'Hallelujah, Christ arose' song."

"He's singing real good now, Mom. Rafer's all right. I believe that."

"I believe that too, honey. I do."

CHAPTER 28

It was a hot Saturday, two weeks after Rafer had left us. On our way to the swimming hole, Sawdust and I stopped by Paw-Paw's place.

"We're headed to the creek," I said. "Sawdust said I should ask you if you want to come with us today."

"Now, it's interesting you should ask me that, Zack. Because I was just thinking, it's been too long since I've lain on the bank, half in and half out of the water, just soakin' in sun and God's good air."

He just looked at me, waiting I guess, to see if I was serious about my offer. I was. "C'mon then. Let's go."

I still thought he'd back out. But he was stepping off the porch, coming alongside me and the dog. Sawdust was beside himself. He always loved Paw-Paw. Who didn't? And the old guy himself was going to the swimming hole with us!

Along the way, Paw-Paw talked openly about Rafer's passing and the funeral. He'd surprised a lot of people by showing up. Most of the townsfolk hadn't seen him in years. When Dad shook his hand and said it was such a shame for someone so young to die, Paw-Paw just up and said it. "He's not dead, Del. He's just not here." Dad couldn't help frowning, but I don't think that bothered Paw-Paw in the least.

Now, walking the trail with Sawdust and me, he told me not to worry about my dad. I wasn't convinced.

"He just seems like such a hard case to me," I confided.

"None of us is a hard case to God, Zack. We're just sinners, needing grace, needing the power of the blood. What's that around your neck?

"It's a nail. Bent in the shape of a cross. Rafer gave it to me."

"Hold on to that, son."

"I will." I looked at him. "I'm planning on giving it back to him one day," I said simply.

"I'm planning on watching you do that." He smiled.

Sawdust smelled the creek before we saw it and took off ahead of us. I suppose he wanted to make sure everything was in order for our frolic. When we came around the bend, he was running up and down the pier, waiting for the jumping and flying and splashing to start.

"You go on up and jump in, Zack," Paw-Paw said.

I tossed my T-shirt to the ground, raced up the tree, took the rope, leaned back far, and jumped off.

I hadn't thought about what to holler. I just opened my mouth. "Rockin' Robins ... live forever!"

Sawdust met me in the air and crashed into the water with me. Crawling out together, we ran over to Paw-Paw who was at the base of the tree, looking up it.

"Do you think I can do that, Zack?"

"I don't know." I shook my head. "I mean, aren't you kind of old?" I didn't know just *how* old, but he had to be up there.

"I'm seventy-two."

"You know better than me, sir." I was young enough not to tell him what to do or not do.

"I don't think I will, then," he said. "To everything there is a season. It's just as much fun watching you and Sawdust."

He stepped over to the water and sat down on the bank.

Sawdust and I must've jumped ten times before we sat down and relaxed with the wonderful old man.

"Can I look at that cross nail?" he asked.

"Sure." I took it off my neck.

He turned it over in his hand. "Rafer stopped by and showed me this when he first got it at the church. Didn't say nothing, but I knew where he got it. I got one myself years ago."

"Really?" I was intrigued.

"At a different church. The same thing, though."

"You still got it?"

"Nope."

"That's too bad," I said.

"No it ain't. I gave it to someone else."

"When was that?" I asked.

"Oh, that must've been sixty or so years ago now."

"Who was it?"

"A good friend," he said.

"What happened to him? I mean, did y'all keep in touch?"

"No, we didn't," Paw-Paw said, a little sadly. "He just disappeared. I guess his family had to move or something. I don't know why everybody keeps moving anyway. We all end up in the same place eventually. We all leave this world."

We were quiet then, just resting, thinking. Our hands were cupped behind our heads on the thick grass, looking up at the Alabama clouds. Sawdust dozed.

"You know," Paw-Paw said, "you and me and Rafer are all the same age."

"How do you figure that?"

"When we see him again, we'll all be in our glory bodies," he said, like it was the simplest, most sensible truth there is. "That'll mean we're all through with time."

"So, I guess you can't get old in heaven."

"Well, we'll all get old. But old up there don't mean what

it does down here. There's no aging. You just are who you are… forever."

"With God," I said.

"That's right." Paw-Paw sighed. "What's it like swinging out on that rope, Zack?"

"It's cool. It's kinda like flying."

"If it's kinda like flying, then I don't need to do it."

He sang then, soft and slow, beautiful. It was just a couple of lines, about a day without rain clouds, a day that would brook no sorrow, not even the most tender nature of regret.

They told me two years later that Paw-Paw fell asleep in his porch chair and never woke up. I don't believe that. I think he'd just grown so light that the Earth couldn't hold him anymore. So he took flight, rendezvousing with his old cross-nail friend.

And with mine.

EPILOGUE

The outfield grass is lumpy, uneven under my feet. Grown wild, it's overlong in some patches and undergrown in others. It's not really grass anymore, not an outfield anymore. It's just a field.

My left trouser pocket vibrates. I pull out the phone.

"This is Pastor Zack."

"Hey, you sound a little down." It's Donnie. "You all right?"

"Oh yeah, I'm fine." I consciously strengthen my tone. "What's up, Donnie?"

"Listen, I was just in the new Food Lion in Gadsden, and... you're not gonna believe this, but I thought it might be him, so I asked him."

"You asked who? What are you talking about?"

"It was Brinks, Zack. You remember Brinkerhoff, the Falcons' pitcher?"

"No way. Riley Brinkerhoff?" It was hard to believe. The boy had disappeared after that season.

"The man himself, I swear!" I could hear Donnie's genuine laugh.

"What... how did you know it was him?"

"That was the easy part," said Donnie. "He looks exactly—I'm telling you, exactly—like the kid on the mound, only bigger. Taller and wider." He laughed again.

"So you just walked right up to him and said, 'Hey, I remember we smoked you in Little League thirty some years ago.'"

"Not exactly. For one thing, I don't remember smoking anybody. Rafer put some serious heat under Riley's backside, but the rest of us just kind of tagged along to watch the fire trucks."

I laughed out loud. "So, I'm sure he didn't know who you were."

"Oh yes he did!"

"You gotta be kidding."

"Yes, sir, he knew who I was," Donnie said, his voice rising.

"Did he remember your name?" I was incredulous.

"Well, it's not so much that he remembered anything," said Donnie evenly. "I said he knew who I was. I mean he knows I'm the youth pastor at Black Creek. He knows your name, too."

"Hold on," I said, gesturing with my hand as if my friend could see me. "Did he remember playing us? Did he remember playing us and Rafer?"

"Absolutely... only after I brought it up, though. 'That was *you*?' he says. '*You* were on that team?' Then he says, 'Were you the kid that ripped my heater into the next county?'"

"And you said, 'Yeah, that was me.'"

"Right!" said Donnie. "Exactly. Then he got that look. You know that look that says, *I can't believe I let a lightweight like you beat me.*"

I smiled, imagining Donnie playing with the man's mind in the checkout line.

"So then I told him it wasn't me, it was Rafer. He said he never really knew the kid's name. He just remembers the ball's disappearing act over the fence!"

"That's pretty cool," I said, my eyes scanning the ancient little infield and outfield around me. "I remember that act too."

"He remembers you. Said he read about some of the ball you played at Southern Choctaw."

"No kidding."

"His family moved to Georgia. He played at Marietta High. He coaches at Kennesaw State now."

"What's he doing around here?"

"He's got a nephew living in Silas. He says he's ready to tear up the Little League."

"Uh-huh." Now I got it. "And he wants us to pick the kid up?" Donnie and I coached the Little League Cardinals. "Sounds good to me." I was back in my 'winning is everything' mode. Coaches are just little kids who want to win one more time.

"Well, the thing is..." Donnie hesitated, and I was afraid he had something bad to tell me. "The thing is he wants to meet with you about his nephew."

"Okay. I hope you told him we can probably draft him. Right? If he's half as good as Riley was... How old is he?"

"He's eleven."

"That's great! He can play for us two years. It's perfect."

"Well, what he said was, the kid has some issues," said Donnie.

"What kind of issues?" I was suddenly extremely interested. I mean interested in the boy, not the player.

"He doesn't talk much," he said. "They can't figure him out. He passes all the tests for normalcy. Riley says he might just be really, really quiet. Anyway, he knew you pastored CrossPoint and he wondered if we could visit the boy and his family. I told him we'd do that. I hope that was okay."

I was struck then by a truckload of emotions, a rush of spectacular memories of when everything changed; everything blossomed from one dying boy's touch.

"Zack?" said Donnie. "Are you still there... Zack?"

"I'm here. Can I call you back later?"

"No sweat," Donnie said. "That's all I was telling you, anyway. I'll talk with you tomorrow."

"Thanks, Donnie."

Putting the phone back in my pocket, I spoke aloud.

"Is it all right if I thank you again, Lord? You're not tired of hearing that? 'Cause I think I would be."

Things travel in circles. People, events, history's episodes are cylindrical. We try to flatten them out, to deconstruct them. But God likes circles. We might as well try to deconstruct God. Sometimes we do—try to do it, I mean.

The circles are going somewhere, though. They're not stagnant. I think God's truth is a spiral, moving unstoppable through the time and space of this world and any that are beyond.

My trousers buzzed again.

"Hello."

"Hi, honey," Rebecca's voice was still like spring. Remaking me.

"What are you up to?" I asked.

"I'm trying to get Sawdust to understand that weeing is for outside." This was the fourth Sawdust. He was just six weeks young, and a ball of fire. "Are you ready to come home? We can grab something to eat."

"Yeah... I just thought I'd swing by Dad's on the way home. Just for about ten minutes."

"That's cool. See ya then, honey."

"Bye, Precious," I said.

Dad was alone these days. He said he was fine. It was always hard for him to admit he needed anything or anyone, but I know he missed Mom. *Maybe today. Maybe today he'll lay aside the weight. Step onto the fields of grace.*

I sat down at the old home plate, covered over with sparse grass now. Alone, with no one anywhere near me, except the Holy Spirit, I sang.

> *Up from the grave he arose, with a mighty triumph o'er his foes;*
> *He arose a victor from the dark domain,*
> *And he lives forever with his saints to reign.*
> *He arose! He arose! Hallelujah! Christ arose!*

Then one of my favorite new ones. Softly, I whispered a song about the cross, and its offer to us to come and die. And live.

For a few more moments, I let the ball field and God take me back, to the season of dying. It happened to both Rafer and me. And to my mom. I'm not talking about when a heart stops or breathing ends.

Somebody once told me that change, real change, is not possible. I don't believe that. I believe everyone changes everyone. Because everyone touches everyone.

I am forever close to Rafer, though he has always been ahead of me.

I envy Rafer. For he has already been touched.

ABOUT THE AUTHOR

In 2009, Rusty Whitener's *A Season of Miracles* was one of four finalists in the Christian Writers Guild Operation First Novel contest, and Whitener's screenplay of the same story won second place in the prestigious Movieguide Awards in Beverly Hills. Whitener has won many awards for his screenplays, including his adaptation of missionary Paul Long's memoirs and Gayle Roper and Chuck Holton's novel *Allah's Fire*.

A pastor for twelve years in the Presbyterian Church in America, Whitener earned his Doctor of Ministry degree in 2004 at Gordon-Conwell Theological Seminary. Presently, he is turning his dissertation on worship into a book. Whitener has published an article on the burgeoning popularity of contemporary worship music, and a stage drama based on characters C. S. Lewis created. He has also written a weekly column in *The Southwest Times* and *The Patriot* for ten years.

A lifelong baseball enthusiast, Whitener lives with his wife, Rebecca, in Pulaski, Virginia. His website, www.rustywhitener.com, gives insight into his writing quest and reflective temperament.

If you enjoyed *A Season of Miracles*, check out www.aseasonofmiraclesbook.com for videos that touch on the novel's themes.

A movie version of *A Season of Miracles*, produced by Dave Moody of Elevating Entertainment, is presently in preproduction.